Beta Rising

Angelina Fasano

Pynhavyn Press

This book edition is published in 2018 by:
Pynhavyn Press

TM

http://www.pynhavyn.com

First Edition: October 2018
Copyright © 2018 Angelina Fasano
All rights reserved.
ISBN-13: 978-1-942622-19-2

Cover Design: SelfPubbookCovers/kreativecovers
Wolf graphic from Graphics Factory, used under license.

DEDICATION

For Annamarie, my greatest masterpiece and the reason I do everything I do.

ACKNOWLEDGMENTS

This book has been a labor of love for many people, and I would like to thank them now. First and foremost, I would like to thank my editor, Rene, for reading and rereading this story a hundred times. I would like to say thank you to Pynhayvn Press for taking a chance on new authors, and giving them the ability to control their own content. I would like to thank my husband, Tony, and my dad, Eric, for holding down the home front so that I could finish my story. Finally I would like to thank my partner in crime, Hailey, for all the overnight writing jams.

CONTENTS

CHAPTER ONE...1
CHAPTER TWO 16
CHAPTER THREE 32
CHAPTER FOUR...50
CHAPTER FIVE...59
CHAPTER SIX...76
CHAPTER SEVEN...90
CHAPTER EIGHT 100
CHAPTER NINE..111
CHAPTER TEN..126
CHAPTER ELEVEN 142
CHAPTER TWELVE 161
CHAPTER THIRTEEN 174
CHAPTER FOURTEEN..188
CHAPTER FIFTEEN 196
CHAPTER SIXTEEN...208
CHAPTER SEVENTEEN...221
CHAPTER EIGHTEEN 232
CHAPTER NINETEEN..245
Teaser for Survivor's Call. 249
ABOUT THE AUTHOR...253

CHAPTER ONE

He hit my midsection with the speed and ferocity of a Mack truck sending me flying backward through the air. I took a deep breath, closed my eyes, and braced myself for the inevitable crash to the floor.

I landed on my back with an audible thump. "Ouch," I sighed, knowing without a doubt that when I rose, there would be a veritable bruise on my butt.

My attacker strolled up to me, and I opened my eyes to peek up at him from my compromised position.

"That had to have hurt," he commented, his face guarded as he assessed my level of anger.

I wasn't mad as it turned out. Just disappointed that he had managed to get the drop on me.

"Yeah, it sure did," I replied, pulling myself up to a sitting position and drawing my knees up closer to my body.

"Sorry." He bent down, offering me a hand that I grudgingly took and pulled me up to my feet.

I studied him for a second, took in the way his brown eyes regarded me tenderly. Subconsciously, I reached out and tucked a strand of his long dark hair behind his ear, my fingertips brushing his cheek. He closed his eyes and drew in a deep breath.

I blew out a disappointed sigh. "You know, Daniel, this isn't what I thought you had in mind when you asked me if I wanted to come over and fool around."

Daniel laughed, and his brown eyes met my own gray ones. "Oh? And what exactly did you think?"

I returned his gaze unflinchingly and shrugged, stepping even closer, so that we stood just inches apart, and hooked an arm around his neck. "Something more intimate?" I offered.

Daniel looked me up and down, his grin quickly fading to a frown as he pulled my arm out from around his neck. "You're nowhere near ready for that," he told me.

I rolled my eyes, taking a step back and away from him. "So, I've heard," I mumbled. "Just to clarify, I find it ironic that you trust me enough to lead an entire nation of werewolves, but you don't think that I am capable of deciding if I am or am not ready to... you know."

Daniel cocked an eyebrow at me, a gesture that I found to be both sexy and irritating as he pursed his lips. "You can't even say the words 'have sex,' but you want to argue with me about this?"

Of course, I knew that Daniel, my boyfriend for the last six months, made a valid point. I was nowhere near ready to move our relationship to the next level, but it still irked me that he couldn't be like other girl's boyfriends and at least make me think that he wanted to take the next step.

As if reading my thoughts, he snaked his arms around my waist and pulled me back to him. "Trust me, Christa. When you are ready, I will be the first one to let you know." He grinned as he bent to kiss me.

I lifted myself up on my tiptoes, anxious for the feel of his lips on mine.

The door opened, and we sprang apart, both of us glancing anxiously up the darkened stairway, hoping that whoever descended hadn't noticed our little embrace.

Thundering steps indicated that someone moved fast as he rushed down the steps, and a moment later, Brock, the muscular behemoth that he was, stepped into view.

He inclined his bald head towards me. "Hey boss," he commented before turning to Daniel. "Daniel," he nodded. "Whatcha guys doing down here?"

If he had seen us, he gave no indication as he made his way into the room.

We were in the basement level of Les Loups-Garous, the club Daniel owned. The name meant "the werewolves," which fit since a pack of werewolves ran it. A pack whose Alpha happened to be me.

Daniel shrugged at Brock. "Christa and I were training."

Brock sauntered over to Daniel and, with a smile, punched him in the arm. "Getting in some mat time with the old Alpha before you run off to Pennsylvania to calm down that feral werewolf in Lana's pack?" he asked.

My eyes darted over to Daniel, narrowing as I saw him stiffen. If we wanted to know for sure that Brock hadn't seen us, this was as good a confirmation as any. If Brock knew about Daniel and me, I doubted he would have ever had the nerve to mention Daniel's old girlfriend in my presence.

Keeping our relationship a secret was imperative, not only because I am his Alpha, but also because I happened to be True Alpha, which meant that I controlled the Alphas of every werewolf pack in the world. I had a lot of power and, as such, I would have to take a mate that had power of their own, most likely an Alpha, or a really strong Beta, from another pack. If I took a weaker mate, then it would put an open target on both of our backs.

Daniel, obviously, wasn't an Alpha. Hell, Daniel wasn't even a Beta, what our kind considered an Alpha's right-hand man.

Not that Daniel's just one of the ranks. Daniel is an Omega, an extremely rare wolf who has the ability to calm other werewolves down when they are out of control, or as we called it, going feral. Still, it was a lesser rank, and I wouldn't endanger Daniel's life, nor would I put my pack in jeopardy just so that I could be happy with the man I loved.

Alphas must put the best interest of the pack before their own happiness.

Of course, that wasn't the only reason we kept our relationship secret. The mundane world pulled us apart, as well.

Daniel is twenty-four, and I'm only eighteen. Daniel owns a club in our hometown of Kennington, Massachusetts. I am a senior in high school. At my age, that is a pretty huge age gap between the two of us, a gap that people like my grandparents and father probably wouldn't look kindly upon.

Needless to say, we both knew our down-low relationship was probably going to end eventually, but we chose to continue while things were still relatively calm.

Although I knew that someday we'd have to part ways, it didn't mean I wanted Daniel traipsing out to see his old girlfriend. Especially since we hadn't really discussed where he and Lana had left things. Even more so since I hadn't been aware that Lana was having a problem with a wolf in her pack, and I hadn't been informed that Daniel would be handling it.

"You're going to help a wolf in Lana's pack?" I asked, hoping that I kept my voice level enough to hide my anger from Brock.

Daniel averted his gaze, a common subservient gesture among werewolves. "Yeah, Aidan got a call yesterday from Lana stating that Emory, her Beta, had started acting strange about a week ago. Yesterday, Emory shifted and started attacking members of her pack. Lana hasn't been able to get him to shift back or calm down, so Aidan decided that I needed to go lend a hand."

I felt my back stiffen again, as I resisted the urge to scream. I may be the True Alpha, but I constantly felt that Aidan over-stepped his boundaries. He kept making decisions about my pack without coming to me first, and it was starting to piss me off. The pecking order existed for a reason. I was the True Alpha of the werewolves by birthright. Of course, there were 25 other Alphas in the world, Lana being one of them, but *I controlled* them all. Not Aidan.

Immediately, I softened realizing that my annoyance came from my inner wolf. She could be a real bitch sometimes. Annoying as it was, I knew Aidan was just trying to help.

I understood why Daniel needed to go. As an Omega, it was his job to calm unruly wolves. That didn't mean that I liked it, or that I'd easily let him off the hook for keeping it from me.

"Huh," I huffed.

"Yeah," Daniel replied.

Our clipped tones must have alerted Brock, because he cleared his throat. "Everything okay, Boss?" he asked me.

I offered him as reassuring a smile as I could muster. "Everything's good, Brock. Just a little surprised is all. Tired of being left out." I took a deep breath to calm myself because I had started getting worked up again.

I sauntered over to the fridge tucked away in the corner and got myself a bottle of water before shooting Daniel a look and continuing. "Anyway, it's nice to hear that Daniel will be going to visit Lana. From what I understand, they're quite close."

I could see Daniel squirming, and I knew that I should cut him some slack, but the she-wolf had gotten the best of me, and I couldn't help myself.

Brock crooked me a grin. "I'm sure he's excited," he paused and winked at Daniel. "Kid's got a way with the ladies, I'll give him that. As long as I've known him he's always had a fine female by his side, but Lana..."

As Brock trailed off and looked to the sky, I felt my grip on my water bottle tighten and my blood boiled. Brock didn't know it, but he was dangerously close to pushing my wolf over the edge.

I prayed that he would drop the subject when he spoke again. "Let's just say, he'd be stupid if he ever let that one go."

I noted the wording, my head cocking to the side before my eyes narrowed again. "Daniel," I spoke carefully. "Is Lana your girlfriend still?"

Daniel paled.

Brock laughed. "Of course, she is. I talked to her earlier, and she was just telling me how bad it sucks that she and Daniel are so busy that they haven't gotten to speak to each other in months."

I looked over at Daniel again, and if I thought that he was pale before, he'd gone downright ghostly at this point.

I knew that Daniel hadn't been talking to or visiting Lana, but it stung anyway, hearing that Daniel hadn't actually gotten around to breaking up with her.

Daniel took a deep breath and fixed me with a level stare. "It's complicated."

Of course, it was. I'd already had one run in with Lana that had nearly cost me my life, and I needed her support. I doubted that I'd still have it if Lana knew that Daniel had been avoiding her because of me.

Even still, I felt my grip tighten on the water bottle again until the pressure caused the top to pop off.

If our strange conversation concerned Brock, he kept it to himself. Knowing Brock, though, it was more likely he was just unaware of the tension. A short, stocky, Harley riding teddy bear, Brock would take a bullet for me without hesitation, but when it came to matters of the heart, he was oblivious.

Daniel eyed me warily, waiting for an explosion. We had an audience, though, and I wouldn't make a scene.

I changed the subject tactlessly. "Right. Well, Brock, did you need something, because Daniel and I still have some more training to do before he sets out on his adventure?"

"Yeah, Aidan sent me down here to get you. We found Brendan's headquarters, and he said there's some stuff you need to see."

I saw Daniel's back go rigid. As for me, well, my heart hammered in my chest, beating against my rib cage with irrational fear at the mention of Daniel's brother, Brendan.

Brendan had been a rogue werewolf. Long story short, he had killed my mother and had a plan to kill me so that I wouldn't become Alpha. He would have succeeded, too, if not for some quick thinking by my wolf and perfect timing from Daniel.

Daniel had killed Brendan, but his name still brought up painful memories. He had toyed with my emotions, making me think that he was in love with me before luring me into a trap

6

and attacking me.

Daniel recovered before I did. "What kind of stuff?" he asked.

Brock frowned. "I don't know, but he said you'd better come quick."

Daniel and I frowned at each other and the three of us made our way up the stairs, passing the first story, which housed the bar and dance floor of the club, so that we could go up another set of stairs that led to the top level of Les Loups-Garous, a pent-house type apartment that Daniel lived in.

Aidan is my Beta. Not calling any one place home, he spent a lot of time traveling to visit other packs, making sure that there were no other rogues plotting against me. He is also Daniel's father, and at the current time, he'd decided to live in the guest bedroom, which also acted as an office, of Les Loups-Garous.

We approached his closed door, and I could hear his smooth voice as he thought aloud. Once again, I bristled, knowing that his voice sounded so familiar to me, but never able to place it.

We paused at the door, and Daniel went to knock. Me, personally? I barged right in. As Alpha, I didn't need Aidan's permission to enter, and I was still pretty peeved that he had decided to send Daniel to aide Lana without discussing it with me.

I'd been Alpha for the last six months, and Aidan had blessedly been out and about for the first three, which had really given me an opportunity to build a rapport with my pack.

He'd been back for the last three months, and in that time we'd butted heads more than a few times. He aggravated my wolf with the way that he kept trying to order my pack around without my consent. I knew he just wanted to help me, especially since he had far more experience leading than me; he'd been my mother's Beta, after all, and had acted as Alpha until I had taken my rightful place.

Still, it irked me, and I couldn't wait until he disappeared again.

If my sudden entrance surprised Aidan, he didn't show it. He stood behind his desk staring down at a scattered array of papers. He peered up at me, his face remaining damnably neutral, a trait that I noted he'd passed on to his son.

It wasn't the only trait that Aidan shared with his son. They were both tall with shoulder-length brown hair although gray laced its way through Aidan's. When I'd first met him. I had described it as greasy, but I quickly learned that he only appeared that way because he'd been traveling in wolf form for months.

They had the same facial features, save for the eyes. Daniel's eyes were dark brown, so dark that sometimes they almost looked black. Aidan had dark blue eyes, a trait that he had shared with his other son. For an old guy, he was damned good looking, but he had a pompous air about him that always set me on edge.

"What's going on?" I demanded, not caring that I'd come off sounding like a petulant little kid.

Aidan pursed his lips. "Good evening, Christa." He started, his drawl slow and steady.

"If you say so," I answered. I couldn't help the sass I was throwing his way. Aidan and his son had a way of bringing out the worst in me.

Not that Aidan cared. He continued as though I wasn't the rudest person on the planet. "I do," he smiled at me from thin lips. "I'm sure Brock told you that we located the rogue's base of operation."

Aidan never outwardly said his youngest son's name. Even though I thought Brendan had been a dirt-bag, it still always got under my skin that Aidan could so easily dismiss his own flesh and blood.

"Brendan." I crossed my arms, staring at Aidan defiantly as I silently dared him to ignore my correction.

My affirmation caught Aidan off guard. "Hmm?"

I resisted the urge to roll my eyes. "Brendan. His name was Brendan. You found Brendan's base of operation."

Aidan picked up on my not-so-subtle tone, and his eyes narrowed for a fraction of a second before his face slipped back to neutral. "Very well, then. We located Brendan's base of operation."

I paused, waiting for Aidan to continue before I realized he wasn't going to offer any more information until I outright asked for it.

Impatiently, I tapped my foot. "Well," I demanded, "What did you find?"

Aidan's lips pursed, again, and he seemed to consider his words carefully. "I think you should sit down."

I sighed in exasperation. "No thanks, I think I'll stand."

Aidan frowned. "Very well then, you can stand." He walked around the front of his desk and flopped into a chair. "I'm going to sit, though."

His entire demeanor had changed. His arrogant air faded away, giving way to exhaustion. I wasn't the only one who noticed.

"Are you okay, Dad?" Daniel asked, stepping in from the door way and coming to stand next to me. "What did you find?"

Aidan closed his eyes and pinched the bridge of his nose. "Apparently the rogue," he started, and I scoffed. Aidan peered up at me and understanding my frustration started again. "Apparently *Brendan* was far more delusional than anyone could have possibly imagined."

I found that hard to believe considering that he'd killed my mom and tried to kill me, but I stayed silent as Aidan continued.

"He seemed convinced that he would please me by killing Karina and when that backfired, he thought he would redeem himself by killing Christa. He thought that if he could pave the way for me to become the True Alpha, then I would welcome him back with open arms."

Aidan sounded so heartbroken that I had to take a moment

to reevaluate his motives. Maybe the reason he had so much trouble saying Brendan's name was that he felt guilty about the way Brendan had turned out. I know that I would have if I were in his shoes.

Daniel looked appalled. "That's insane. Where would he even get an idea like that?"

Aidan regarded us levelly. "Exactly. It was insane. He also didn't come up with the idea on his own." Aidan paused again, and I could feel a chill running up my spine. Something was up. Maybe I should have sat down after all.

"What do you mean?" I asked.

"We found manifestos, tons of them, written by Brendan. But there was more. Correspondence between Brendan and another rogue. Brendan signed all of his letters. This other guy didn't. He used a mark," Aidan reached behind him to his desk and grabbed a paper, looking at it briefly with disapproval before handing it to me.

I took the paper, staring at it as Daniel peered over my shoulder, and froze. The letter was addressed to Brendan. It commended him for all of his hard work, but warned him that whoever had written it was not ready to come forth and lead the rebellion, yet. It was signed with a mark, one I recognized.

A backward R with three slashes through it, I had only seen it one other time, when Brendan had desecrated my Alpha's throne with it.

It was the Rogue's mark.

My world swam.

Daniel looked up from the letter. "What does this mean?" he questioned. Aidan didn't answer.

I did.

"It means that the war is coming."

And then my knees gave out.

Later that night, I sat in my bed thinking about the terrible truth that had just been revealed. It was too much to comprehend. Brendan hadn't been the rogue, after all. He'd only been a pawn for someone else.

I thought about Brendan. He'd broken my heart and nearly killed me, but the silver-lining had always been that he was gone and with him the threat of a rogue werewolf gaining power and starting a war.

Now, it seemed that Brendan was just the beginning, and a much more powerful enemy was lurking somewhere out in the world, waiting for the right time to bring a battle right to my front door.

My thoughts were interrupted by the ping of rocks hitting my window.

I didn't bother to get up and look; I already knew who it was.

I'd fled Les Loups-Garous without so much as a word to Daniel, sneaking out of the room he'd put me in while I was passed out. I'd had no trouble slipping out undetected since the bar had been open and happy hour in full swing.

Now that the club had closed, and Daniel wasn't busy deejaying to the masses, he'd come to find me, but I wasn't in the mood to talk to him. Despite everything we'd just learned, I couldn't shake the anger I felt toward him in regard to keeping the Lana thing a secret from me.

Daniel knew that I was ignoring his early morning rock flinging. He tried a couple more times before pausing and then yelling up to me.

"Come on, Christa. Please talk to me."

I stayed on my bed, pointedly silent.

Daniel threw a couple more rocks, and then began singing at the top of his lungs.

"Come on, baby, come to your window!!!"

Well, one might call it singing, I called it yelling. More importantly, the slur of his words indicated that Daniel was drunk. Also, he'd sang the lyrics wrong.

I blew out a sigh. The ping of rocks hitting the window

would hardly alert anyone to Daniel's presence, but his yelling sure would.

From the room next to me, I heard my brother, Jackson, throw open his window. "What the fuck, Daniel?" he hissed, before tossing something at Daniel. The object must have hit, because I heard a thud before Daniel yelled again.

"Tell Christa to come down, man," he implored.

I heard my brother mutter "Jesus Christ," before his window slammed shut. A few seconds later he stormed into my room.

"You better handle your wolf, Christa, before I fucking put him down."

I winced at my brother's casual cursing. I was by no means a saint when it came to foul language, but I definitely didn't use profanity as often as some of the people around me.

Vulgar language or not, Daniel had struck a nerve with this whole Lana thing. "I have a gun on the shelf in my closet. Loaded with silver bullets, and ready to go," I offered.

Jackson stared at me in disbelief for a moment before shaking his head. "I don't know what your boyfriend did to piss you off, but he's gonna wake up Dad, Nana, and Pops, so you might want to go down and talk to him." Jackson paused for a moment and crinkled his nose. "Actually judging by the smell, he's pretty drunk so you might want to have him come up here and sleep it off."

Jackson was the only person who knew about Daniel and me, and only because it had become too hard to hide it from him, especially since we lived in the same house, with his room right next to mine, and unfortunately, this particular interaction had become commonplace.

He was also the only member of my family who knew I was an Alpha werewolf. I'd been forced to tell him the truth after he'd fallen victim to Brendan, who had orchestrated Jackson's kidnapping, beat him mercilessly, and then carved the Rogue symbol into Jackson's chest. He'd left Jackson for me to find, broken and bloody atop my Alpha's Throne. After that, I'd had no choice but to tell Jackson who I was and why this had happened to him.

What had happened to Jackson tore at me. He's my little brother, and I want him to be safe. He isn't a werewolf. In order to keep family from fighting for power, if a child is destined to be an alpha, then none of their siblings will inherit the werewolf trait. A thought struck me, and I gasped. Since finding out that Brendan was the rogue who had been trying to destroy my family and me, I'd always wondered how he had managed to do it, especially since Brendan had been with Daniel and me when Jackson had gone missing and when he was found.

In light of the new information about Brendan just being a pawn, and not the rogue leader, I finally put the pieces together.

If Jackson noticed my epiphany, he gave no indication, for which I was thankful. I wasn't in the mood to go into details about what had happened earlier in the day.

My brother stared out my window. Clicking his tongue in disgust, he turned to me. "Christa, Daniel just peed in Nana's flowers." He looked out the window and then back at me. "He just flopped face first into the pissy flowers."

I sighed in exasperation. "I can't just leave him like that, can I?"

Jackson grinned and shook his head. "Nah. If you left him there, you'd have to explain him to Nana in the morning, and I'm pretty certain that wouldn't go well."

I afforded Jackson a small smile. "I'm going down there to get him. Will you help me? I don't think that I'll be able to drag him into the house and up the stairs by myself."

Jackson pursed his lips. "Yeah. I guess." He wagged a finger at me. "But you owe me."

I shrugged. "What's new?" This wasn't our first rodeo, after all.

Jackson and I made our way down the stairs and out the front door, tiptoeing all the way so that we didn't wake anyone.

We went around to the side of the house, where my grandmother's prized flowerbeds played bed to my unconscious boyfriend. I bent down and whispered into his ear.

"Time to get up now, Daniel."

He groaned in response.

I stood back up and tapped him in the ribs with my foot. He didn't stir.

Looking over at Jackson, I shrugged. "Nothing to it but to do it, I guess."

Jackson nodded in response. "I'll get his feet, you get his head."

We set to our task, shivering from the cold wind that had blown in with the winter and was still present now in March. We lifted Daniel and began our slow journey toward the front of the house.

The wind blew again, and I froze, loosening my hold on Daniel as I did.

Jackson grunted, understandably frustrated. He had to pick up the slack or Daniel would fall to the ground.

"What the hell? I can't carry this dude on my own, Christa."

"Shh." I hissed. I needed to concentrate.

I sniffed at the air again, and the hairs on the back of my neck stood up. I could sense something in the yard with us. Something not human, but not werewolf either.

"Put Daniel down," I told my brother, lowering Daniel's head until he was back on the ground. I kneeled down next to him, a protective feeling crawling up my spine.

Something had invaded my territory, and whatever it was didn't belong in the human world or mine.

Jackson had finally caught on that something wasn't right. "What's going on, Sis?"

I couldn't answer. I scanned the area, searching for the source of the unusual scent. Frantically, I looked back and forth, up and down. I just couldn't pin point where it came from.

Finally, I saw a shadowy figure out in the street.

Whatever it was, it stood on two hind legs. It stood tall, coming in at around six feet. From where I stood, I couldn't make out any details, but my keen survival instinct told me that I should be concerned.

"Jackson," I said quietly. "Back up carefully, go inside, and call Brock. Tell him to come now."

Jackson didn't waste time, immediately backing up. A few seconds later, I heard the sound of the door closing.

I stared at the creature in the street. It didn't move, but some part of me knew that it stared back at me.

I needed to get inside until reinforcements came, but I couldn't leave Daniel defenseless, and I couldn't very well carry him on my own. I needed him to wake up.

Shaking him slightly, I looked down at Daniel. "Please wake up," I begged, but I might as well have been talking to a statue.

I tried again to no avail.

Looking back at the street, I saw the creature cock its head to the side, but it made no other movement.

I shook Daniel again. Still nothing.

The creature in the street looked up at the sky.

I stared at it mesmerized.

It howled, and I screamed covering my ears, as the most horrible sound I'd ever heard split through the air. The howl made my skin crawl, carrying both the sound of a feral werewolf and the shrieks of a madman.

Nothing about that sound could be called natural.

Preoccupied, I staring at that creature, praying that the awful sound would end.

I still stared at the creature in the street when something slammed into my left side like a battering ram.

CHAPTER TWO

The hit the creature landed on me put Daniel's earlier attack to shame. Daniel might have been like a Mack truck, but this thing hit like an adult-male sized, speeding freight train sending me rolling backward, head over feet. I rolled a few times before finally stopping.

I shot up fast, not bothering to assess the damage to myself. Pain exploded through my midsection, but it didn't matter as thoughts of protecting Daniel race through my brain.

I darted a glance over to where Daniel lay in the grass. The creature hadn't noticed him, probably because his focus stayed on me as he circle me. It didn't make a move towards me, instead just walked around me, assessing me.

Up close, I took in what the creature looked like. It wasn't easy to process. Neither man nor wolf, but rather some sort of mix of the two, it stood up right on its hind legs, like I'd observed before. Fur covered his body and arms, which were very muscular, but still maintained a human look, despite the fur, until I looked down to where hands should be. Instead of hands, the creature had giant paws equipped with razor sharp claws.

I found the creature's face most startling, something straight out of a horror movie, with yellow eyes and a snout that protruded from its face, complete with sharp, saliva dripping teeth.

As I'd noted before, this monster stood tall, towering over my human form, but I would put down money that if I shifted we would be a pretty even match.

A new problem presented itself when the monster from the street joined his buddy, and the two them closed in on me.

I had to think quickly. One wolf-man stood in front of me, the other stood behind me. If I moved fast enough, I could dodge to either the left or the right and shift, but I wasn't sure how fast these guys really were.

Daniel's body sprawled to my right, closest to me and my house. This presented a problem because Daniel was close enough to me that if I chose to go that way, I ran the risk of shifting and landing on top of him, all two hundred and fifty pounds of my wolf.

On the other hand, if I chose left, it might lead my attackers away from Daniel, whom they still hadn't noticed, and even more, I might be able to lure the creatures away from my house altogether.

It weighed the risk, considering that I had no idea what these things were, or if they were predators like we were. Would they even chase me?

Still, it seemed like the soundest choice.

I geared myself and prepared to jump left, but the appearance of a third creature on my roof gave me pause.

It hopped down from the roof gracefully, landing lithely on both feet.

His companions may not have noticed Daniel, but he definitely did. He walked slowly towards Daniel's undefended body, and I made my decision.

I tensed, and before my attackers had a chance to respond, launched myself sideways and through the air towards Daniel and his very own attacker.

I shifted in the air before landing, luckily, in between Daniel and the wolf-man, teeth bared and snarling.

My wolf, on four feet, was easily six feet tall, two hundred and fifty pounds of snow-white fur. An impressive, intimidating sight.

Or so I'd thought.

The wolf-man cocked his head to the side, and if I didn't know any better, I'd say he grinned.

Whatever he did, it caught me off guard. The gesture seemed entirely too human for his ugly mug.

I felt a little offended that this thing and his companions

weren't running for the hills at the sight of me. I was nearly as tall as they were, and I definitely outweighed them.

I toyed with the idea that maybe they didn't realize what they were up against anymore than I knew what they were.

Behind me, I could hear the other two monsters approaching, snapping their jaws as they came, but I kept my eyes locked in a stale mate with the one in front of me, and I wasn't going to turn around.

I didn't need to, the one in front of me shot a look at the two behind me, and I heard them whimper before shuffling back.

I didn't care about them. This guy had looked away.

Check mate, bitch. I thought to myself, before sinking into my hindquarters and pouncing toward the creature in front of me.

Check mate, my ass. The wolf-man back handed me casually as though swatting at a fly. Flying backward through the air, I hit the wall of my house with a painful crack.

I yelped, knowing without a doubt I'd broken a rib or two.

I recovered quickly to discover that these new monsters did, in fact, like to hunt.

The one who'd hit me turned toward me, abandoning Daniel for a moment, while the other two flanked him on either side, making a V-formation.

I recognized it. It was one of our favorites, too, cornering a lesser animal and attacking as a group.

I watched as they approached me slowly, in unison, taking their time.

They were playing, and I didn't like their game.

These things had not behaved at all like I expected. Some things were so strange. Their strength outmatched mine, and despite their oafish appearance, intelligence lurked. More concerning, they didn't care about looking away when challenged.

On the other hand, they behaved so much like us. They clearly traveled in packs, and hunted efficiently. We used the V-formation because it effectively cornered our prey. If the hunted went forward, it hit the leader. If it went to either side, one of the flanking wolves would be able to dart out and stop it.

I almost found humor in this odd turn of events. The predator becomes the prey.

Cornered like the animals my pack and I hunted. It seemed a crappy way to die.

With no other options, I did the only thing I could think of.

I threw back my head, and I howled.

It was clear that my howls grated against their nerves similarly to the way theirs did mine because they were distracted momentarily.

I felt my lip pull back in some approximation of a wolfy grin. With their attention on me, they hadn't noticed what I'd already scented until it was too late.

The answering howls gave me hope. My pack had arrived.

The leader regained his composure and nodded to each of his companions. They glanced briefly at me before each tore off in either direction to meet my pack.

They were in for a treat. I had no doubt my pack would tear them apart.

The leader stared at me again, and this time his face held no intimation of humor. I knew without a doubt that he wanted blood.

Too bad for him, it wasn't going to be as easy as he thought. I would fight him, broken rib and all.

More importantly, the snarling sound from behind him indicated that Daniel had woken up

And boy, was he pissed off.

My opponent turned and looked at Daniel, clearly surprised to see him, but not altogether worried about him.

I met Daniel's eyes, and nodded, the gesture simple but conveying so much between us. Daniel's returning nod told me he understood.

The creature's attention stayed on Daniel, clearly deeming

him the bigger threat. The joke was on him. I didn't think that Daniel or I would be able to take this guy down on our own, but together we were a force to be reckoned with.

The two of us pounced, Daniel attacking the creature from the front, jaws clamping onto his throat, while I hit his back, burying my claws deeply into his muscle.

The wolf-man howled in pain, the sound causing me to tense, thus embedding my claws even deeper into his back.

Disoriented, the creature began backing up. Too late, I realized his aim as he began slamming me repeatedly into the wall of my house. Each time I hit, the house shook, the force knocking loose pieces of the exterior and sending stucco raining down on me.

The pain grew unbearable as I felt my ribs protest every time my body came in contact with the house, but I would not loosen my hold on the monster I fought. Without a doubt, I knew that Daniel would not be able to fight this guy on his own. He needed my help, even if I was getting pretty banged up.

The monster tore at Daniel, while he kept backing me into the wall. I met Daniel's eyes again, and I could see fear etched on the features of his face, something I wasn't used to from him. The moment of realization proved enough for the creature to get the best of me and this time when I hit the wall behind me, I felt my hold on him slacken. I fell to the ground in a useless heap, breathing shallowly.

I heard a howl of outrage as Daniel realized that I might be seriously hurt, and then another more grating howl from the wolf-man as Daniel's teeth tore into his neck with vicious ferocity.

Despite the fact that Daniel's teeth were buried in him, the wolf-man did not falter as his fists and claws beat in Daniel's back, tearing away fur and flesh every time he pulled away.

My heart thundered traitorously as I realized that Daniel was the one in mortal danger. I tried to pull myself up off the ground. Tried to summon enough strength to attack, but every time I tried to get up, my legs gave out, and I flopped back down onto my stomach.

The monster tore into Daniel again and I heard him cry out in pain. In return, I began to whimper, fearing the worse for the man I loved.

I would not lay here and watch Daniel Hawthorne be torn apart. I steeled myself, took as a deep a breath as I could manage, and began to stand on my wobbly legs. I'd just started to take a step toward Daniel and his opponent when I heard the most lovely sound.

Ping ping. The sounds of bullets tore through the air. A sickening thud indicated that one hit Daniel's adversary and a few seconds later the two of them crashed to the ground, Daniel rolling off the monster's lifeless form as soon as they hit, and shifting back to human form.

As soon as I saw him, limping and bloody, but upright and mostly safe, I collapsed onto my belly once more, shifting back to human form as I went down.

No sooner did I hit the ground then my gun-slinging savior hit her knees beside me. Her light, almost honey-colored brown eyes assessed me carefully and with utmost concern. I wasn't surprised to see her instead of Daniel at my side. I knew that he held back the rest of my pack, the ones who hadn't set off after those crazy weird hybrid wolves. He'd made the right choice. As a still semi-new alpha, the last thing I needed was for my pack to see me in a compromised situation, lest one of them decided to get ballsy and try to finish me off.

"Shit, Christa, are you okay?"

I winced and shook my head. "No Des. Not particularly," I managed to groan out to Destiny Dissaro, my best friend and an agent of The Lunata, the secret group of ninja-human bad-asses tasked with helping werewolves keep their existence secret, as well as helping police any of us who got out of line.

I ached right down to my bones, a deep, relentless throb which ensured that I would be down for a minute.

Unfortunately, I didn't have time to lie in a helpless heap in my yard. The front door started creaking open, and considering the commotion that had just taken place, I didn't think that Jackson would be the only one coming out.

I panicked slightly, my only thoughts being that I lay belly down in the yard with no clothes on. Shifting into wolf form had pretty well shredded the clothes I'd come out in. Worse still, an equally naked group of men and women surrounded us.

I shot a help me look at Des, who quickly stuffed the gun she held into the waist band of her pants before she gave out two sharp whistles that had the werewolf in me groaning.

Without any other words, the members of my pack shifted back into wolf form and took off towards Les Loups-Garous, presumably.

Only one wolf stayed behind, his looming black form slinking into the shadows around the corner of my house, where he could remain unseen, but still watch me with no trouble.

Des looked down at me with sympathy. "You know what you gotta do, kid."

I grimaced. I did know what I had to do. I'd run this drill a thousand times since becoming the Alpha and coming to terms with the fact that as such, I'd put a huge target on my family's back.

"Fuck." I whimpered as I steeled myself and shifted back into wolf form, begrudgingly lifting myself up onto all fours just as my father and grandparents came around the side of my house.

"What the hell is all this racket!" My grandmother yelled, her gray hair still wrapped up in curlers while her slippers sloshed through the wet grass and her robe trailed ominously behind her.

My father and grandfather were at her heels, clearly concerned, but also clearly less alert.

Des kneeled down, pulling a leash from her back pocket and holding it out to me. I bristled and growled. Even though I knew the drill, it didn't mean that the wolf in me delighted at the thought of having a leash slipped around my neck.

Despite my distaste, I let Des put it on. She looked up at my grandmother and smiled.

"Hello, Mrs. Ellsworth. I didn't mean to cause such a ruckus. My dog here took off out of my backyard. I've been chasing her for hours, and apparently, she was chasing some kind of pack of wild dogs or something because she just got attacked by a bunch of them. I didn't know what to do, but luckily some guy came by with a gun, and he shot at the pack of dogs, and they took off, leaving my poor Snookums alone." Des paused to consider, and I growled at her stupid pet name. "Actually, maybe I should be concerned that some guy came by with a gun. What kind of person just runs around at this hour at night shooting off pistols?"

Des looked up at my grandmother, her face as earnest as could be, and I felt a bit of pride well up in me. Des may be a lot of things, but stupid wasn't one of them, and she tried hard to make sure everyone knew that. For her to be standing here, pretending to be clueless just to protect me and my secret, well, it meant a lot.

My grandmother, bless her heart, face as dead-pan as could be regarded Des levelly and said, "Criminals, Destiny. Criminals are the kind of people who run around at night shooting off guns. You're lucky he didn't look at you and decide that he wanted to kidnap or murder a pretty girl tonight."

Expression glib, Des nodded. "You're right, Mrs. E. I can't believe I was so naive."

My grandmother pursed her lips and stared at Des a moment longer before turning on her heel and heading back to the house, my grandfather trailing behind her.

My father stayed back, waiting until both of his parents were safely back in our house before he looked Des over once and then fixed his gaze on me.

He pointed two of his fingers on one hand at us, the gesture reminiscent of scissors and frowned. "I don't know what the two of you are up to, but if you're going to keep this secret about werewolves from my parents, and the rest of the world for that matter, you'd better come up with some better cover-up stories."

If I were in human form, my jaw would have dropped. As it was, the expression on my wolfy face must have been shell-shocked enough, because my dad pursed his lips at me, making him look strikingly like my grandmother at that moment, and shook his head. "Your mother would have never let this happen. And even if she had, she would have had a much better story. Now go on and get to whatever pack meeting, collateral damage assessing thing you're going to have to get to," he finished, waving us off as he turned and made his way back into the house, all the while muttering about how the whole lot of us were amateurs.

I looked up at Des, whose face held as much blank shock as I felt. My father's words rooted me to the spot, confusion and surprise warring for prevalence in my mind.

Somehow, and without me ever knowing, my dad knew about me and the pack. Not only did he know, and never said a word I might add, but he seemed okay with it -aside from the fact that he clearly thought I was doing a terrible job as Alpha.

For the second time in one night, I felt the world swirling beneath me, and then go completely dark.

I woke up in Daniel's bed at Les Loups-Garous, surrounded in the warm cocoon of his silky sheets. Of course, he wasn't in here with me. That went against his whole "protecting my innocence" code. I looked over at the big chair in the corner of his room, empty as this bed felt, and concern washed through me. I'd thought for sure that Daniel would have stayed by my side, yet he wasn't here.

I sat up, looking around and wondering where he could be before I spotted him sitting in the ivory bench on the balcony outside his bedroom, staring up at the moon while he absentmindedly took sips of his signature drink, a bloody mary.

I watched him a moment, appreciating the way the silver light of the moon danced across his shoulder length brown hair. Once again, my mind reminded me that he was too beautiful for me to ever truly comprehend.

I sighed, my heart aching with fear that someday Daniel might realize how much I paled in comparison to him, and that he would leave.

The alpha wolf in me flared with irritation, reminding me once again, that it didn't matter how I saw myself, what mattered is that Daniel saw something in me that I couldn't.

I sighed again and stood, happy to note that someone, probably Des, had managed to wrestle my unconscious body into a pair of faded blue jeans and plain white tee-shirt, before I tip-toed across the bedroom to the French doors that opened onto Daniel's balcony.

I silently stepped outside, not wanting to interrupt Daniel's quiet time with idle chit-chat and made my way over to where he sat.

He smiled up at me, patting the bench next to him, inviting me to sit. I obliged, cuddling myself close to him, as he wrapped his arms around me.

The two of us sat like that, staring up at the moon, in contemplative silence for a few minutes before Daniel leaned forward and kissed me gently on the cheek.

"I'm sorry I didn't tell you about Lana. I just didn't know how. Everything is just so... precarious, you know? I feel like we're just stuck here, you and me, barely floating, barely being able to be together. Be us. And we have to keep playing these roles. I wanted to officially break it off with Lana, but I wanted to make sure it seemed like it was for the right reason, you know like because we'd just grown apart. I didn't want her to think it was about you. I just thought that we had enough enemies, no reason to make more..." Daniel trailed off, looking me in the eyes, his expression earnest.

I smiled, trying to convey as much understanding in my face as I could, before I reached up and gently stroked his cheek.

His hand snaked up and caught my caressing one, holding it to his face, and for a moment, Daniel's uncertainty caught me off-guard. I resisted the urge to wince, knowing that my anger with him and caused his hesitancy.

I leaned forward and kissed him gently on the lips pulling away just slightly so I could look him in the eyes. "I know, D. None of this is easy, and we're trekking through it the best that we can. And I understand why you have to go, I just wish you would have told me."

Daniel looked away, ashamed. "I should have. And I wanted to. I just couldn't find the right time. I love you, Christa. In this shitty world, full of shitty people, you are the one thing that keeps me fighting. I hope you know that."

I pulled Daniel into me, holding him in a tight embrace, more because I didn't know what to say to his comments than because I craved the contact. Something about his words unnerved me. And for a moment, I feared for him in a much different way than I had earlier during the fight with the weird monsters.

Daniel was a beacon of strength to me and to the others. If he felt this way, it made him dangerous. He sounded suspiciously like a werewolf that was about to give up on humanity. And werewolves that give up on humanity go rogue, and eventually have to be put down.

I didn't express my fears to Daniel. Instead, I just continued to hold him for the space of another heartbeat before I pulled myself away from him.

"I love you, too," I told him simply, hoping that my tone didn't betray to him that a part of me was suddenly very afraid of and for him.

If my voice held any uncertainty, he didn't catch it. He just beamed at me, soaking in the words I had spoken.

We stared for a moment longer before I again broke the silence. "We have to have a pack meeting," I told him. "We have to talk about those weird creatures that attacked us."

Daniel nodded in agreement and then shot me a puzzled look. "You don't want to talk about the fact that your Dad knows what we are?"

I closed my eyes and pinched the bridge of my nose, sighing deeply. "I can only deal with one thing at a time. Right now, it's the pack. When I get home, or maybe tomorrow, I don't know, I'll probably need to have a real heart-to-heart with my dad. Right now, we need to call the pack together for a meeting."

Daniel shrugged and took a sip of his bloody mary. "The pack is down stairs already. So is half of The Lunata. Apparently, this is a big enough issue that even Zee showed up."

I grimaced. Des and her boyfriend, Casey Jones, were the agents from The Lunata assigned to watch over our pack, but Hannity Zee was the leader, the Alpha. He and I had a very strained relationship, as is common when you put together two people of power from opposite ends of the spectrum. Often times his methods and mine clashed. More specifically, I constantly tried to find a way to keep peace with humanity while still keeping the existence of werewolves anonymous, and Zee thought that we were all soulless mutts that needed to be put down. Sure, he pretended that he thought most of us were okay, but I kind of felt that deep down he really didn't like a single one of us, and on several occasions, I stated my opinion to his face.

Like I said, our relationship was strained.

"Well, damn," I muttered, not really knowing what else to say.

Daniel shot me a lop-sided smile. "Play nice," he told me, most likely remembering our last encounter, in which Zee had muttered that the world would be a lot better if there were only humans, and I responded in kind by telling him that I thought that the world would be a better place without *him*. And then I called him a word that doesn't bear repeating. It wasn't one of my finer moments, especially since I let the she-wolf in me override my common sense.

I rolled my eyes and returned his grin with a playful one of my own. "I'll try."

Any thoughts I had of trying to play nice immediately left me as we made our way down to the bar area, and meeting spot, of Les Loups-Garous, and I realized that the pack meeting had started... without me.

"What the he-," I started, but immediately I knew what, or rather who, was responsible. "Aidan." I hissed before busting into the room loudly as to make my presence known.

I stomped up to the podium where Aidan casually droned on about how more than ever The Lunata and the packs all around the world needed to come together as a united front to fight this new threat.

I felt anger start from the top of my head and curl all the way through my body and into my toes.

It wasn't even because I thought that Aidan was wrong. I absolutely agreed with what I had heard from him so far. It just infuriated me that, once again, Aidan had over-stepped his boundaries and done my job.

"Great point." I cut in, causing Aidan to pause and look down at me with his usual blank stare.

"Oh good," he drawled, his voice bored. "You're awake."

I managed a tight-lipped smile, a feat considering that I wanted to tell Aidan where he could go shove himself and stepped up next to him on the podium.

"Yeah, I took some pretty wicked hits to the ribs, I needed a minute to heal before I came down. How kind of you to start a meeting in my absence." I told him, trying to keep the venom out of my voice.

I don't think I did a very good job at it, though, because Aidan's eyes narrowed a fraction of an inch before he wiped his face blank once more.

"Anything for you, my dear Alpha," he stated before

turning his attention back to the horde of people crowded into the bar. "I humbly hand over this meeting to our worthy leader, Christianna Sharpova-Ellsworth, Alpha of the North American Pack and True Alpha by birthright."

Aidan stepped out of the way, and I positioned myself in front of the mic set up on the podium, steeling myself to give a speech, probably similar to what Aidan had already said, but mine none-the-less.

I didn't get a chance to talk before I began being bombarded with questions.

"What were those things?" Someone from my pack shouted.

"Why did they attack you?" Someone else shouted.

"How do we stop them?"

"What do they want?"

The pack threw a slew of questions, each one a bullet that tore through me because I didn't know how to answer.

Finally, one question rang out; a question that boiled my blood.

"Are your kind morphing into something more nefarious?"

I didn't have to search to find the person who had asked the question. I could tell by his disgusted tone. Still, my eyes searched until I landed on Hannity Zee, his graying black hair and goatee just as greasy looking as the last time I had seen him; his black pinstriped suit just as perfectly pressed.

He met my narrow-eyed gaze with his own look of disdain. "Well?" he pressed.

"No, Zee. Whatever those things were, they did not come from us," I told him, surprised that I managed to answer so calmly.

"Well, Christa. What are they then?" Zee wasn't the one who had spoken. I looked over, my heart saddened when I realized that the question had come from Casey, Des's partner and boyfriend, and I'd thought my friend, as well.

To be fair, his light brown eyes held no accusation, no

condemnation, just genuine curiosity. He ran a hand through his wavy, light brown hair and spoke again. "If you know anything about these things, you have to tell us. I wasn't there, but Des said she'd never seen anything like them. She said they felt evil and unnatural."

I darted a quick glance at Des, whose amber colored eyes were stared down at the floor, and made a note that she did look visibly shaken-up. It alarmed me because Des never let anything get to her.

I took a deep breath, trying to find the words that could answer as many of the questions posed as I could.

Unfortunately, my mind drew a blank. "I don't know. I don't know what those things are. I don't know why they attacked us, or where they came from. All I know is that Des is right. Whatever they are, they felt unnatural. They operated like a werewolf pack. They hunted like a werewolf pack, but the way they moved, the way they looked, and the way they sounded were seemed different from anything I'd ever seen."

Hannity Zee, who had remained blessedly silent, chose that moment to speak up. "One of mine knew what they were. Or at least, he thought he did," he started, his voice slow and even.

My patience had already worn thin, and I didn't feel like beating around the bush, which I felt Zee was trying to do.

"Well, what are they then?" I asked, sharp enough to convey that I didn't feel like playing games today.

Zee shrugged. "Oh, that I can't tell you. You see, your mutt-loving father had him tossed in prison before any of us could find out. Since the day he killed Jamie Hawthorne, he hasn't spoken a word about what he knows."

At that moment, several people spoke at once.

Me personally, I narrowed my eyes and said, "What did you just call my father?"

Meanwhile, Casey had gone white while he stuttered out his own response. "Do you mean my father?"

But more importantly, Daniel and Aidan had shifted when

Zee had mentioned Jamie, Daniel's mother and Aidan's wife, and were speeding towards Zee in a way that left no doubt that they intended to kill.

My pack looked to me for direction, wondering if they too should shift and attack or not, and the present members of The Lunata drew their guns, pointing them at any person in the vicinity they deemed may be a threat.

Too shocked to think, I froze.

CHAPTER THREE

I may have been struck stupid, and my two main backups may have been irrationally barreling toward Hannity Zee, but Des, sharp as ever, jumped into action.

Her face set with irritation she yelled over at me. "Christa, call off your wolves!" In the next breath she threw herself between Zee and the two wolves. "Drop your weapons! Don't force them to feel threatened!"

Spurred on by her quickness, I began orchestrating my pack. "Daniel! Aidan! HALT!" I screamed before turning to Brock and his partner, Rowan. "Jump in between the Hawthornes and Zee. Keep them from turning this place into a blood bath!"

Daniel skidded to a stop, unable to resist my command. Aidan pressed forward, seemingly unaffected by my authority. Uneasily, my inner wolf told me his resistance could lead to problems. I brushed her aside, knowing that I needed to focus my attention on keeping Aidan from starting a war between us and The Lunata.

Drawing as much Alpha power as I could from my pack, I trained my eyes on Aidan's back and spoke again, "Aidan Hawthorne, I said stop."

Aidan jerked to a stop, turning and training his dark blue wolf eyes on me.

Our gazes locked, and his intent could not be misread.

Aidan Hawthorne was trying to challenge me.

The Alpha wolf took over, and cocking my head to the side in amusement, my lips split into a small smile before I shifted.

I jumped off the podium and sailed through the air, landing lithely on all fours right in front of Aidan.

Staring him down, I puffed myself up so that I looked down at him as opposed to being eye to eye.

In this form, I could feel that Aidan's challenge wasn't

meant to undermine me. He was half-feral, the mention of his dead wife driving his reason away.

I needed Daniel's Omega to come and help calm Aidan, but reaching out through my pack, I realized that even though Daniel had listened to my first command, he had not regained his higher reasoning. Brock and Rowan had already pushed him out of Les Loups-Garous and were trying to convince him to shift back to his human form while he backed himself to the tree-line surrounding the club, growling menacingly.

I was on my own this time, so I did what the werewolf in me urged me to do. I stared Aidan down, trying to draw as much strength from my pack as I could and lending it to him, my wolf pleading with his wolf to do what was right.

At first, I could see no humanity in the aged wolf before me, and a thought at the back of my mind reminded me that when a wolf goes feral, eventually someone has to put it down.

I steeled myself, knowing that someone would probably be me.

I stomped my feet, redistributing my weight to buy myself some time, all the while my wolf still pleading with Aidan's to shift.

Aidan's feral wolf stared stubbornly back at me, and I sank my weight back into my hind legs, preparing to lunge at him.

My movement halted when I glimpsed a flash of realization spark in Aidan's eyes. He blinked, turned to glare at Zee with bared teeth, and then glanced back at me with a whimper.

Relaxing from the lunge position, I took a careful step towards Aidan. He backed up, his haunches brushing against Zee as he did, and I could have sworn I saw Zee shudder and still as though frightened.

As well he should have been.

Aidan blinked at me a couple of more times, each one bringing more and more humanity into his wolf, before he sank down onto his hind legs into a seated position and shifted, his whimpers transitioning to sobs as he transformed from wolf to human.

He continued to cry as his human arms wrapped around his legs and he buried his face against his knees.

Crisis barely avoided, I sprang around Aidan so that I could shift behind the bar, where I had a stash of clothes hidden. I ducked low, throwing on my spare clothes without any unwanted attention and then quickly shot up. I looked over at another member of my pack, a particularly prickly kid around my age.

"James," I barked. He gave me his full attention with no hesitation and I pointed to the back of the club where a closet held emergency supplies as well as the usual janitorial stuff that one would expect.

"Grab Aidan a blanket from the closet so he's not sitting here naked," I told him before turning my attention to Des, who looked like she was ready to bolt from Les Loups-Garous without a moment's hesitation.

Figuring I might as well kill two birds with one stone, I offered her a way to step away from all the excitement without looking weak in front of her superior.

"Des, Daniel is outside, still in wolf form, and about to bolt into the woods. Will you step out and see if you can coax him into calming down? Brock and Rowan are out there now, but I'm not sure how much they're really helping since right now he's only seeing them as threats."

Des watched me for a second, shoulders hunched in a defensive pose before I saw her take a deep breath and shake herself out. "What do you expect me to do?"

"Appeal to his human side as his friend. Any wolves I send out there are going to feel like a threat to him, and that includes me at this point."

Des looked skeptical, and I couldn't blame her. I wasn't confident she was the best person for the job, but on the flip-side there really weren't any other options. I'd meant what I said. Sending a werewolf wouldn't do any good, not even I could go.

Looking around the room, I knew that sending another member of The Lunata who didn't know Daniel would be a disaster; they would only see a werewolf about to go feral, and The Lunata killed feral werewolves. I supposed I could have sent Casey, but that seemed a bad idea considering that the mention of Casey's murderous father had set this whole situation into motion.

No. All things considered, Des was the only one who would be able to help Daniel now.

I implored her with my eyes, begging her to help us. She stared back at me stubbornly, but after a moment I saw her face soften and she rolled her eyes.

She pushed her self away from the bar where she leaned and shook her head at me. "Fine," she started, breezing past me. "But you owe me."

I grinned at her back as she made her way out the door. "You're the best, Des."

I waited a moment before I focused my energy into reaching out through the pack bond that connected me to my wolves so that I could see what happened. I knew that I only had a few spare seconds to check in on Daniel before I needed to turn my attention back to the horde still loitering around Les Loups-Garous, but I wanted to make sure that I hadn't just made a bad situation worse by sending my best friend in the world out to try and calm down the wolf of the guy I'd been secretly dating..

It was such a secret that even Des didn't know about it.

My quick glance showed me enough. I saw that Brock and Rowan had managed to wrangle Daniel into a corner where he wouldn't be able to make a run for the forest unless he tried to go through them. He leaned back, and crouched low to the ground, ears flat as he growled at them.

The trio heard Des approach and Brock and Rowan nodded in her direction, never taking their eyes off of Daniel.

Daniel quit watching them and darted a suspicious look at

Des, snapping his jaws as she took up a position next to Brock.

She put her arms up in a non-threatening gesture and cocked her head at Daniel. "Easy, pup," she started, her tone even and soothing. "Remember me? I'm your pal, Destiny. You love me. You think I'm an angel."

Daniel's wolfy eyes narrowed in disbelief and I swore that he cocked his furry eyebrow.

I smiled, realizing that Des had started to get through to him, and turned my attention back to Hannity Zee and my incredibly pissed off pack.

"What are you playing at?" I hissed at Zee.

Zee looked back at me with a cool expression. "I'm not 'playing' at anything. I am merely stating a fact. A member of my organization tried to warn us against this threat, but was imprisoned before he could give us any solid information. And now he's not telling a soul what he knows."

I clenched my jaw and took a deep breath. "What's the point in bringing him up if he's not going to be able to help us?"

Zee smiled and looked over at Casey, who stared intently at the door that Des had walked out of, clearly wondering if she was okay. "I think we might have someone in our midst who could convince him to talk," he told me slyly.

I turned my attention to Casey, who still hadn't notice that he had become a focal point and noted that Zee might have been on to something. Who better to get this guy to talk than his own son?

I chewed on my bottom lip while I mulled over what Zee suggested before I spoke. "What do you say, Case? Do you think you'd be able to convince your dad to share what he knows?"

Casey slowly turned his attention from the door to me.

"No," he answered simply, his tone flat and expressionless.

"What do you mean 'no'?"

Casey shrugged. "I mean that I'm not going to ask him to tell us what he knows. He's crazy anyways, obviously, and he probably doesn't actually know anything. I don't bother him. He doesn't bother me, and I don't have to be reminded that he savagely murdered someone's mother in cold blood."

I stared in disbelief, amazed that Casey wouldn't even try, just in case maybe his dad actually did know something.

"Are you serious?" I asked, trying not to lose my temper and audibly failing as my rising voice betrayed me. "What if he isn't wrong and is the only person who can help us crack this?"

"Well, then I guess we're all fucked, Christa." I could tell by the tone of his voice that I'd struck a nerve and that Casey barely managed to keep his own temper in check.

"But-" I started, unable to voice my rebuttal because someone interrupted me.

"Stop now, Christianna." This time Aidan spoke from his position on the floor. His face showed that he still felt distraught, but his voice stayed as damnably calm as it ever was. "We do not need Cooper Jones to help tell us what these monsters are."

I put my hands on my hip and looked down at Aidan in disbelief. "Oh really? And I suppose you have some amazing, better idea?"

Aidan managed a small smile that didn't reach his eyes. "Yes. We retrieved the body of the one your werewolf-hunting friend shot and brought it down here. It's as dead as can be, but I think if we were to take it somewhere safe and study it, we might be able to find the answers we seek."

Seeing as I'd passed out from exhaustion and surprise, I hadn't know they'd dragged that creepy corpse here, but I grudgingly admitted that Aidan had proposed a good idea.

I pursed my lips and considered what we should do, all the while knowing I;d ultimately go with Aidan's suggestion. If Casey wouldn't even try with his dad, then Aidan's plan was really the only plan.

I just couldn't give him the satisfaction of knowing he was right that easily.

I let the moment drag on much longer than necessary

before I blew out an exasperated sigh.

"Okay then. I guess we can set up some sort of lab down in the basement and try to figure out what the heck these things are."

Aidan's face scrunched up, indicating that he agree with my idea. His words cemented my observation. "Les Loups-Garous isn't really setup to run experiments the likes of those that we are suggesting."

Fatigue washed over me and gave way to annoyance as the adrenaline from the fight with the monsters and the almost-fight with The Lunata wore off. "What do you think we should do then, Aidan?" I hissed, my voice dripping with venom as I spoke his name.

As usual, Aidan seemed unaffected by my curtness. "Lana's compound in Pennsylvania has long been equipped with a lab where her father, the Alpha of her pack before her, used to do experiments."

I tensed at the mention of her name and resisted the urge to scream. As far as the world knew, Lana and I had no reason to dislike each other, and that included Lana. She had no idea that I'd technically stolen her boyfriend, and throwing a hissy fit about her would only cause suspicion. A suspicion that could reveal the forbidden nature of my romance with Daniel.

"Oh and what? Lana is some sort of bio-chemist?" I asked, figuring that at the rate things were going for me, it would be just my luck that she turned out to be one.

"Don't be silly, Christianna. You've met her. You know her only interests are staying fit and protecting her pack. But as I said, before he died, her father was a scientist. He made sure that the compound there stayed well-equipped, as well as staffed with highly trained professionals. Professionals that Lana has kept on the pay roll."

I tried to figure out if I had any other options, but deep down I knew I didn't.

"Fine. I'll send the creepy wolf-man corpse to Pennsylvania

with Daniel. Lana can deal with it."

I smiled to myself, knowing that Lana may be a badass, but this monster would still scare the bejesus out of her.

Aidan smiled in appreciation, probably just relieved that I hadn't tried to fight him about this before he spoke again. "I may not be a bio-chemist myself, but I know a fair deal about the subject and could accompany Daniel to Pennsylvania and over-see the project. As long as you are amenable to it, at least," he offered.

I may not have been thrilled about having to turn to Lana for help, but the prospect of being rid of Aidan's over-stepping presence cheered me considerably.

I tried not to sound too enthused when I answered. "Sounds like a plan to me. You can travel with the dead monster and Daniel out to Lana's headquarters, and we'll stay here and try to figure out the other stuff that you told me about earlier," I hinted, hoping that he caught on that I meant the fact that we had just discovered that Brendan may not have been the rogue leader after all.

Aidan's keen glance in my direction told me that he caught on. "It's a plan, then."

A gruff cough from the left alerted me to the fact that someone didn't find our plan as great as we did.

I turned to face Zee, the cougher, and pursed my lips. "What?"

Zee stroked his salt-and-pepper goatee and returned my look with one of his own. "I feel it's only right that a member of my team accompany them and assist with the experiments."

I didn't have chance to tell Zee to pound sand myself before Aidan spoke up. "This is pack business. It's of no concern to you or yours."

Zee had been slouched, so when he stood to his full, almost six-foot height, I could tell that he was trying to seem intimidating, a risky move in a room full of werewolves. "I disagree, Aidan Hawthorne. These creatures are not your pack, and as such that makes them as good as rogues where we're concerned. And rogues are a threat to humanity. Which makes them our problem, just as much as yours."

I could tell my Beta geared up to argue, but I cut him off before he got the chance. Whether or not I liked The Lunata, Zee made a good point.

It wouldn't hurt to have an extra pair of eyes watching Daniel, Lana, and Aidan, just to make sure that there no funny business occurred.

"Aidan, I agree with Zee. They should send someone, too. The Lunata are going to need to know what these things are, what their weaknesses are, if they are going to be hunting them."

Aidan glanced at me with surprise, obviously wanting to argue, but also not wanting to argue with me in front of the pack, for once. "Fine, Christianna." He turned to Zee. "And who do you propose you'll send?"

Zee's almost constant tense face cracked into some approximation of a grin. "Well, me, of course."

Aidan cocked an eyebrow. "You? And who will you leave in charge of your troops?"

Zee shrugged, unconcerned. "Destiny."

Aidan stared at Zee, his poker-face betraying no emotion. "Very well." He turned back to me. "Do you have any objections?"

I had to bite back my elation. Objections? Heck no. The way I saw it, I had just rid myself of two pains in my ass. "Nope."

"It's settled, then," Aidan said, looking back at Zee. "We leave tomorrow morning at 6 a.m. Meet us here."

Zee nodded his understanding. "I'll be here."

I felt like the meeting had gone pretty smoothly, all things considered. Too bad, I didn't remember that in my life, things never ran smoothly. No sooner had the issue inside been resolved, than the problem outside escalated.

Through the pack bonds, I felt Daniel's fight-or-flight reflex kick-in, and in that moment, he inadvertently pulled me into his mind, allowing me to watch the scene in the parking lot unfold.

Daniel stared at Destiny, still growling in his wolf form. She stood stock still, clearly trying not to upset him anymore than she already had. She had one hand up in a calming gesture, but her other hand had moved to her back, where I knew she had a gun stashed.

"Easy, Daniel. Remember, I'm your friend," she spoke softly, trying not to let any fear color her words.

Daniel growled, and stomped the ground in front of him with one of his giant black paws.

Des, her eyes still trained on Daniel, nodded. "Come on now, Bud. We take care of each other remember. We're family."

Daniel's ears cocked up from the flattened position on his head. Des took that to mean that Daniel had begun to listen to her, but I could feel through the pack bonds that this wasn't the case. Daniel had taken issue with her bringing up family, especially since this whole ordeal had been caused because of the mention of his mother.

The miscommunication would prove disastrous. Des took a step forward, thinking things were okay, and meanwhile Daniel read her action as a threat.

Daniel tensed, and quicker than I could register, pounced toward Des.

Des reacted just as quickly. Stepping back and pulling the gun from her back in one fluid motion, she aimed it at Daniel.

She squeezed off two quick shots, both tearing through Daniel's torso and knocking him down.

I tore myself away from watching the scene through the pack bonds so that I could sprint out of the bar to where Daniel lay in a heap in the middle of the parking lot.

Since I had been frozen in place while watching the interaction in my head, I'd been the last one out of the bar, most of the rest of the occupants running out as soon as they heard gun shots.

I pushed my way through the crowd, to where Daniel, now sitting up and in human form, was glaring menacingly at Des. Brock and Rowan were between them, shielding Des from Daniel as best they could.

Des and Daniel looked over at my approach.

"What the hell happened?" I shouted.

Daniel lifted the arm on the side that hadn't been shot and pointed at Des. "She fucking shot me!"

I glanced over at Des, whose flushed appearance showed that she'd been shaken a little more than she let on "Yeah, well, you were coming in for the attack, and at the end of the day it's a lot easier for a werewolf to recover from a gunshot or two than it is for me to recover from a fucking mauling!"

I closed my eyes and took a deep breath, trying so desperately not to lose my cool, and walked over to Destiny.

"Are you okay?" I asked her.

She nodded, but wouldn't look me in the eye. "Mostly. My nerves are pretty well shot, but other than that, I'm okay."

I knew that Des felt terrible for having to shoot Daniel, and I felt terrible for having put her in that position. I put a hand on her shoulder and gave a gentle squeeze. "I'm sorry, Des."

Des smiled thinly. "Not your fault. But if you don't mind, I'm going to get the hell out of here. I know Zee needs to talk to me about whatever happened in there. Honestly, after everything that has happened tonight, I just want to go home, take a bath, and forget about this shitty day."

I totally understood and waved her off as kindly as I could before walking over to Daniel and kneeling. "Are you alright?"

Daniel, who sat in a puddle of quite a bit of his own blood, nodded slightly, although I didn't buy it. He looked really pale, and he'd started to shake, probably from shock.

"Can you stand?" I asked.

Daniel answered with another nod as he attempted to stand. He barely made it to his feet when he looked down and if possible, paled even more. I followed his line-of-sight and my stomach turned uncomfortably as I saw that Des's bullets had torn a rather large chunk of flesh out of Daniel's right abdomen.

Daniel swayed, and I barely had time to register what was happening before he hit the ground, passed out.

I found it to be quite the turn of events, Daniel lying unconscious in his bed while I sat on the chair in the corner terrified that he had been hurt, yet angry that he couldn't have controlled his temper a little better. I mean, he was the Omega, after all. His entire purpose in my pack was to keep things like this from happening.

I suddenly understood why Daniel's anger all those times that I'd found myself in this position. I blamed myself for not being able to keep him safe, and I blamed him for not being able to keep himself safe. It presented quite the conundrum, one I couldn't seem to reconcile in my mind.

The she-wolf reminded me that Daniel was a big boy and had been taking care of himself long before I stepped into the picture. Without a doubt, he would take care of himself long after I was out of it.

I don't know if the insight had been offered to comfort me, but I found it to be more of a bleak outlook than anything else.

At any rate, the role reversal really opened up a new perspective for me. I promised myself that I would do my best to keep out of trouble so that Daniel would never have to experience this feeling of angered worry again.

Daniel had been out for hours. I found myself thinking about all the times that I had been in his position, lying in bed after nearly getting myself killed. I pondered whether took me as long to wake up, and I wondered how he had done it, quietly sitting there waiting for me to wake up so that he could both know that I would be okay, and to berate me for being so careless with my own life.

The she-wolf's internal voice snarled in my ear reminding

me that Daniel constantly overreacted and informing me that I'd turned into a drama queen. We're werewolves. Danger comes with the territory.

The other half of my psyche wasn't wrong. I'd known for quite some time that, as an Alpha, danger followed me, but that didn't mean that I couldn't wish that sometimes things were simpler. Easier.

Nothing in my life could be easy, it just wasn't in my cards. I'd been born into this role, a True Alpha like my mother before me, her mother before her, and so on. As a child, I knew what destiny had planned for me, but somewhere between my mother's death and moving to California, I'd forgotten. Not forgotten, actually. Someone had pushed the memories out of me, someone who probably meant to do me harm. For the life of me, I couldn't remember that person's face. I only had a vague memory of his voice, and it wasn't clear enough for me to recognize it if I heard it again.

When all the repressed memories had broke through, and I remebered what I was, it had scared the bejesus out of me. Daniel had been there for me, helping me grow and become a better Alpha. In the process we had fallen pretty hard for each other.

Our relationship presented its own complications, and eventually those complications would end us, but for now we did the best we could to be there for each other.

Daniel stirred, and I focused my attention on him, instead of my own troubled thoughts.

He mumbled something, but his eyes remained closed.

I wasn't sure if he'd really said anything or not, but either way I got up and stood next to him, bending down so that I could hear him.

"Did you say something?" I asked.

Eyes still shut, Daniel licked his lips and muttered incoherently.

I bit my lip and leaned down even closer to him. "I'm sorry,

I don't understand."

Daniel moved his head to the left, his neck cracking with the movement and cleared his throat before opening his eyes and staring at me. "Your friend fucking shot me," he stated, clear as a bell.

I grimaced. "You pounced at her!" I retorted, trying not to sound defensive, but failing miserably.

Daniel sat up in the bed, the sheet falling away from him and revealing his lean muscular torso, with only a small scar left to indicate what had happened to him just a few hours earlier. "Whatever," he grumbled.

Two emotions warred inside me. I felt ecstatic that he had awoken and seemed fine, but irritation that he had decided to be so nonchalant about the fact that he'd attacked Des soured my happiness.

"Not 'whatever', Daniel!" I shot back, my voice biting with barely contained anger. "No one could get you to calm down. You were more than half-feral and you attacked a human. And not just any human, a member of The Lunata. You could have killed Des, and you're lucky that she hadn't aimed to kill you!"

Despite the ire in my words, Daniel's jaw stayed stubbornly set. "If her damned boss hadn't mentioned fucking Cooper Jones, none of this would have happened."

I took a deep breath, trying to calm my fried nerves. "You're right. Zee should have thought that one through a little more, but he wasn't trying to upset anyone. He truly believed that Cooper Jones could help us solve our little monster problem," I paused and sighed dejectedly. "Too bad he was wrong."

Daniel's head cocked, some of his irritation washing away from his face. "Why?"

I shrugged. "His entire plan to get Jones to talk was based on getting Casey to appeal to him."

"And?"

"And Casey flat out refuses," I exclaimed, my own

frustration lacing my words.

Daniel stared at me disbelievingly. "Why would Casey refuse to talk to his Dad? What happened while I was..." Daniel trailed off, but I knew what he meant.

I blew out another defeated sigh and relayed what had happened to Daniel. He listened with rapt attention, his earlier hostility abandoned, for the moment. When I finished, he leaned back and heaved his own exhausted sigh.

"So, my dad, Hannity Zee, and I are going to transport a dead monster to Lana's labs to try and figure out what these things are all because Casey doesn't want to confront his old man? Wow." In all its irritating glory, Daniel's anger returned, immediately grating against my already frazzled emotions.

"Yeah, Daniel. That's the plan. I don't like it any more than you do. Especially because it means you'll be with Lana that much longer." I couldn't help the ice in my voice and I saw Daniel flinch before his shoulders sagged, clearly not wanting to fight any longer.

As if confirming my observations, Daniel's eyes met mine, an apology evident on his face. "I don't want to fight with you, Christa. I was stupid. I couldn't let go of my anger and it put Des in danger. I'm sorry."

Knowing that I didn't want to fight, but still so on edge, I couldn't help the bite in my response. "Yeah? Well don't tell me. Tell her."

Daniel flinched, and I groaned while running my hands over my face. "Sorry. I think I'm just too emotional after everything that has happened tonight to think rationally," I offered, my voice flat to my own ears.

Daniel nodded, and then closed his eyes for a brief moment before blinking them open and fixing his fatigued stare on me. "Trust me I get it. I wish our lives could just be easy. I wish we could just..." he trailed off for the second time in our conversation, exhaustion evident in the sag of his body.

I could feel my own tiredness taking over me. I stood,

reaching my arms up to the ceiling in a much-needed stretch. "I know, Daniel. But I don't think that's ever going to happen for us." I leaned down, kissing him softly on the lips, hoping that the sweetness conveyed that I couldn't stay mad at him. "For now, though, we have to take what we can get," I murmured against his lips.

I straightened and offered a small half-smile. "It's late, and I need to get to bed. And you need to rest so that you can recover enough to leave tomorrow morning," I told him, reaching down and grabbing his hand gently. "Good night," I whispered before turning to walk away, my hand still resting on his.

Quicker than I'd thought he could manage in his current state, Daniel's hand shot out from under my hand and grabbed my wrist. He pulled me back towards him, his hand abandoning my wrist as I came closer and moving to my back as he pulled me in even tighter.

I bumped into the side of the bed as he pulled me towards him, and he pushed himself up, catching my lips with his. My breath caught, not just from surprise, but from the ferocity of his kiss. This was a much different kiss than what I had grown accustomed to over the last six months. Those were sweet, tender. This reminded me of a time not long ago, when moments like this were stolen and we were trying to lie to ourselves about how we felt. This kiss held fire, and passion, and need.

As his other arm came around me, pulling me from the side of the bed and onto his lap, I felt a swirling tornado of emotion form inside me.

I held onto him as though only he kept me alive, my weariness forgotten in his sudden onslaught of passion. He pulled away from me, suddenly, and just for a moment before he crushed me to his chest and his lips moved to my ear, brushing ever so slightly against the lobe. My lips quivered, and my breath becoming shaky while I waited for what he would do next.

"Will you stay with me tonight?" he asked, the warmth of

his breath hitting my neck and sending shivers down my spine.

Despite that warmth, despite the tingling in my body telling me to say yes, I froze, My body going completely rigid against him.

Daniel, noticing the change, pushed away just enough to look at me, his hooded eyes piercing through me. "Well?" he asked, voice husky.

Well, indeed. Despite my bold advances earlier in the night, Daniel had been right. I was nowhere near ready for what he was offering.

He continued to study me, and I had no doubt I looked like a deer caught in headlights as I stared back with wide eyes. I could feel my mouth trying to move, trying to formulate words, but none were coming out.

Daniel cracked a seductive half smile, and I felt my legs turn to jelly at the gesture. "Come on, kid, you're wounding my pride. Its just a yes or no question." His tone held a hint of mock hurt, although a flash in his eyes told me I may have legitimately hurt him.

I owed him an answer. With a deep, shaky breath, I gathered enough strength to respond. "I...uh... I'm...um..." I stuttered shamefully before finally spitting out what I need to say in a jumbled rush. "Idon't...er...thinki'm...um...readyforthat."

Internally, I groaned, feeling like a damned fool.

Matters were made worse when Daniel pursed his lips together for a fraction of a second and then laughed at me.

I pouted. "What's so funny?"

He bit his lip trying to stifle another laugh. "It's just that I think you misunderstood what I meant. I know you're not ready for *that*, as I've already pointed out. I would just really like it if you stayed here with me."

I narrowed my eyes. "You were laying it on pretty thick for someone who wasn't trying to..." I trailed off, feeling even more stupid than before.

Daniel shrugged, a slight bit of remorse for confusing me

touching the humor in his eyes. "I got carried away."

"Hmpf." I exhaled, sagging a little as his arms tightened around me again.

"Hmpf? Well, will you stay?" he asked again, no humor remaining in his voice.

I paused for a moment, before rolling onto the side of the bed next to him and cuddling in close. "I guess," I told him. "But no funny business," I added with a bit of playfulness.

Daniel's responsed somberly as he flicked off the bed side lamp and draped his arm over me. "I wouldn't dare."

CHAPTER FOUR

After all the excitement, we maybe got three hours of sleep before we had to wake up so that Daniel could set off on his adventure with his dad, Zee, and the dead creature. I'd awoken reluctantly, feeling in no way refreshed from what I could only describe as a nap.

And even though I was awake, barely, I still snuggled in the warm comfort of Daniel's bed while he rushed around getting his things together. I watched him as he moved about, worry filling my mind while I thought about how long he would be gone. No one had any idea. Daniel told me it could take a day or two, or it could take months.

Me, personally? I silently prayed with all the faith I could muster that it would only take a day or so. Pathetic as it sounded, I couldn't shake the fear that Daniel would see Lana and some forgotten feelings would resurface.

After all, wasn't our entire relationship proof of the fluidity of Daniel's emotions? He hadn't even officially ended it with Lana before he ran off with me.

I chewed my lip while I thought, and the she-wolf in me once again bristled, her haughty voice in my head telling me that Lana paled in comparison to what we were. The True Alpha.

Maybe she was right.

Or maybe, sometimes, even being the most powerful entity in our world wasn't enough to keep love from fading.

Daniel paused meeting my eyes from across the room, and his lips lifted in a smile. "You're awake." Trying to push my dark thoughts away, I smiled back. "Barely."

Daniel laughed and threw me a sweatshirt. I sat up and pulled it on over my tank top, stretching out as I did.

He came over and sat next to me on the bed. "Did you sleep okay?"

I nodded. "Yeah. I slept fine."

"Really? You tossed and turned a lot."

I shrugged. "That's weird, I didn't notice."

Daniel put his hand on my thigh. "I did. I barely slept. I just stayed up watching you."

I blushed, hoping I hadn't done anything embarrassing like snore or drool. "Oh. Maybe I have a lot on my mind."

Maybe was an under-statement. I knew I had a lot on my mind, between this new rogue threat, the crazy new monsters, and Daniel leaving to visit his not-quite-ex-girlfriend.

As if reading my thoughts, he pulled me in to him. "I love you, Christa. As long as we remember that, as long as we stay strong for one another, we're going to be okay."

His words washed through me, spoken with so much honesty that I felt my fears ease. I held him back, clutching him as tightly to me as I could.

"I know, D. "It's you and me against the world, even if the world doesn't know it."

Daniel kissed the top of my head before pulling away from me slightly. "The world doesn't need to know it. Only we do."

I smiled at him, my heart filled with so much love for this man that I wished that I could shout it out to the world, but I knew I couldn't. "You probably need to get going. I'm sure your dad and Zee are already downstairs, waiting on you."

"I know. I was just about to leave when I saw you were awake." He stood, still looking down at me. "But, I do have to go." He bent down and kissed me softly before turning and grabbing his overnight bag from the floor.

I called to him as he reached the door. "I love you."

He paused and turned around to look at me. "I love you, too. More than you could ever know."

And then he slid out the door.

I shot straight up, my heart pounding in my chest as I tried to recall my nightmare. No details emerged; the only indication that I'd fallen back asleep and subsequently dreamed of something terrible being the feeling of dread coursing through me.

And the sound of my mother's voice, whispering a warning.

Don't let it break you.

The advice echoed, and while I knew it to be important, I couldn't remember why. Wracking my brain, I yawned and looked over at the alarm clock, blanching as I saw the time.

"Damn."

It was 10 a.m. I knew I would be in trouble when my family realized I wasn't home. My dad may have, somehow, known what I was, but I felt fairly certain that he wouldn't condone an all-nighter at Daniel's house, and that was without knowing the extent of our relationship.

I grabbed my phone and looked down at the screen. "Double damn." I whispered, noticing the several missed calls from my dad.

I still wore the sweatshirt Daniel had given to me earlier in the morning, and I'd slept in my jeans, so I only needed to put on my shoes. I pulled them on quickly and tore out of the bedroom at a solid run, sliding to a stop as I pulled open the door to the stairs that led down into the bar.

I took them two at a time, barely pausing at the bottom before I took off across the club in a sprint.

I didn't even notice anyone sitting down there until I reached the entrance and began fumbling with the deadbolt to get it open.

"Where are you off to in such a hurry?"

I froze, my hand twitching against the deadbolt as my body filled with dread. I closed my eyes, working on slowing my breathing, but not daring to say a word. I hoped that I was still stuck in a nightmare, because there could be no possible way *he* was here.

"Well?"

Triple damn. I turned slowly and looked in the direction of the voice. It took a moment for my eyes to adjust to the dim light in the bar, but once they did, I saw him sitting at a booth, his blue business suit contrasting oddly with the sparkly red upholstery of the bench seat. His hands were folded together on the Formica tabletop, his face unreadable.

"Speechless, Christianna?"

"Uh... Hi, Dad." I sounded guilty. I knew I sounded guilty, but I couldn't understand how the hell he was here.

His hands unfolded, and he lifted one in the air crooking a finger as he beckoned me over to the table. I continued puzzling over how he got into my bar as I made my way over to him.

I watched him the whole time, hoping to see some emotion tinge his face, so that I knew what sort of lecture he had in store, but damn him, his poker-face could rival Aidan Hawthorne's.

I reached the table and slid into the booth across from him, avoiding eye contact at all cost.

"I was on my way home." I offered softly.

He didn't say anything, and I looked up at him. He didn't look at me, instead he glanced around the bar, drinking in every detail.

"It's been a long time since I've set foot in this place," he murmured.

I bit my lip and waited for my dad to turn his attention to me, all the while trying to figure out what I would say to him.

My dad still didn't say anything to me, and I started to feel very much like I'd interrupted a very private moment for him.

When I cleared my throat, he reluctantly turned his attention to me.

"I'm sorry. The pack meeting finished so late that I ended up staying here on the couch in the office." I'd never been a liar before finding out I was an Alpha werewolf. I told myself that I had to tell a lot of stories to protect the pack's secret. Even still, I cringed internally as that particular lie slid through my teeth.

If my Dad could tell I'd lied, his face didn't show it. "I figured as much," he started before he started looking around again. "Your mother spent a lot of time here, obviously. After she died, I swore I would never step foot here again." He stopped and fixed his gaze on me once more. "I'm not mad at you."

Confusion washed over me. "If you're not mad, why are you here?"

His lips pursed. "You didn't come home. After whatever happened last night, I wanted to make sure you were safe."

"How did you know what I was? How did you get in?" I asked, the questions coming out unwarranted.

"I have a key," he stated, answering my second question first. His head cocked to the side as he regarded me levelly. "And of course, I knew what you were. I was with your mother for a long time. She kept her secret at first, but after she realized that she wanted to start a life with me, she felt she owed it to me to show me the truth."

I noted his wording, still confused. "You mean she told you about the packs and what she was."

He nodded. "She tried telling me at first," he chuckled, and I got the feeling that my dad was a million miles away replaying memories from long ago. "Imagine what I thought. I was terrified. I thought this woman that I was falling in love with was insane. I offered to help her. I told her that I could get my mother to pay for the best psychiatrists in the world. She was so offended that I thought she was crazy, that I didn't believe her words. So she showed me."

My eyes went wide. "Mom shifted in front of you?"

"Oh yeah. If I was terrified when I thought she was nuts, I can't even describe how scared I was when she morphed into a giant wolf right in front of me. I would have peed myself if not for the fact that I thought I was stuck in a nightmare."

"But, eventually you accepted her and what she was."

"Eventually." My dad paused to take a deep breath. "I'm not going to pretend that I accepted it right off. After the shock wore off, and I realized that it wasn't a dream, I left her."

My mouth popped open and shock jolted through me. "You left her?"

"I was scared, Christa. And looking back, I'm not proud of it. I'm even less proud of what I'm about to tell you." He swallowed, the words clearly difficult for him.

"After a couple of months of the worst heart-break you could ever imagine, I came to my senses. We got back together and got married, then after a while, you came along. I accepted what your mother was. And I always knew there was a good chance you or Jackson could end up like her, but I prayed every day that you guys had somehow escaped that fate."

Anger washed over me. He talked about what I was like it was a curse. He talked about what my mom had been like she was a monster. "Then you never accepted what she was. What we are." I spat, not bothering to hide the accusation in my voice.

My father's face twitched, hurt washing over his features. "No, Christa. I accepted who she was. But I saw what you didn't get to. This life," he paused and swept his hand through the air, gesturing around the bar. "It takes a toll on a person. Protecting this secret, protecting her pack, it consumed her. Eventually, a bit of madness did touch her, and she started to become paranoid. She began locking herself away, hiding here for hours for fear of her life. She said that she could feel unrest ripple through the pack magic. Eventually, this life cost your mother hers."

"You don't think our secret deserves to be protected?"

He shook his head. "Of course I do. I just wish it could be someone else's burden."

I gritted my teeth, knowing my dad just wanted to protect me, but so angry that he didn't understand. "I don't. This is *mine*, just as it was hers."

"It is yours. It didn't matter how far I took you away, it found you. I'd just hoped that I could have saved you from it."

I stood, my temper no longer under my control as the she-wolf took over. "You knew what you were doing! You knew that by taking me away, you would make sure that I could never shift! Did you know that if I'd never shifted, I would have eventually died?"

Just as quickly as my anger took over, my father's broke through his calm facade. He slammed his fist on the table before rising himself. "I did what I thought I needed to do to protect you! I did it out of fear, and I was wrong for it. But I couldn't bear to watch you suffer the way she did. I couldn't bear to watch my daughter crumble the way my wife did! I couldn't sit back and allow this *world* to consume you like it did her. And I couldn't allow you take your own life because of it!"

My anger dimmed as understanding washed over me. He didn't know. He still thought my mother had killed herself. I slumped down onto the seat as the bitterness flowed away from me.

"Mom didn't kill herself. She was murdered."

Surprise from my words washed over my father, visibly arresting him. "No. You're mistaken. The little Hawthorne boy, the younger one, he was there he..." He trailed off as he saw my shaking head.

"He killed her. And he tried to kill me, too. If it wasn't for the wolf inside of me, and Daniel, he would have succeeded. He wanted to overthrow us. He's dead now."

My dad recovered quickly. "I always knew something was off about his story, " he stated, as he, too, slid back into his seat. He rubbed his hands over his face and then spoke again. "So, it was him. I guess you're safe now, at least." He glanced at me hopefully. I felt a jolt in my stomach as I realized I had to tell him the truth.

"No. I'm far from safe. He was just a pawn. There's someone out there, a rogue. Someone who is trying to gather support from the packs to start a war."

He stared at me for a long time, his face giving nothing away, before he spoke again. "If there is a rogue out there, it means you are no longer safe in your grandmother's home."

"None of us are safe. Even without the rogue, there's another threat. Some type of monster that none of us have ever seen before." I launched into telling him about the events from earlier, what had lead to all the commotion. I left out the parts about Daniel, staying away from telling him anything that would shine a light on our relationship. I wasn't ready for my dad to know.

I saw my dad's jaw clench as he considered what I said. He seemed to be warring with the thoughts in his mind. Finally, he sighed again and reached across the table to grab my hand. "Then I guess it's time," he whispered.

"Time for what?"

"You and Jackson are my greatest loves. I would do anything to protect you. Your mother warned me that there might come a time, someday, that I would have to choose. She said there might come a day when I wouldn't be able to protect you both, and I would have to make a choice."

Dread filled me. "What are you saying?"

"I love you, Christa."

"I love you, too, Dad. But I still don't understand."

"I tried to keep your mom with me, when I should have let her go, Christa. I thought that being with me would keep her safe, even when she told me that there was a safer place for her in the middle of the unrest she felt. I ignored her pleas. I should have listened. I won't fail her again." My father stood and came around to stand next to me, before bending and kissing the top of my head.

"You are no longer safe in my home. And because you are no longer safe, Jackson is no longer safe. I can't help you anymore. The things you face, they are beyond my ability to defend you against. For me to allow you to stay with us, I would be condemning you to certain death. But there is a place, a fortress for your kind. It was specifically built to protect the True Alpha and her pack in times of need."

"Are you kicking me out?" I asked in disbelief.

He shook his head. "No. I'm insuring your survival. And with your removal from our home, I am insuring Jackson's survival."

Tears filled my eyes. I knew that my father didn't want to toss me out. I knew that he only meant to protect me, but his words hurt nonetheless.

"You think I would let anyone hurt Jackson or you or anyone in our family?"

"No. Not at all. But I also know that none of us can keep you safe any longer. You're always welcome to be with us, but the truth is, you need to be surrounded by your pack. They are the ones that will keep you alive where we would fail."

My chin quivered, but I understood what my dad meant. He would always be there for me, but he couldn't help me any longer. "Where is this place? Where should I go?"

My dad looked around and groaned, no doubt taking in the scene of the dingy bar around him. "Here, Christa. Les Loups-Garous is the safest place for you to be. It's the Alpha's home. It was where your mother's family lived before she gave it to Aidan Hawthorne, and he turned the second floor into a bar. It's the home of the True Alpha, and as much as it kills me to let you go, I know that it's time for you to go home."

I wiped the tears from my cheeks and stood, kissing my dad on the cheek as I did. I could not allow myself to be sad. I understood the sacrifice my father made. He wanted to be able to keep me with him. He wanted to be the one who could protect me, but knew he couldn't. Despite his personal feelings, he resigned himself to do the one thing he knew he could to keep me from harm's way.

With that acceptance, my father and I spent the rest of the morning discussing my permanent relocation to Les Loups-Garous.

CHAPTER FIVE

My phone rang in the middle of me telling Brock where to put the giant box of clothes he carried up the stairs. I pulled it out of my pocket as I pointed to a corner of the office I was going to be gradually turning into my room.

"Hello?" I answered.

"Christianna, I'm sending Eloise to the store to pick you up some groceries. I don't know what the Hawthorne's keep in the fridge there, but I'll not have you eating take-out every night."

I cringed at my grandmother's stern voice, still just thankful that she'd accepted my moving out with such grace.

She'd argued a bit when my father and I first told her that I'd decided to rent a room at Daniel's apartment. After pointing out that I was eighteen, and would be graduating soon, she acquiesced, but not before giving me a set of stipulations.

One said stipulation was that Eloise, my mother's maid, would be coming twice a week to keep the apartment clean since she apparently thought that Daniel kept his apartment like some sort of slum.

The other condition was that I had to come every Sunday for dinner. I had no problem accepting it, especially since my grandmother's maids had always served the most mouth-watering food I'd ever tasted.

"Okay," I responded to her.

"Okay? Well, what do you need? I'm not a mind reader, and neither is Marguerite."

I flinched at my grandmother's mistake. "Eloise," I corrected.

"What? Oh, yes. Eloise. Poor Marguerite is dead."

Eloise was Marguerite's replacement, and my grandmother still hadn't gotten over it. She'd adored Marguerite, most of the time, even though she constantly complained that Marguerite was incompetent. Unfortunately, Marguerite had been murdered by Brendan as a warning to me.

Hearing her name caused the guilt I still barely held back to resurface.

"Well? What do you need?" My grandmother asked again, breaking through the sadness I felt.

"Uh, I don't know. I haven't had a chance to check the refrigerator."

My grandmother tsked. "Well, are you at home?"

I looked around the cozy upstairs apartment, not quite ready to call it home, but knowing what she meant.

"Yes."

"Then go look in the refrigerator."

I suppressed a sigh and walked down the hall to the small kitchen area that housed a few cabinets, some counter space with a microwave, a little white refrigerator with an attached freezer, and a small electric range and oven.

I threw open the cabinets and saw that they were completely empty. Turning to the refrigerator, I pulled it open and saw more of the same. Damn her, my grandmother had been on to something.

"There's no food at all," I told her.

I heard my grandmother tsk again and I could envision her eye roll in my mind. "Very well, then. I will tell Eloise to buy all the essentials. I love you. Good-bye."

Before I could reply, she hung up the phone. I stared down at it in awe. "Love you, too," I mumbled.

I walked back down the hall, where Brock made his way up the stairs with another box. "Same room, Boss?" he asked.

I nodded. "Yeah."

Brock snorted. "You should kick Danny-boy out of his room and make him turn this shit-hole office into his room."

"Maybe later. Gotta take baby steps, you know?"

Brock nodded. "So he still hasn't called you back?"

"Nope. Boy, is he gonna be surprised when he comes home

and realizes he's got a roommate." I kept my tone light-hearted, but in reality, I sweated bullets. It had been three days since Daniel left and my dad and I decided I would move into Les Loups-Garous. In that time, Daniel hadn't called once.

Brock laughed and bounded back down the stairs.

The radio silence had me on edge all by itself, and the added stress of moving into his apartment without his knowledge or consent had me flinching every time the phone did ring.

I stepped into the room that had formerly been an office and looked around. I'd moved the desk to the corner of the room and crammed in a small twin-sized bed with an even smaller dresser. The over-packed room didn't allow much space for moving around, but most of my clothes and pictures fit in so it would work for now.

I supposed that I could have just stayed in Daniel's room in his absence, but it felt weird to move into his apartment and sleep in his room, especially since he still had no idea that I now technically lived here.

Brock came back up the stairs, another box in his hands. "This is the last one, Christa," he told me, setting it down on top of the others in the corner and turning to hand me the keys to my car, a red 1969 Mustang that my grandfather had been letting me use. Yesterday, he'd gifted it to me permanently, for which I was grateful, when my father and I had announced my plans to move out.

We'd told everyone that I spent so much time at Les Loups-Garous because I had a part-time job doing their books. I obviously did not actually work at the bar, and seeing how being an Alpha left little time to get a job, I wouldn't have been able to afford a car if my grandfather hadn't given me the Mustang

I took the keys from Brock and stuffed them into my purse on the dresser, checking the time on the alarm clock. It was six thirty on Monday night, and Les Loups-Garous would be opening in an hour and a half. Normally, Daniel deejayed, and Brock acted as a bouncer, but we'd had to switch some staff around with Daniel gone. For the time being, Brock would fill in as the deejay, and Rowan, Brock's right-hand man, and best friend, would man the doors by himself.

"You hungry?" I asked him, my own stomach growling.

"Yeah. What do you have in mind?" he asked.

"I can make grilled cheese and tomato soup," I offered. Eloise had come and gone with more groceries than the tiny kitchen could hold, but I couldn't be ungrateful. At least, I could feed the masses, and by masses, I meant Brock.

"I'll take four, please," Brock stated, catching me off guard.

"Four what?"

"Four sandwiches."

I blanched, wondering how in the world he could eat four grilled cheese sandwiches, but setting to my task anyway.

I'd just started making Brock's fourth sandwich, the first three of which he consumed as soon as they came off the stove, when the phone rang.

"Hello," I answered without even looking at the caller I.D, my attention focused on flipping the sandwich before I burned it.

"Hey," Daniel's voice broke through the line freezing my hand mid-flip.

"Hey," I answered carefully, afraid that my tone would give away the apprehension I felt about telling him I'd moved myself into his home.

"Is everything okay? I just saw that you called like fifty times." His voice carried a hint of annoyance mixed in with playfulness.

"I did not call fifty times. It was only like thirty. Forty tops."

Daniel's responding laugh fell short when Brock yelled over to me. "Woman! Sandwich! I must eat before I open the bar!"

"Is that Brock?" Daniel asked slowly.

"Yes," I answered, equally as slow.

"Are you making him food?"

"Yes."

"At your house?"

"Er. No. Funny thing, I'm, uh, making him food at *our* house."

Daniel coughed, and then the line went silent. I waited a moment before speaking, hoping he hadn't hung up. "Are you still there?"

Daniel's exasperated sigh broke the silence over the line. "Yes. I'm a little confused about a couple of things. First of all, what the hell is going on? And second, why are you making Brock food?"

In my typical fashion, I chose to answer his second, easier question, first. "He was hungry. I was making food. I offered him some, and he accepted."

"You don't make me food."

"Well, maybe I will now."

"Now that you're living in *our* house?" Daniel's careful tone effectively hid any emotions he must have been feeling.

"Mmhmm."

The line fell silent again, and then Daniel burst into a hearty laugh. "Okay. Very funny. Seriously, where are you guys? Bah, making Brock food! Do you even know how to cook? Living together? What a weird thing to joke about!"

He laughed heartily for a while more, before I cut in, my hurt feelings coming through. "I can cook."

"Yeah, I bet. Probably grilled cheese." He continued laughing, evidently still believing this whole thing to be a joke.

I huffed. "As a matter of fact, it is grilled cheese," I told him, feeling irritation boil up inside. "And, none of this is a joke. I *am* living at Les Loups-Garous now."

Daniel stopped laughing. "You're not joking?"

"No. Not even a little bit."

"Okay. So let me get this straight. I went out of town for a while, and you took the opportunity to move into *my* house without my knowledge?"

"Well, yes. But when you put it like that, it sounds creepy.

It wasn't like that."

"What was it like then?

"My dad told me I had to come live here now because I was no longer safe at my grandmother's house."

"I see. So I'm assuming you and your dad had your little talk?"

"Yes."

"And he said you needed to live at Les Loups-Garous?"

"Yes."

"Right. Why don't you start from the beginning and let me know how you guys came to this conclusion?" I winced, the irritation touching his words leaving me feeling unwelcome.

Either way, I owed him an explanation. I huffed out a short breath before launching into the details of the conversation with my dad. It took a while to relay the whole thing, and blessedly, I didn't have to relay the story in front of Brock. As soon as I had finished making his last sandwich, he grabbed it and took off down to the bar, mumbling about how long it had taken in the first place.

Daniel listened without interruption, and when I finished, he seemed a lot less anxious than he did when he had first realized I wasn't kidding about me living here.

"Your mom told your dad a lot," he stated.

"No kidding. Is it less weird now?"

"Yeah. After you explained, it made a lot of sense. Les Loups-Garous was originally built for the True Alpha."

"My dad told me it was a fortress, but to hear you confirm... I mean, wow. How safe can it be? It's Les Loups-Garous, you know? It's the club all the kids like to sneak into."

"Hey," he started, and I could hear the offense in his tone. "You were one of those kids not so long ago."

I blushed, thankful that he couldn't see me through the phone. "I know."

"Besides, for an Alpha, there's no safer place. Think about it. It's guarded by wolves almost constantly, for starters. Not to mention, when it goes into lock down mode, it's pretty impressive."

"Really?" I asked, trying to hide my disbelief.

"Really. Bars slide down the windows, There's reinforced outer doors for all the exits. It's pretty legit."

"Well, I hope it never gets bad enough that I need to lock the place down."

"Me, too." Daniel paused before switching gears. "So, you told your dad everything? Even about us?"

I paused before answering. "No, I kept that to myself. Didn't want to give him a heart attack."

Daniel laughed. "I figured. I doubt he would have urged you to move in if he'd known you were moving in with your boyfriend."

"Yeah, he probably would have reconsidered," I took a deep breath and chewed on my lip thoughtfully. "Look, Daniel, this doesn't have to be weird. Me living here, I mean. I've already cleared out space in the office and made it into my own room. I won't invade your privacy, I promise."

"You didn't have to do that. I'm not even there, so you can sleep in my room for now. And, when I get back... well, it's not like we haven't slept in the same bed before."

"Eh, I don't want to give anyone the wrong impression. We wouldn't want people guessing what's really been going on." I took this opportunity to tactlessly change the subject. "Speaking of getting back, any progress on that front?"

Daniel sighed. "Yes and no. As far as Lana's wayward Beta goes, I've been able to get him to calm down, but I can't convince him to shift. As far as the wolf-man goes, well let's just say it's not going. They've run a ton of experiments, but nothing that's even giving us any leads to what these guys are, or what we're up against."

Despite the disappointment filling me, I tried to keep my voice steady. "So, I guess you're going to be gone a bit longer."

I'd failed at keeping the tears out of my voice, and I knew

that Daniel heard the sadness loud and clear.

"I'm sorry, Christa. I wish I were there."

"I know. I just wish we had some idea when you were going to be back."

"Me, too. But, hey, it's getting late so I should probably let you go. You have school tomorrow."

I rolled my eyes. "I know. I'll go to bed. I love you."

"I lo-" he started to respond. "Shit, someone's coming, I gotta go." He finished, and the line went dead, not before I'd heard a silky voice saying Daniel's name. Lana.

I stared at the phone in silence, the tears I'd barely been holding back spilling over as I realized that he'd hung up on me without so much as a bye, and all because Lana had interrupted our moment.

I cleaned up the mess I made in the kitchen, trying to reign in all the emotions swirling within me. After I finished straightening up, I went and laid down in my bed, hoping to get some sleep since I had to go to school in the morning. I only had a couple of more months until graduation, and even though I didn't have a clue what my future held, I wanted to finish school strong, just in case I chose to go to college someday, or whatever else.

I'd played hooky today, effectively giving me a three day weekend, but I didn't want to make a habit out of not going.

I laid in bed for about a half an hour, the faint sound of music floating up from the club below me, and wondered how the hell Daniel slept through all the noise. The club wasn't the only thing keeping me awake. I couldn't get over the fact that Daniel had hung up on me.

My cell phone pinged with a message, and I reached over to my nightstand and grabbed it.

You awake? The message came from Des. I hadn't seen her much since a couple of days ago, and I desperately wanted to. But a quick glance at the time told me that it was already ten o'clock at night, and I needed to get some sleep. I couldn't pull an all-nighter the way she could.

The phone pinged again with Des's follow-up text. *If you are, come downstairs.*

I wanted to see her. Wanted to complain to her about all my frustrations, but in all honesty, how could I? She didn't know about Daniel and me, and it wasn't something I felt like I could tell her, at least not right now.

I sighed and readjusted my pillow before rolling onto my side. I couldn't go down there tonight. Not when the hurt still felt so raw. Not when my emotions were such a jumbled mess.

The phone beeped again, and heat flashed through me. Man, Destiny could be persistent when she wanted to be. I grabbed my phone already thinking that I would just tell her that I couldn't come out tonight because I'd decided to try and be responsible etc... etc... etc... The name on the screen gave me pause. This message hadn't come from Des. It had come from Daniel.

Sorry about earlier. I'll call again when I can.

That was it. No, explanation, no reassurance that he still cared about me. Part of me knew that hearing Lana's voice, and the distance between us, caused my irrational thoughts. The other part of my brain, though, the part that was drowning in so much hurt, had started over-powering my rationality.

He was *sorry.* I clenched my jaw, anger bubbling up inside me. Not yet, he wasn't! If he wanted to gallivant around Pennsylvania with Lana, I would let him.

With my light brown hair and gray eyes, I may not have been the most beautiful girl in the world, but I knew I could go down there and find someone to make me forget about Daniel Hawthorne. Or to at least keep me company for the night. And maybe, somehow, Daniel would hear about it, and he would get jealous.

Not completely in control of my higher reasoning, I hopped out of bed, threw on a pair of ripped jeans and a plain black tank top, brushed my hair and teeth, and threw on some eyeliner and mascara.

I looked myself over in the mirror. I didn't look knock out gorgeous or anything, but I looked clean and presentable, which seemed good enough for me.

I slipped on my black Converse sneakers and then headed down the stairs, taking them two at a time with renewed energy.

I burst through the door from the stairs into the bar, coming out right next to the deejay booth, and climbed up next to Brock.

He looked over at me hopping up into the booth, a spark of interest flashing before he shook his head. "Is that you, Boss?"

I shot him a concerned look. "Of course, it is."

His eyebrows shot up, and his face pulled into a frown. "Oh, I didn't recognize you."

I stared at him for a moment, trying to figure out how he wouldn't have recognized me. I opened my mouth to ask, when Des came running up, her soft brown eyes lighting up as she saw me.

She climbed into the booth and threw her arms around me. "It is you! I told Casey, I think that's her, and he said, 'I don't know, something's different.'" I could detect the faintest hint of alcohol emanating from Destiny, and I looked down out of the deejay booth to see Casey standing there, arms folded, and watching everything as though he

just waited for the chance to spring into action.

I still puzzled over how these people, my friends, hadn't recognized me. "Do I look stupid or something?" I asked.

Both Brock and Des stared at me in confusion. "No. Why?" Des asked.

"Both you and Brock said they barely recognized me, and Casey said I looked different. I didn't do anything special. I wear these jeans and this shirt all the time."

Des laughed. "You look awesome. I think it might be the extra-dark eyeliner and mascara, but it's really making you look like a punk-rock goddess."

I blushed as Brock shrugged noncommittally. Casey looked

up at us and shook his head. "No. It's the waves of hostility rolling off of you. It makes you look fierce and dangerous."

Des looked down at Casey before meeting my eyes and rolling hers. "Ignore him. He's been on one ever since Zee left."

Casey pursed his lips. "We need to be extra diligent, Destiny. Without Zee, it's up to us to keep everything under control."

Des grabbed my hand, and we climbed out of the booth. "I'll keep that in mind," she told Casey before pulling me over to the bar.

We ordered a couple of girly drinks and watched as Macy, the bartender working tonight, and one of my werewolves, mixed them up.

"Trouble in paradise?" I asked Des, inclining my head toward Casey.

Des shrugged. "He's just worried about Zee. He feels like there are better ways to figure out what these monsters are and what we're up against. He doesn't think we should have thrown Zee into the wolves' den."

Macy handed us our drinks, and I took a sip. Without thinking, I shrugged at Des. "Well, he's right. There was a better way, but he refused to talk to his dad." I didn't mean to sound so accusatory, but I did nonetheless.

Destiny fixed me with a level stare, surprising since I would have bet money that she was drunk, or at the very least buzzed. "That's not fair. That may seem like a little thing to ask of someone, but it's not. That's asking Casey to go and face the man who quit being his father when he murdered someone in cold blood." Her voice was harsh, and I felt myself flinch.

"You're right. I'm sorry."

She offered me a small smile. "No worries. Let's just talk about something else." Des paused to take a sip of her own drink. "How are things going with you? How do you like being Daniel's roommate? Have you found a date to prom?" I flinched again at the mention of prom.

The penultimate high school experience, senior prom, and I found myself both dateless and dreading it. I had asked Daniel, off-handedly if he wanted to go. He'd flat out said no, explaining that he wasn't big on dances, and he didn't want to have to come up with a cover story as to why we were going together. And, he'd added, he was too old.

Considering that the last time I went to a dance, my date tried to kill me, I wasn't too keen on the idea of going to prom, especially if my boyfriend didn't want to accompany me.

I took another sip of my drink and frowned at Des. "Eh. I'm okay. Daniel's not here, so I don't know what it's like being his roommate, and I already told you, I'm not going to prom."

Des frowned back at me. "Look, I know that the last date you went on didn't go well," Des started echoing back my own thoughts in her words. "But, there are plenty of non-homicidal-maniacs who I am sure would love to go out with you. Isn't there someone out there in all of Kennington that makes your heart beat just a little faster?"

Yes. Daniel. And not just a little faster either. He could make my heart beat so hard I sometimes feared that it would tear free and explode right out of my body. But I couldn't tell Des that.

Staring at her though, so open and honest, I reconsidered. Maybe I could tell Des. Maybe she would understand. She'd been my best friend since kindergarten, and even living across the country from one another couldn't destroy that. I knew that she had once harbored her own crush on Daniel, but since partnering up with Casey, and then subsequently falling for him, she seemed to have gotten over it.

I could tell Des. She would keep our secret safe. I opened my mouth, resolved to let her in on what had really been going on, and finally able to get some advice on the current situation when Des began speaking. "You're not still pining after Daniel are you?" she asked. "Because, I mean, he's cute and all, but doesn't he have, like, an actual girlfriend? One of those other

Alphas? And, like, he's so old."

I gritted my teeth at her casual mention of Lana and bit back my confession. No, I couldn't tell her the truth. I couldn't tell her that things had escalated far beyond pining. I couldn't tell her that I had fallen madly in love with Daniel, the kind of love that threatened to destroy someone if things went badly. I couldn't tell her that I felt pretty certain Daniel loved me the same way.

Instead, I smiled at her. "I don't know what you're talking about? I have never pined after Daniel. And I'm not sure if he's still with his girlfriend. It's none of my business." I kept my tone light, but in reality, just saying the words at all hurt. I really didn't know what was going on with Daniel and Lana, but my imagination did enough to effectively shatter my heart where I stood.

If I seemed like I hid something from her, Des didn't notice, instead grabbing me by the shoulder and turning me to face the dance floor.

"One of these guys," she stated grandly, gesturing to the mass of people grinding away to the sound of music. "One of them could be the man of your dreams. Or at the very least, a date to the prom."

I nodded while Des's eye squinted against the dark bodies, no doubt trying to find a guy she found passable enough for me to approach.

I turned back to Macy, threw back my drink and downed it, and indicated that I needed another one.

I should have stayed in bed.

I woke up for school the next morning, head pounding and drenched in sweat. Des, true to her word, had combed through the masses, introducing me to every single guy in the bar. None of them panned out, partly because I wasn't interested, and partly because they were all twenty-somethings. Apparently, in Des's excitement to find me a guy, she'd forgotten that we weren't technically supposed to be in the bar, and were only there because Daniel, Brock, and the rest of the staff at Les Loups-Garous had turned a blind eye to our fake Ids.

Feeling like I had been hit by a truck, I dragged myself out of my bed and down the hall to the bathroom.

I turned on the shower, allowing the temperature to rise to as hot as I could stand, before stepping in and letting the water wash over me.

I stood there for a long time, the heat and steam from the shower doing wondrous things to ease the tension in my head. Eventually, though, I turned the water off and stepped out.

I went through my usual routine, getting ready for the day, and even though I still didn't feel great, I felt like I could make it through school.

I popped an aspirin before stuffing my wallet into my backpack and heading for the door.

I'd just made it out the door of the bar and was headed for my car when the phone rang.

I glanced down at the caller ID, sighing as I answered Daniel's call.

"What's up?" I asked, a little harsher than I'd meant to.

"How are you feeling?" Daniel asked with a hint of amusement.

"I feel fantastic. Never better. Why do you ask?"

"The funniest thing happened to me this morning. I woke up, saw that my phone was flashing with a message and listened to it."

I groaned, vaguely recalling drunk-dialing Daniel around one in the morning, before I passed out in my bed.

"I tried to call earlier, but either you were still out or getting ready and didn't hear me," he pressed on.

I fumbled with keys, trying to unlock the door to my car. "I must have been in the shower."

"Yes. It was an interesting message. You sounded obliterated, just drunk as hell. I called Brock to confirm, and he said you and Des were up all night, main-lining tequila. And he said that Des was trying to hook you up with any guy there that would be interested in taking you to the prom."

I groaned again, the taste of tequila haunting me. "That was Des. I told her I wasn't interested in going, but she wouldn't listen."

"Well, if your message is to be believed, you are very much interested in going. And you have a laundry list of concerns when it comes to me, also. So, tell me, it is true? All the things you said, did you mean them?"

Triumphantly, I unlocked the car and climbed in, starting it up with no problems, and wracked my brain trying to remember what I said in that damned message. I shifted the car into drive and took a deep breath. "You're gonna have to be specific, D. As you've already pointed out, I was super drunk, so I don't remember what I said."

"Apparently, you think I'm off rekindling my romance with Lana. Let me be perfectly clear, so there is no confusion. I ended things with Lana as soon as I got here. She's well aware that, with everything that is going on, I'm not interested in maintaining a relationship. At least that's what I told her. Secondly, don't ever question what you mean to me. I would die before I'd ever see you hurt. And finally, if you want to go to the god-damned prom so much, I will take you. No one else will take you, I won't have it."

Despite the fact that I had adamantly told Des I didn't want to go, just hearing him tell me that he would take me if I wanted to go lifted my spirits a little.

"Well," he pushed. "Do you want to go?"

I almost shouted out. Of course, I wanted to go with Daniel, but the way he asked made me falter. It wasn't the romantic, earth rocking proposal that a girl wished for. His words held a resigned, uninterested offer. He didn't want to go. He just didn't want me to go with anyone else.

I sighed. "No, it's cool. I don't really want to go."

Daniel stayed quiet for a moment, and I could just picture his exasperated expression. "Okay," he said slowly. "Then we won't go." I wasn't sure, and maybe I was just being hopeful, but I could almost detect a hint of disappointment.

I shook it off. He couldn't be disappointed, he had made it clear several times he didn't want to go.

I could see the school looming in front of me and knew that I needed to wrap this conversation up. "Look, Daniel, I appreciate the offer, but it's okay. I don't want to go. You don't want to go, and there's no point in making a big deal out of it when neither of us wants to do it."

"Are you sure?" he asked.

"Yeah. Just forget about it."

He paused again, the silence weighing on me, and I once again wondered if maybe deep down he wanted to go with me. I let the thought go.

"Look. I just got to school. I need to go." I said before he could speak again.

When he spoke, Daniel's words were guarded. "Okay. Well, I'll talk to you later, I guess."

I shrugged, unable to stop myself even though I knew he couldn't see it. "Yeah, I guess." I tried to keep the annoyance out of my voice, but I just couldn't.

Daniel caught on, his next words sending a pang to my heart, even though I knew he hadn't intended to. "Please don't forget, Christa. I love you, and only you."

I closed my eyes, fighting against the well of emotion building inside me. I could feel it already, a distance between us that had nothing to do with the actual distance between us. It felt like something had started to break between us, and my heart clenched desperately as I tried to fight against that feeling. Pushing it back with a deep breath, I spoke, my voice coming out flatly. "Yeah. Me, too. I'll call you later. Bye." I hung up before he could say anything and pulled my car into a parking spot before turning it off and leaned my head against the steering wheel, the tears that I'd barely been holding back finally breaking free and dripping down my face.

CHAPTER SIX

T he week passed uneventfully for which I was thankful. I spent most of my time hanging out with Des in my apartment, watching television or studying. I'd had a few scattered conversations with Daniel, mostly just reports about what was happening at Lana's headquarters. Each conversation became more and more disheartening since things didn't seem to be changing. Emory, while calm, wouldn't shift and Lana's crack team of scientists, led by Zee and Aidan, hadn't gotten any closer to discovering any secrets about the strange new creatures.

We were at a standstill and the stagnation began to wear away at me. Tensions rose high around Les Loups-Garous, as we all waited for something to happen.

Even my conversations with Daniel were short and awkward. Each time he'd call me with nothing new to report, my retorts would become more and more clipped and sarcastic. At first, Daniel had tried to push through the unfriendliness I offered, trying to break through my sour mood. After a few unpleasant conversations, though, he too became cold until we could barely speak to each other without it ending in a shouting match.

It was a mess. I contemplated the whole situation while I sat on my Alpha's throne, a huge flattened rock that overlooked the Moon Bay Cliff, a breath taking view of canyons and cliff ledges that silhouetted against the moon in a hauntingly beautiful way.

This throne and Moon Bay Cliff were also the base of werewolf magic where all our power originated from.

For me, this place was more than just the seat of werewolf magic. It provided refuge from a world that seemed hell bent on breaking my spirit. This place was my kingdom and my birthright as the True Alpha.

The cool wind whirled around me, and I pulled my coat tighter around myself, wishing that I could stay as calm as I felt right now all the time. I closed my eyes allowing the steady flow of power from the Alpha's throne to wash around me. Here, I found the most peace I'd felt since first learning that another rogue hunted me. A more powerful one lurking somewhere in the world and plotting against me.

I replayed the last awful conversation I'd had with Daniel over in my mind. He had called with his usual report of nothing, and I'd snapped. He tried to calm me down, whispering that soon enough, everything would work itself out, and we couldn't lose faith in each other. We couldn't lose faith in our love. I'd snorted bitterly and told him not to call me again until he had something helpful to report and hung up on him.

That had been two days ago, and he hadn't called me since. I'd tried calling him to apologize, but he kept forwarding my calls until eventually, I couldn't even leave a voicemail. The rejection, though well deserved, pained me so deeply that I feared it would leave a visible scar. I'd hurt him, and he seemed hell bent on making sure he returned that pain in full.

It was because of that last conversation that my heart leaped hopefully in my chest when my phone rang shattering the silence around me. I looked down at the screen to see that Daniel was calling.

I answered hastily, an apology already forming on my lips. "Daniel, I'm so sor-" I began before his words cut through mine, his voice cold and emotionless.

"I have something new to report."

I faltered, blinking fast while I willed my heart to stop beating so thunderously against the grief rising in my chest at Daniel's toneless inflection. He was mad. Really mad.

"Daniel, I'm-" I tried again, ignoring his initial statement. We could get to that, later.

Or maybe not. Daniel sliced through my apology once more, not even allowing me to breathe life to it.

"I have something new to report," he intoned once more, his voice still flat. "You asked me only to call you once I had something new. Do you want to hear it?"

I flinched, taking a shaky breath. "Yes," I whispered weakly.

"Emory will not shift. Lana believes that we have tried long enough, and it's time for us to free Emory."

I had a feeling that I knew what Lana's idea of "freeing" Emory entailed, but dread still colored my words as I spoke again. "What does that mean?"

"Lana has ordered Emory to be executed at midnight."

Daniel knew me. He knew how compassionate I always tried to be, but still, he delivered his words without a touch of sympathy. He spoke as the true soldier that I knew he could be, completely emotionless. Cut off from the man I loved. In the back of my mind, I realized that my moment of cruelty had hurt Daniel more than he allowed to show.

I shook my head. "She can't do that. That's not her choice to make."

"She's his Alpha. She can make that decision if she feels it's what must happen." His defense of Lana ruffled me, and I felt my anger rise washing away the regret I felt about hurting him.

"No. She can't," I growled. "Emory may have been hers, and she can forsake him if she chooses, but her wolves are still mine, and I decide who lives and dies. Not her. He is *mine*."

"If you decide to spare him, he becomes your responsibility. What place would you find him in our pack? He is a Beta, and Betas are generally not content to be one of the ranks. Would you toss out my father to make room for him?"

I snorted in irritation knowing that Daniel's words rang with honesty, but unable to reconcile giving up on helping Emory after only a short time.

"Of course not. But I can't condemn him to death. He may be her Beta, but he is a werewolf. My duty is to protect our kind. I owe him a chance."

Daniel's cool indifference finally broke, his anger boiling over as he shouted through the phone. "Owe him? You don't even know him! You owe him nothing!"

"As long as he is a werewolf, I owe him a chance. He may not want to join as part of our ranks, but we can deal with that later."

Daniel sucked in deeply, and I could hear him breathing raggedly as he fought for control over his anger. "If you will not allow Lana to free him in the only way she knows how, what do you suggest we do?"

I chewed my bottom lip as I considered his question, reaching to the she-wolf inside to help me find the answer and not liking the only conclusion she could come up with. Even worse, I knew Daniel wouldn't like it.

"Have her break her ties with him. Bring him to me, and I'll see if we can use the power in Moon Bay Cliff to save him."

"Condemn him to life as a rogue? Don't you think that's a fate worse than death?"

"If we can save him, then he can make the choice to stay a rogue, or join as part of our pack until a position opens for him elsewhere."

"And what if you can't save him, Christa? Would you risk your life for his?"

I sighed, praying that it wouldn't come to that, but understanding the definite possibility. "If I can't save him, then we can discuss his execution. But we will try one last effort before giving up."

"Fine. But know that I don't support this. I have felt his instability. He's dangerous," Daniel said softly, and I felt that hope rise in my chest once more. Hope that I hadn't damaged things between us beyond repair.

My hope deflated quickly with his next words. "Good luck. I hope you don't die."

The line went dead, no goodbye, no opening given for my apology. No guarantee given that he would even come to help me save Emory.

Nothing but silence.

Shaking slightly from the realization that I may never again have to fear that someone would discover the truth about Daniel and me, mostly because there was no more Daniel and me, I pushed myself away from the Alpha's throne and strode across the dirt clearing surrounding me. Heading for the forest that bordered the cliffs, I made my way back through the path that would lead me to Les Loups-Garous.

I couldn't wallow in sadness over the apparent end of my first real relationship. Sunday night had arrived, and I had a dinner to attend.

I stepped through the foyer of my grandmother's house, my flowing black skirt swirling as my black heels clicked against the shiny hardwood floor.

I'd had to make a quick detour at home to change into something more appropriate for dinner with my family. My grandmother would have never allowed me to sit at her dinner table in the faded, ripped jeans and black hoodie sweatshirt that I'd been wearing at Moon Bay Cliff.

I could hear the chatter of my family as I approached the dining room, and grimaced as I realized they were all already seated, probably waiting for me so that they could begin their first course.

I breezed into the room trying not to draw attention to the fact that I had arrived ten minutes late and took my seat between my dad and Jackson.

All conversation paused as my grandmother flicked her glance at me. "You're late."

I nodded, mumbling my apology.

My grandmother pursed her lips, an expression I had seen often. "Are there no clocks to tell time in your new home?"

To anyone else, her tone would have suggested sarcasm, but I knew that any snark had been unintentional. My grandmother just couldn't see any other reason why I'd been late.

"There are clocks, I was just out on a hike today, and I lost track of time."

She studied me for a moment before craning her neck toward the entrance to the kitchen.

"Eloise, she's here. You can begin serving us now," she told the girl with no further comment about my lateness.

I sighed in relief, glad that I'd managed to avoid another argument with someone I loved tonight.

The evening stayed pleasant as my family and I ate dinner. We spoke about the week, with everyone wanting to know if I enjoyed the freedom of my own place.

I answered as honestly as I could. "It's okay, but it's pretty lonely when you consider that I went from living with a house full of people to now living with a roommate that's barely ever home."

My grandmother tsked in her usual way. "You can always come home, you know? Your room is always ready." I smiled at my grandmother. Her tone may have been very formal, but the love that fueled her offer reflected in her eyes.

I glanced over at my father and noticed the regret in his eyes. As kind as my grandmother's words may have been, my father and I knew the truth. This house would probably never be my home again.

"Thank you, Nana, I'll definitely keep that in mind."

She offered me a tight-lipped smile before taking a sip of her wine and looking at my grandfather. The two of them started chatting to one another about current affairs and I tuned them out a bit, not overly interested in what they discussed.

I finished my dinner in silence, listening to my family's easy conversations as Eloise came in every few minutes to check on us and offer me wine, which I consistently declined.

After dinner, my grandparents informed me that they were going to a movie, and said goodnight, leaving me to spend the evening with my dad and Jackson.

Hours had passed since my conversation with Daniel, and I just prayed that he'd upheld his end of our arrangement. I mulled it over, chewing nervously on the inside of my cheek, while we watched television. Around eleven, Jackson excused himself, saying that he had to get up early for his swim practice and needed to get to bed.

I stood as he did, meeting his arms and grasping him in a tight hug. "Take care of yourself, sis," he whispered.

I nodded. "Will do. I mean I've got a whole army of legendary monsters just waiting to jump in and protect me, so I think I'll be okay."

Jackson eyed me carefully; no doubt taking in the exhaustion and sadness I tried desperately to keep hidden. "Whatever is going on between the two of you, I'm sure you'll figure it out," he said, his voice just barely a whisper.

I blanched in surprise, awed by how intuitive my brother seemed to be lately and gave him another quick hug.

"Me, too," I whispered back, blinking to fight the sting of tears in my eyes.

My father, thankfully oblivious to the exchange between Jackson and I, also stood, putting his hand on my shoulder.

"Well, kiddo, independent werewolf or not, I think it's time you started heading home, too. It's getting late."

I nodded my agreement and allowed my dad to lead me to the front door. We said our goodbyes, and I took off headed back to my new home.

I took the roads slowly. It may have been early spring, but the streets were still icy, and an eerie layer of fog had settled blacking out any light that the full moon would have offered and making visibility a real issue.

I pulled down the quiet street that would lead me to Les Loups-Garous, doing my best to make out the road in the thick fog. Adding to the eeriness, sinister looking forestry lined each side of the street. In fact, forest surrounded Les Loups-Garous.

I couldn't see anything. I slowed even further hoping that if

I stayed slow and straight, I could make it the next mile and a half without incident.

I should have known better. Something large and dark flashed across my windshield, running across the street, from one side of trees to the next. The hugeness of the shape caught my attention, the familiarity of its size sending shivers down my spine.

Knowing that I probably didn't want to wait around by myself to figure out if the dark shadow was what I thought, I picked up speed, realizing the danger, but also knowing that I had a better chance of surviving a car accident than an ambush from more of those wolf-men.

I kept my attention focused mostly on the road ahead, although I checked my rear view mirror occasionally to make sure no one chased me.

I could just make out the club ahead of me, and I sighed in relief. My tension subsided as thoughts rushed through my mind, comforting me in my time of fear. I'd made it. I was safe.

Everything was going to be o--

A strong force slammed in the passenger side of the care, interrupting my thoughts. The Mustang flipped it into the air, turning over before it slammed down on the driver side and rolled over the embankment.

The car repeatedly flipped, narrowly missing trees as it tumbled further into the deep forest. Terror thundered through my chest as the frame of the car crushed in on itself with each turn. The airbag deployed, smashing into my face with a sickening crunch and robbing my lungs of air, while my head banged unceremoniously into the driver's side window shattering glass into the car and all over my face.

My mouth widened into a scream, but no sound came out. I couldn't breathe. Two thoughts just kept repeating in my mind.

I should have checked the side mirror.

I never got to say I'm sorry.

Almost as quickly as it began, the car made tumbled one

last time, landing sideways on the passenger side before skidding for another hundred feet and stopping.

Shaking from the burst of adrenaline, blood dripping from all over my body, and breathing shallowly, I managed to reach around and wriggle free of the seat belt.

As soon as I freed myself from the suspension the belt had offered, I fell sideways in the car, landing so that I laid against the glass of the passenger window, which pressed against the ground.

With some painful maneuvering, I managed to position myself so that my feet pushed against the passenger side of the car, and I was able to pull my self out of the driver's side.

I looked up seeing the smashed window and grimaced as I remembered the sound of the glass breaking and showering across my face. Several jagged pieces of glass edged the window, and I hoped with all the strength I could muster that I would be able to just open the car door because climbing through that window was going to hurt like hell. After just enduring what I had, I felt pretty sure that I'd already pushed the limits of my pain threshold.

I tried the handle and frowned. The door had been smashed in; no way in the world would I be able to open it.

I eyed the window with dread, studying it for places where I could put my hands and slide my body out with minimal damage.

Gritting my teeth, I pressed my hands against the window, wincing as I lifted myself head first through the opening, and the broken shards bit into my palms.

I rolled out, plunging to the ground gracelessly but sustaining minimal cuts to my torso. Unable to glance at my hands, I feared seeing the mangled mess I knew they were.

On shaky legs, I stood, taking in the scene around me.

The car was totaled, and judging by the way it looked ,I felt lucky to be alive. Glancing around, I saw the car had ended up in the middle of a meadow surrounded by trees on all sides.

My body ached, throbbing in ways that I had never experienced. Blood ran from the cuts on my forehead, and I could feel the streaking trails all over my face. My clothes were torn, bloody, and absolutely destroyed.

I took a step toward the trees, my movements jerky. I paused, taking a painful breath, and steeling myself for my trek through the forest and back to Les Loups-Garous.

Each step I took set my nerves on fire, the pain piercing so deep that I felt that I might pass out.

Despite the agony, I pushed forward, adrenaline carrying me to the tree line. It was slow going, but I took each torturous step with steely determination.

I reached the border, wondering how far away from the road I had rolled, and what kind of hike I would have to endure before I reached help.

I set my shoulders in defiance. The hike didn't matter. I needed to get out of here before whatever hit me caught up.

Twigs snapped in front of me, and I froze as I realized that it was too late. My assailant had already caught up.

Another twig snapped, and then the huge body of one of the wolfmen stepped into the clearing directly in front of me. I allowed myself one shudder of terror before I took a step back, not taking my eyes off the giant monster, my eyes locked on his. I knew better than to turn around or cower from a wolf in hunt mode.

Especially since I wasn't sure how I managed to still be standing, let alone how I would outrun a predator.

He took another step forward, and I took another back. On and on, we repeated our deadly dance, my heart beating traitorously in my chest as I wondered how long I could keep this going before he grew tired of the game and attacked. In my current broken state, I wasn't sure I would be able to shift, and even if I could, I knew for certain I wouldn't be able to fight.

My concerns didn't matter. With a strange twitch of his mouth, almost like a smile, the beast stopped.

I only spared a moment for confusion before I realized what had happened, and bone-chilling terror froze my heart.

Mr. Creepy had herded me into the middle of the clearing, and as I looked around, wolfmen stepped out of the surrounding forest from all directions. Taking a quick head count, I shuddered. There were at least twenty of them against me.

My odds were non-existent. Not to mention, I was surrounded. "Well, fuck," I whispered as they braced for their attack.

Time slowed. I waited for the onslaught of teeth and claws to tear through me, but nothing happened. I glanced around quickly. They stood stock still, just staring at me.

I didn't understand why they weren't attacking. My battered human form assured their victory. They had me surrounded. I had no place to run, and even if I tried to shift they would be able to get to me before I completed my transformation.

What were they waiting for?

A twitch of movement caught my attention, and I looked over to the wolf that had herded me into this trap.

He eyed me hungrily, head cocked as he waited for whatever signal he expected.

I didn't have to puzzle it out for long. With a gust of cold wind, the fog swirling around us shifted, sliding away from the moon, and suddenly the whole clearing was visible, lit by the glow of the full moon.

With terrifying synchronicity, the wolfmen threw their heads back and howled, their salute to the moon tearing into my body and grating against my ears. Shuddering from the violence promised in their battle cry, my body twitched of its own accord, instinctively beginning to shift in an attempt to save me from certain death.

I fought against my own instincts, knowing that changing would only speed the monsters' attack. Panic overwhelmed me. What was happening? Had I been injured so badly that I couldn't control myself?

From the back of my mind, my she-wolf whispered to me. She told me to let her have control. She said we might die, but at least we could take a few of the beasts with us.

I sighed and resigned myself to trusting my she-wolf. She may be unpredictable ninety percent of the time, but in most life or death situations, she usually made it out alive.

I quit resisting and allowed my wolf side to take control as I felt the shimmer of werewolf magic wash over me transforming me where I stood.

The wolfmen around me quit howling, all of their attention focused on me. The howled once more then charged, coming in at me from all sides.

I didn't just stand there waiting like a deer in headlights while they came. With my wolf side telling me what to do I tore towards the first monster I could reach colliding with his giant paw as he smacked me with bone-crunching strength.

I hit the ground hard, slow to get back up after such a powerful hit. The wolf inside me bristled. She'd been sure that we would have held out longer than this.

Pain shot through me as I willed myself to get back up and looked around the clearing. The wolf who had hit me circled me, waiting to defend against my next useless attack.

The rest of the monsters backed away, still guarding the perimeter, but not concerned with their leader's ability to demolish me. Somehow, I understood that they wouldn't be joining this fight. They were just here to make sure I didn't escape.

I rose to my feet again and forced myself into another offensive attack, lunging at my opponent with as much force as I could muster in my broken body.

He slapped me hard across my muzzle, driving me down. I hit the ground, and my body shifted back to human without my consent, my will too weak to keep my wolf form.

I looked up feebly at my opponent, and he backed away several feet from me, crouching down onto all fours.

I didn't understand his intent until it was too late.

He rushed me at a full sprint before pouncing in the air, his positioning perfectly poised to land right on top of me.

I wanted to look away, I didn't want to witness my own demise, but pure fear left my eyes locked on him.

He was so close, his body closing the distance between us quickly, and I prepared myself for the death that was coming swiftly for me.

Out of nowhere, the most beautiful of sounds filled the air. A snarling howl so full of rage that I felt my heart lighten.

Daniel was here.

His howl tore through the silence, echoed from all around the valley as my pack tore into the line of wolfmen surrounding the perimeter.

Elation flooded through me. My own attacker still closed in, but at least, I would die knowing that I would be avenged swiftly.

Time sped up again as I watched the wolfman finish the distance between us. I braced myself for him, and before I could blink, he was on top of me, jaws snapping at my face.

Another snarl nearby drew his attention and he looked to the side.

A flash of brownish-red fur sped into my vision slamming forcefully into my attacker and tearing him away from me.

Relief washed through me before confusion set in. I'd been so absolutely certain that Daniel would be the one to throw that monster off, but the flash of color I'd seen definitely hadn't been Daniel's black wolf.

I rolled to my side, watching as the wolfman that had just been seconds from obliterating me rolled around, locked in a battle with the brownish-red wolf that I most certainly didn't recognize.

Thundering steps on my other side alerted me that even though this mystery wolf had saved me from one monster, other predators waiting to destroy me filled the valley.

I turned, eyes blurry as my vision swam, and snarled, the inhuman sound strange to my human lips before more waves of relief rolled over me.

I knew this wolf, his black fur as familiar to me as breathing. I smiled as he slowed to a stop, anguish twisting across his lupine features as he took in my appearance.

He reached me just as a tremor rocked through my body, sending my back arching into the air and stealing away my breath as I screamed silently in agony.

My body fell back to the ground, and I struggled to breathe, fighting to get the air into my lungs as my breath came faster while my heart beat more rapidly. He nudged me, whimpering as he watched my whole body violently shake.

My vision swam, and when I focused again, Daniel's human face peered down at me instead of his wolf's. The fear in his eyes told me all I needed to know.

I was dying, and he couldn't save me.

He bent over me scooping me up into his arms before he took off at a sprint towards a part of the tree line that my wolves had already cleared.

I wanted to speak, but every time I tried, blood just gurgled in my throat, rising up and spilling out of my mouth.

Daniel looked down again, and I saw that desperate fear twist his features. "Please," he whispered, voice cracking as the tears began to slip down his cheek. "Don't die, Christa. I can't lose you. I love you."

I felt my lips twist into a slight smile before a huge shudder tore through me, sending me into a coughing fit that produced only blood.

The world shivered, my eyes unable to focus, and then everything went dark.

The last thing I heard was Daniel's heart breaking cry as he screamed out.

"No!"

CHAPTER SEVEN

I tore through the forest, heedless of the branches and foliage snaking out around me, trying to catch me off guard to send me flat on my face.

I'd never seen the forest like this before, the trees so thick they blotted out the sun. The surrounding scenery struck me as hauntingly beautiful, but I couldn't stop to appreciate it.

I only had enough time to stop what was going to happen before it became too late.

My feet carried me far and fast; my objective so clear that I had no doubt I would succeed. I flew into the meadow, looking around at the damage as sorrow washed over me.

It was empty.

I stood alone, utterly and completely. My chest constricted, and I fell to my knees, head sagging as sobs heaved from within me.

Soft steps approached, and I looked up to see a stunningly beautiful woman. Her white dress and curly brown hair flew behind her, and her gray eyes observed me with affection.

I resisted the urge to throw myself into my mother's arms.

She knelt down beside me, placing a delicate hand on my cheek and forcing me to meet her gaze.

"When the time comes, you must not let it break you," she said softly.

She stood, leading me with her, her hand on my elbow, before she swung me back toward the direction I 'd just run from.

I turned back toward her. "What time? What do you mean?"

She smiled, her eyes sad, and shook her head. "It's time to wake up now."

I grabbed her in panic, needing to know what she meant. "What time, Mom?" I begged, but she stayed damnably silent. She gently pulled herself away from me and urged me toward the way I'd come.

I sighed deeply, knowing that she had given all she could offer, and took a step back into the woods before glancing back at her.

She frowned, before speaking again. "Don't let it break you," she repeated before my dream melted away.

I vaguely registered that something near me beeped. Beep. Beep. Beep. The sound kept time with my heart, loud but reassuring. As I gained more awareness, I deciphered more sounds. People breathing, whispered conversations.

I opened my eyes, the blast of bright white light forcing me to close them immediately. Stars danced under my eyelids and I blinked rapidly to fight against them. I opened my eyes again, straining against the offensive light blinding me until I found that I could focus on my surroundings. My mind struggled to place me, even though I felt the tingle of familiarity roll through me.

I looked to my side toward the sound of beeping and saw a monitor with green spikes. Next to the monitor stood an IV pole and bag, its lines flowing downward and I lifted my hand to see that it connected to me.

I blinked again. A hospital. I was in a hospital.

What in the hell?

A sound at the door alerted me to someone's approach, and I looked up from my hand.

Daniel stood frozen in the doorway, his expression unreadable as he clutched a cup of coffee. He met my eyes, holding me prisoner with his stare, and dropped the cup, the sloshing sound of the liquid hitting the floor leaving no doubt that the coffee had spilled.

In one moment he stood across the room; in the next he

was right beside me, his knees hitting the floor as he buried his head into my chest and began to sob, chanting my name over and over like some sort of prayer.

I lifted my arm, ignoring the throb of pain, and ran my fingers through his dark brown hair, wondering what on Earth had him so distraught. I didn't give voice to my questions, not wanting to interrupt whatever battle raged inside his mind.

After what felt like an eternity, he took a shaky breath and looked up at me, bringing his hand up to cup my cheek. "You're alive," he breathed in awe, his eyes alight with joy.

I shrugged, not understanding his clear overreaction. "Well, yeah. Why wouldn't I be?"

Daniel looked at me in confusion, clearly studying me for signs of something. "Don't you remember?"

"Remember what?"

"You were attacked."

I raised an eyebrow at Daniel. "Yeah. I know. Slimy wolfman bastards ambushed me. But, I mean, you guys got there in time. I may have had a few broken bones, but obviously, I'm fine."

Daniel looked away from me, but not before I saw grief flash in his eyes. "We didn't get there in time," he whispered.

"Of course you did. I remember you guys tearing into the valley. You..." I faltered as Daniel's head started shaking from side to side. "You saved me. You picked me up and started running, and-"

Daniel's gaze locked hard on mine, anguish and rage dancing dangerously in his eyes. "And you died," he cut in, his voice cracking.

I opened my mouth to speak, but I couldn't seem to find the words. After a long moment of silence, I finally managed one small denial. "No."

"Yes. You died before we even made it to the road. I had already called the ambulance, and they met us once we cleared the trees. They kept trying to pronounce you dead, but I wouldn't..." Daniel paused as he shook away some terrible memory. "I couldn't let them. I made them bring you here. And then I had to fight with the staff here because they kept saying they couldn't save you. They kept saying that thirty minutes was too long, that you were already gone. But I wouldn't let them say no. I made them help you, and they shocked you- and shocked, and... and.. I haven't been able to sleep, every time I close my eyes I hear them yelling 'clear.' Every time I close my eyes, I see your lifeless body jump as they shot you through with electricity." He paused in his rambling to look me over, the joy at seeing me alive battling with the guilt he felt for not being there sooner. "Then you breathed."

I took a moment to let it all sink in. "I was dead for thirty minutes?" I asked.

He nodded and grabbed my hand. "Even when you breathed, they told me it might have been too little too late. They said that the trauma to your body was too severe. The accident alone would have killed you. The airbag deploying broke your nose, and smashed into your torso with enough force to break a couple of ribs. Your left arm was broken, the shoulder dislocated. The fight with that monster made things worse, you cracked a couple more ribs, and those pierced your lungs. Your brain was hemorrhaging, too many consecutive blows to the head. They told me that even if your body healed, you might never wake up."

"How long have I been here?" I asked.

"Almost two weeks."

I closed my eyes, trying not to hyperventilate as I realized how much time had passed. I took in Daniel's ragged appearance, the dark circles under his eyes, and the fatigue written all over him. "Have you been here the whole time?"

He nodded. "I had to be here in case you woke up."

"You haven't gone home at all?"

He shook his head. "I had to be here. The others they came and went in rotation. They kept telling me to go home, but I had to be here."

I rubbed my hands over my face and took a moment to really look at Daniel. He looked terrible, and something didn't seem right. He wasn't his usual calm, collected self. I'd been hurt tons of times, and he'd never seemed so... terrified.

I shifted over in the bed and gestured for him to lie next to me. He hesitated for a moment before getting up off his knees and sliding in next to me, holding me so close I felt that maybe he thought if he didn't hold me tightly I would disappear.

"It's okay, Daniel. Everything is okay. Let's just get some rest, okay?"

"I can't leave."

"I know. You can sleep in here with me. If anyone says anything, I'll tell them to mind their own business."

Daniel chuckled, sleep already starting to take him in his exhausted state. Before he fell out of consciousness, I felt him place his hand against my heart, feeling for the steady beat. "I wouldn't survive if I lost you, Christa," he murmured. "You have the power to destroy me. You almost did. Please, please, don't do this again."

I kissed him softly on the lips, hoping that offered enough reassurance as he drifted off to sleep, but unable to sleep myself.

His words cut through me, echoing back my own fears. Daniel shouldn't be afraid of me leaving him. I'd always been the one hesitant to give him too much of my heart for fear that he would end up destroying my soul.

What a pair we made, both of us hoping we could hold each other just far enough away that when this thing between us eventually had to end, we wouldn't end up devastated. Both of us knowing that we were fools. We were already past the point of avoiding getting hurt. Now the only thing left to do was figure out what we could do about it.

I yawned, sleep taking me even though I hadn't thought I could.

A few days after waking, I sat in Daniel's Jeep as he drove us home. My body still ached, but my werewolf genes had done a superb job mending my broken body.

I stared out the window, sulking. I'd spent two weeks in the hospital from my injuries. Luckily, all of the teachers at school were kind enough to give me home studies so that I wouldn't have to spend my summer catching up just to graduate. Mostly, the hit my pride had taken at being so easily defeated hurt worse.

Because of my near-death experience, Daniel and I were at odds about the best way to keep me safe. He felt that I should be on constant lock-down. I felt that I just needed to have constant backup, but that I should be free to live life normally.

As we pulled up to Les Loups-Garous, I let out an angry grunt. Armed guards manned the front doors, which were covered by the steel barricades that Daniel had told me about. Bars covered the windows, leaving the whole building feeling cold and unapproachable. Razor wire fence surrounded the perimeter, closing off the entrance to the parking lot where a make shift guard-post had been set up.

Daniel stopped next to the guard post and rolled down his window. Brock's familiar face peered into the window and smiled. "Hey, boss. Glad to see you made it out alive."

His tone may have been playful, but deep in his eyes, a haunted gleam reminded me that everyone knew I almost didn't make it.

I smiled in return. "Of course, I did. It would take a lot more than an ambush from some simple-minded creeps to take me out of the game."

He grinned at me again, the gesture not quite touching his eyes and hit a button inside his post. With a screech, the gate in front of us slid open, and Daniel pulled forward, still silent.

"You locked down Les Loups-Garous," I stated, trying to keep my voice even.

He nodded back wordlessly.

I cracked my knuckles, frustration coursing through me. "You locked down Les Loups-Garous without talking to me first."

Daniel pulled into a spot, and an entourage of guards surrounded us, flanking us as we got out of the Jeep and headed towards the door. When we reached it, Daniel entered a code into the panel affixed to the steel trap doors.

We walked into the club, all quiet except for a few more guards, and Daniel turned on me. "I did tell you. You just didn't want to listen." He stalked across the floor not waiting for me to answer. I trailed after him, following him up the stairs to the apartment.

"Because this is stupid! Locking me away isn't going to help us. It just makes me look weak."

We reached the landing of the apartment, and Daniel spun around, grabbing me by my shoulders so quickly I didn't have time to react. "I don't care if you look weak," he shouted, desperation cracking through his indifference. He took in my shocked expression and closed his eyes, breathing deeply for control. "I can't lose you."

"The pack needs me to be strong. Now more than ever," I whispered.

Daniel released my shoulders and reached his hands up to his face, fists of frustration forming before he let his hands drop to his side. "To hell with them. With all of them. I'd let this entire building, the whole pack, burn to the ground before I watch the light leave your eyes ever again."

The Alpha inside me bristled. His words were dangerous, and not in a sexy, romantic way. They set me on edge, the fear that whatever was going on between us had already begun to twist him in ways I couldn't save him from. He knew better than anyone. Pack was power. Pack was *family*. The pack came first.

He had taught me that, so I couldn't understand how he could say such traitorous things.

"It doesn't work like that, and you know it. My life means nothing if I can't keep them safe."

"Your life means everything to me!" he shouted, turning away again and bursting through the door of his bedroom.

I followed on his heels, my fear for him trumping any anger I'd felt over the lock-down fiasco.

"Daniel," I started, the words soft. He didn't respond, and I tried again. "Daniel!"

He spun, a predatory look in his eyes, and closed the space between us. I backed against the wall, inexplicably afraid.

"I would die a thousand times," he started, words soft but harsh. "Before I ever let anything hurt you again."

Before I could respond, he pressed into me, mouth crashing onto mine with so much intensity that I felt my knees turn to jelly.

I kissed him back with equal fervor, my hands snaking up around his neck as he backed us away from the wall, pulling me down as he fell to the bed without breaking the kiss.

My fingers clutched at the hem of his shirt as his mouth moved away from mine, and his lips trailed softly down my jaw and onto my neck.

A soft moan escaped my lips, my body wanting this so much it hurt. Urged on by the sound, Daniel's mouth moved further down, brushing across my collarbone hungrily.

I wrestled with his shirt, pushing it up and running my hands against the hard planes of his chest. With just a little urging, he lifted his head away from me as I pulled the shirt off and tossed it away.

His fingers, in turn, reached for my shirt, slowly pushing it up as he looked down at my pale stomach...

And I tensed.

Faster than I could comprehend, I pushed him away from me, springing up and pulling my shirt back down.

Daniel, understandably, looked confused, staring at me as though I had slapped him.

"Wh- what?" he stammered.

I shook my head, not understanding myself why I had stopped him, but just knowing with every fiber in my being that I had to.

We stared at each other, Daniel so shocked while my mind struggled to catch up to what my body had already figured out.

This wasn't right. I'd wanted to experience this moment with him for so long, but not like this. This wasn't about love, or passion, although there was plenty of passion in the way we had devoured each other.

He'd used this as a distraction. A way to end an argument between us.

Daniel watched me warily, waiting for me to answer his question. I met his eyes before looking away and biting my lip. How could I tell him what I'd been thinking? I wanted to be with him so badly, but deep down I knew this situation had gotten out of hand. We'd promised each other that we would take each day together as they came, but both of us had an unspoken understanding that we knew this couldn't go on forever. From the start, we'd known that eventually, this would end. Taking this next step felt wrong like we were abandoning our duty for own selfish desires.

We were out of control, and I winced as I realized that I needed to end this, now.

"I'm not ready," I whispered, instead, shame filling me as I realized I'd been too much of coward to do what I needed to do.

His lips stretched to a thin line, his guarded eyes revealing nothing. He opened his mouth to say something but promptly shut it.

His gaze tore through me, almost as though he could read my mind and knew that there was more to it than just me not being ready. He sighed and ran his hand through his hair. "Right," he said softly, nodding. He fixed his dark eyes on me once more, and I felt as though he saw right through me. "I knew that. I just..." he trailed off, ashamed in himself for letting the moment get the best of him. "I won't get carried away again," he promised.

My heart clenched. I had to end this. There couldn't be a next time. My will wouldn't hold out again.

"Daniel," I started, commanding his attention. "We need to ta-" My words were interrupted by a quiet cough at the doorway.

Startled, I spun around, taking in the intruder and my breath caught.

CHAPTER EIGHT

I didn't know him, but he was, aside from Daniel, one of the most beautiful men I had ever seen. He stood a few inches shorter than Daniel but just as muscular, the black shirt he wore hugging tightly to his toned body. Straw blond hair, much shorter than Daniel's, but still long enough to flop into his face, framed his chiseled cheeks. He was tan, the kind of color that my pale skin could never achieve, no matter how many hours I spent at a tanning salon. He met my gaze with eyes so honey brown that they looked like liquid gold, his stare cutting through me as he smiled with amusement. I tried not to blush under the intensity of his gaze. He looked like a sun god, and I felt incredibly inadequate standing between the sun god and the moon god on either side of me.

His eyes flicked from me to Daniel. "Am I interrupting something, *Omega?*" he asked, the last word dripping with sarcasm.

Daniel's lips pursed as he crossed his arms over his still bare chest. "How long have you been there, Travis?"

The tension between the two of them crackled, palpable and stifling. I had to work hard to force myself to interject. "Do you two know each other?"

That golden gaze flicked to me again, a grin twitching at the side of his mouth before he ignored me completely and looked coolly back at Daniel.

"Not that long. Just long enough to see the two of you staring awkwardly at one another."

Daniel huffed in annoyance. "What do you want?"

The grin spread across his lips, lighting up this Travis fellow's face gloriously. "I just wanted to meet the True Alpha. After all, it's not every day I find myself in the presence of someone so... alluring."

That did it. I blushed, so brightly that I felt like anyone

within a fifty-foot radius would be able to see me and giggled.

Daniel's eyes flicked to me, his eyebrows shooting straight up on his forehead, and his ire at my reaction sobering me.

I cowered away from his annoyed look and fixed my stare back on the newcomer.

"Who are you?" I asked, blessedly not stumbling over the words.

Mock hurt flashed across his face, and he placed a hand on his heart. "Christa, you slay me. I thought for sure you'd recognize the face of the wolf that saved you from certain death."

I blinked in confusion, unable to place this guy. "What are you talking about?"

"Really? I thought it would be obvious. I mean, it's not every day that someone rushes in and saves the day. You really don't recall a certain wolf jumping in to knock that monster off of you?"

My mind rippled, the memory of the unknown reddish wolf flitting across my consciousness. "You-" I started.

Daniel scoffed. "Enough. Quit playing games. You only helped her because she spared your insignificant life."

Travis shrugged. "Maybe. Maybe not. Some might say she didn't save me at all. Some might say she condemned me to isolation."

Pieces started falling into my mind as I realized his identity. "Are you Lana's Beta?" I asked, not believing it. The last I'd heard he hadn't shifted from his wolf form, and while the last time I'd met all the Alpha's and their Beta's had been a blur, I felt certain I wouldn't have forgotten someone so breathtaking. Then again, I hadn't been too focused on committing anyone to memory back then. I was just trying to get through formalities so that I could get on with my destiny.

Travis's eyes shifted, going cold. "I *was* her Beta. I'm no one's Beta now, thanks to you."

I shivered from the chill in his voice, and Daniel snorted

again. "Christa, this is Travis Emory, former Beta of the Eastern- American pack."

I studied Emory carefully, not sure if he was barely hiding hostility he felt about being released from Lana's pack, or just trying to test me the same way his old Alpha would have.

"I'm sorry if you feel like I wronged you, but she wanted to execute you, and I thought it was better to at least give you a fighting chance at life."

He stared back at me, his expression blank before he laughed heartily. "Chill, little Alpha. I'm not mad. Lana and I were experiencing difficulties. I no longer felt like a part of her pack, anyway."

"So you were just testing my patience, then?"

Emory opened his mouth to speak, but Daniel cut him off. "No. He was testing me. He wanted to see what I would do if I felt like you were threatened. He believes that we're hiding a secret romance."

My heart beat hard in my chest as I tried to keep my face neutral. "Well, that's just ridiculous."

Emory kept that amused smile as he responded. "Is it? Because it sure did seem like I was interrupting some sort of private moment when I walked in on the two of you staring each other down and panting."

"We were arguing," I answered, silently congratulating myself for thinking quickly on my feet.

"About what?"

Daniel answered before I could. "We have differing opinions on the best way to keep Christa alive."

Emory's eyes met Daniel's and held them, evaluating him for the truthfulness of his statements. I don't know if he believed Daniel or not, but his eyes cut back to my face. "Tell me little Alpha, what do you think we should do to keep you safe?"

I shot a look at Daniel, my forgotten frustration resurfacing as I flopped down to sit on the edge of the bed. "I don't know. I just don't think locking down Les Loups-Garous is the answer."

"I agree," he answered back.

"You do?" I asked in surprise.

"You don't get an opinion," Daniel said in annoyance.

Emory smiled at me kindly, his whole face transforming as he let his mask of calculated arrogance slide away, and he took a step further into the room. "I told good ole Danny-boy here that, as a Beta, I could see where locking away an Alpha in the attempt to keep her safe would ruffle her feathers. He told me to mind my own business because I didn't know you, and I wasn't part of your pack."

"And I meant it, Emory. Mind your own business," Daniel spat furiously.

Emory shrugged again. "I'm just saying..." he trailed off, darting a glance to Daniel. "I might not be a part of your pack, but maybe she wants to hear what I suggested."

"What you suggested is insane," Daniel answered.

"To you, as an Omega. But maybe to her, as an Alpha, it wouldn't seem so crazy." Emory turned to me. "What d'ya say, little Alpha? Do you want to hear what I had to say on the issue?"

I chanced a glance at Daniel, his lips pursed with barely contained annoyance and knew that I needed to say no.

But the thing was, I didn't know this guy, and he didn't know me, so some part of me thought that maybe, just maybe, his judgment wouldn't be clouded by the same protectiveness that affected Daniel's.

Bracing myself for the anger I knew I would incite in Daniel, I answered quietly, "Yes."

Daniel huffed angrily. "This should be interesting," he barked, and I winced.

Emory smiled like a wolf who'd just killed his prey. "I think that instead of waiting for the next attack to come to you, we should take the attack to them."

I stilled, certain that I had missed some kind of joke. Surely, this guy was off his rocker because his suggestion seemed mental.

Gathering my thoughts, I took a deep breath. "You think that we should attack the monsters that we know nothing about let alone what they are?"

"Don't you? Or are you content to let Daniel lock you away indefinitely? Because that is his plan, you know?"

Daniel strode forward, only stopping when he stood inches away from Emory. "My plan is to keep her alive and safe. Something you wouldn't know anything about. Lana warned me about you. She warned me that you were becoming unpredictable. She told me all about how you felt that we needed to quit waiting for wars to come to us. She told me about how you wanted to launch an attack against *all* rogues to ensure that none of them could rise up."

Emory's lip curled at Daniel. "You know I'm right, Daniel." He paused and regarded Daniel with disgust. "What happened to you? There was a time where you shared my point of view."

Daniel shook his head in response. "I'm not doing this with you again. This conversation is done, Travis. I said you could stay here, down where the other wolves are camped out. Don't make me rescind the invitation."

Emory scoffed and shook his head in return before spinning away from Daniel and heading for the doorway. He allowed me one more glance, no more humor on his face.

"He doesn't treat you like his Alpha. He doesn't even treat you like his equal. You are the Alpha; you call the shots. You know where to find me when you get tired of your imprisonment and decide you want to do something."

He strode out of the room, leaving me staring at the empty space where he'd just been, mulling his words over in my mind.

His suggestion was crazy, but I couldn't help the nagging feeling inside that kept screaming that he might be right about Daniel.

He didn't see me as his equal, and he definitely didn't treat me like his Alpha.

That would never change as long as I kept letting him make decisions for me.

Daniel slammed the door shut drawing my attention away from the empty doorway.

As I studied Daniel, my thoughts wandered to Emory's final words. Was he right? Was Daniel keeping me from being the Alpha I was meant to be?

I shook the thoughts away. Daniel just wanted to keep me safe. His tactics may be undermining to my authority, but his intent wasn't to make me look weak.

He just couldn't bear to lose me.

His passionate but dangerous words from earlier echoed in my mind and reminded me that things were escalating between us. The thought pinged hollowly in my chest. I knew what I needed to do, but I couldn't find the strength to end things between us before our situation got any messier. I really needed some space, some time to evaluate what Daniel and I were doing here so I could figure out if it could continue.

Daniel glanced over at me, his face softening as he took in my contemplative face. "Don't let him get to you, Christa. Emory is a troublemaker. Always has been, always will be."

I frowned at Daniel. "Is he right, though? Should we quit waiting for the enemy to come to us?"

Daniel sat on the edge of his bed, grabbing me and pulling me, so I stood in front of him as he placed his hands on my hips. "I don't know. I just know he's not wrong," he answered, shocking me. I'd been expecting him to go on a rant about Emory being out of his mind. I definitely hadn't expected him to agree.

"Do you really intend to lock me away at Les Loups-Garous?"

He closed his eyes, breathing deeply. "If you'd let me. But we both know you never would. I may concede that Emory is right about us needing to launch offensive attacks, but he is definitely wrong about what he said to you," Daniel paused and met my eyes, earnestness written across his face. "I do see you as my Alpha. I do see you as my equal. And if you don't want to stay locked up here, I can't make you."

I felt tears prick my eyes as his words washed over me, erasing any doubts that Emory had planted. "I really think that there are better ways to use our resources. Plus, we need the club open to generate revenue."

Daniel nodded his agreement. "So, what do you think we should do?"

I bit my lip, mulling over the thoughts that had already been forming in my mind. "I think we could keep guards out, hidden of course, but we could open the club back up. Let's be honest here, predators don't walk straight into the wolves' den. They wait until they can isolate their prey to attack. Everything I've seen from these monsters so far indicates that they are definitely predators. They would never attack Les Loups-Garous directly. In the meantime, we can try to figure out everything we can about these guys and see if we can find their weaknesses. See if we can figure out how to draw them out."

Daniel observed me, considering what I had to say. "They're not the only threat, though. You still have a rogue out there trying to undermine you. How will you handle trying to get to the bottom of that and solving the mystery of these new creatures?"

The gears in my mind were already turning, forming plans that had the potential to help me with *all* my problems. I tabled Daniel's question for a moment, needing more information about something else.

"I'll get to that. But first... I have some questions about Emory."

Daniel's eyes flashed with annoyance, but he didn't interrupt; instead, he waved his hand in my direction.

"What happened between me telling you not to kill him and you guys arriving here?"

"I don't know. Lana and I argued but in the end, she told

me she was planning on sending Emory elsewhere, anyway, so we could just take him and deal with it. She told me that they had been having differences of opinion for a while now and that she felt like he had outgrown his role as her Beta."

"And then you guys left, and he was still in wolf form?"

"Yes. He drove all the way to Kennington in wolf form. We were driving down the street, almost here, when all of a sudden he shifted. Scared the shit out of me. He told me that he'd been waiting to get away from Lana's pack. That he felt something twisted in the pack magic, and that he had a feeling there was a traitor somewhere in her pack. He'd told Lana, but she'd brushed his concerns off as him being paranoid."

Criticisms rushed to my lips, but I held them back as I considered what I would do if I were Lana. Hearing that there might be a traitor in your pack, and not being the one who'd caught on, would be a tough pill to swallow for any Alpha, myself included.

Instead of bad-mouthing Lana, I asked another question about Emory. "Do you think that he was pretending to be feral to get away from Lana's pack?"

Daniel shrugged. "With the way he just came out of it on his own? Kind of."

I stayed silent, thoughts rushing through my mind. Daniel watched me intently. "What are you thinking, Christa?"

Instead of answering, I asked my own question. "Tell me how you guys knew that I'd been attacked."

Daniel grimaced. "Emory. I don't know how he knew, but as soon as I stopped my car in the parking lot, he tore out of the car and shifted, running full speed for the forest. I thought he was running from us, so I signaled the pack to hunt him down. He led us right into the ambush," he paused, and I saw pain flash as he recalled the memory. "He reached you first. He saved you."

"How did he know?" I asked.

"He said he heard the screech of tires and knew someone

was hurt. None of us even realized those things were out there until we were already running through the forest, and then we heard the howls."

"We need to talk to Emory. Where is he?"

Daniel eyed me curiously. "He's down in the basement with the other wolves who are camping out here while we figure out a plan. What are you thinking, Christa?" he repeated.

"I have a plan, but you're going to have to trust me."

Daniel rose to his feet. "Why do I have the feeling I'm not going to like this plan of yours?"

"Because you probably won't. But before I tell you what it is, we need to talk to Emory."

I spun away from him, heading out of the bedroom and marching straight for the exit. I took the stairs two at a time all the way down to the basement level, crashing through the door unceremoniously, Daniel right behind me.

Heads snapped in my direction, but no one said anything. "Emory!" I yelled. "Where is Emory?"

From somewhere in the back, Emory's voice rang out. "I'm over here."

I looked around, spotting him sitting at a round table with three other guys and pushed my way across the basement to where he sat holding some cards in his hand.

He glanced up at me when I reached him, his face reflecting that same amusement from earlier.

"Did you decide that you wanted to take some action?" he asked nonchalance drowning his features before flicking his eyes to Daniel and shrugging. "Guess not."

"I need you to come upstairs with me, right now," I told him.

He looked me up and down before turning back to his cards. "I'd love to, but can it wait, because I'm cleaning house at poker right now?"

I rolled my eyes, and grabbed a fistful of his shirt, yanking him up as best as I could. "No. It cannot." I told him.

He stood, brushing my hand off his shirt and fixed me with a level glare. "Fine," he said, marching past me.

Daniel and I followed him up to the club floor, and we took a seat at one of the tables, Daniel and I on one side, Emory on the other.

He slouched in his seat, irritated by our interruption, but otherwise unconcerned. "What do you want?"

"I decided I wanted to do something," I offered, purposely not providing any more information until I gauged his reaction.

"Oh?" he asked, curiosity peaking his interest.

"Yeah. And we're going to need your help. Daniel says that you felt a traitor in your pack bonds?"

Emory's eyes narrowed slightly. "So?"

"So, there is a rogue threatening me. Trying to take control of the packs. Between trying to figure out what these new creatures are and trying to stop a rogue war, my resources are stretched a little thin."

"How is that my problem?"

"If a rogue takes control of the packs, it's everyone's problem," Daniel cut in.

Emory afforded Daniel one contemptuous glare before focusing on me again. "What exactly is your plan, little Alpha?"

I nodded. "Right. Well, I need someone to help me gather more information about who is behind this rogue mutiny. I also need another person watching for the traitor in Lana's pack, and if possible riding the research team there like Seabiscuit, so that we can come up with some answers. Not to mention, if we're going to open Les Loups-Garous back up, I'm going to need a leader heading my security detail."

Emory shook his head. "If you think I'm going to go back to Lana's pack and play spy for you, you are sorely mistaken."

"Of course I wouldn't send you," I started, apprehension filling me as I spoke the next words. "I'm sending Daniel. I need you to stay here and watch my back."

Daniel's head snapped toward me. Emory looked like I'd

dumped cold water on him.

"What?" they both asked in horrified unison.

CHAPTER NINE

I had to talk fast to get the guys to listen to me, the shocked looks on their faces telling me that they both thought that I'd come unglued. Maybe I had, but truthfully I couldn't see any other options. I needed someone to infiltrate Lana's pack and find the rogue. I couldn't very well send Emory. I mean, he'd been kicked out of the pack; none of them trusted him.

I'd considered sending someone else, but honestly, no one else in my pack had ever really dealt with Lana or her pack, and I need someone who her pack trusted. Lana and Daniel had a long history, one that irked the hell out of me, but a history nonetheless. Daniel had been flitting in and out of her life, and subsequently her pack's lives, for years, and they trusted him.

Given their history, it killed me to send him back to her, but we needed to get to the bottom of this.

My selfish part also admitted that sending Daniel had the added benefit of giving me the space I needed to reevaluate our own relationship.

Plus, Daniel could be super-insistent and annoying when he wanted to be, so I felt that he could supervise the research team and push them into getting answers faster. I trusted he would be quick to relay information about these new wolf-monsters as things were discovered.

Emory was another story. I didn't trust him. I found his whole alibi a little too convenient given my current situation, but I figured I'd operate under that whole keep your enemies close adage. I'd rather he try something nefarious right in front of me, on my own turf, where I had appropriate backup.

Neither of them seemed thrilled to follow through with my plan, but I didn't care. I may not have known or trusted Emory, but he was right about one thing; we had to quit waiting for the next attack to take us by surprise. We had to end this war before it really started.

"Any questions?" I asked once I'd finished relating my plan to them, conveniently leaving out my thoughts about sending Daniel so that I could decipher my torn feelings about him. Emory may have his suspicions about what was going on between Daniel and me, but I didn't need to give him any more ammo to fuel his theories.

Emory cracked his neck, the tendons straining as he thought over what I'd said.

"So, besides babysitting me to make sure I'm not your enemy, what exactly are you going to do while Daniel is busy traipsing around with Lana?"

His words were bait, a way to see if I'd have a jealous reaction. And honestly? I was green with jealousy, but I'd be damned if I would let Emory see that.

I shrugged, placing my hands on the table between us. "I'm going to try to convince my buddy, Casey, to have a little chat with his father."

Out of the corner of my eye, I saw Daniel tense at the reminder of Cooper Jones.

Emory missed the gesture; his attention focused on me. "Trying to force a little family reunion?" he scoffed. "Sounds like an utter waste of time that has nothing to do with solving our actual problems. Just like a female to let sentimentality get in the way of actual work." He paused and pointed his finger at me, spearing me with a serious look. "You may want to fix all your friends' family dramas, but don't expect me to tag along. I have better things to do."

I gritted my teeth at his sexist comment, letting it slide even though I really wanted to punch this guy in his smug face. "I'm not trying to fix any family problems, and you *are* going to help me with it. Casey's dad made claims a long time ago that he knew what those things are. We need Casey to get him to talk."

"Why?" Emory retorted, his tone reflecting his disinterest.

"Because no one else can. He's been in prison a long time, and now he swears he won't tell a soul what those things are.

But I was hoping that maybe his long-lost son might be able to coax it out of him."

Emory chewed on his nail, still slouched down in his seat, and staring off at nothing. For a second, I thought he'd completely tuned me out before he raised his eyebrows at me. "Sounds like some sentimental female shit to me. If the dude doesn't want to talk to his pops, you shouldn't make him."

I opened my mouth to retort, but Daniel cut in. "He's right, Christa. Casey doesn't want anything to do with that lunatic, and I don't want you anywhere near him. Cooper is dangerous. I don't trust this dingbat to protect you," he said, jerking his thumb at Emory.

Emory straightened in his seat, something clearly captivating his attention as he watched me with curious eyes before his gaze flicked subtly to Daniel. "I'm not a dingbat," he mumbled, still deep in thought before I saw his whole face light with realization.

He looked back and forth between Daniel and me, his head flipping between us with exaggerated movement before he put his hand over his mouth in mock-astonishment. "You don't mean... Well, you just couldn't mean..." he paused, and the corner of his mouth lifted in a wicked smile. "You aren't talking about *Cooper Jones*, are you? Well, well. This just got interesting." He met Daniel's eyes with an impish gaze. "Didn't that guy ki--"

"Stop before you get hurt," Daniel growled, the threat in his voice sending shivers down my spine.

Emory threw his hands up in a surrendering gesture. "I'm just saying," he added, slinking back down into his seat.

My lips curled in disgust. "What the hell is wrong with you?" I asked.

Daniel answered before Emory could give me another sarcastic retort. "He's a child stuck in a man's body."

Emory shot Daniel a dark look. "Nothing is wrong with me. I'm just me, take it or leave it. There was a time when you lived the same way."

I rubbed my temples, Emory's constant sarcasm giving me a headache. "I think we're done here for tonight." I rose, scooting myself out of the booth I sat in. Daniel followed me out as I headed across the room for the door that would take us the staircase.

I gazed over at Emory, trying hard not to sneer at him. I'd expected so much more from a Beta. This guy was a disappointment. "We'll meet back here in the morning to hammer out the rest of the details."

Emory smiled joylessly. "Oh goody. I can't wait."

I rolled my eyes, turned away from him, and followed behind Daniel, catching up with him as he swung the door open to start up the stairs.

I paused in the open staircase, turning around to glance at Emory one last time before heading up. His eyes, smoldering like liquid fire, met mine and a chill slithered through me. I detected no trace of his sarcastic humor as he studied me from across the room. He watched me with a guarded expression, all seriousness, as though he were trying to figure me out.

Not knowing what else to do, I shook my head at him, disappointment obvious on my face, then turned and hurried up the steps.

Pushing through the door to the apartment, I strode down the hall, turning into Daniel's room. He lounged in his bed with his back against his headboard and his knees up.

"What is with that guy?" I asked, unable to hide the distaste in my voice.

Daniel shrugged. "That's just Emory."

I huffed. "Well, is he always so frustrating? And what was with all his macho, 'you used to be like me, Daniel,' garbage?"

Daniel shrugged again and patted the bed next to him. I strolled over, sat down, leaned my head against his shoulder and pulled my knees up next to his.

"Emory used to be my best friend," Daniel started.

I looked over at him, surprise written on my face. "How? I mean, he's so arrogant."

Daniel peered back at me, cocking his eyebrow in that disturbingly sexy way of his. "In case you forgot, there was once a time when you accused me of being just as much of a cocky prick."

I winced, a blush spreading across my cheeks at his reminder. "Yeah. But I was wrong."

"Maybe you weren't."

"What do you mean? Of course, I was. Just look at you now. You're probably the kindest, most loyal person I know."

Daniel squeezed his eyes shut and took a deep breath. "Christa, I was a supreme asshole. I thought the world belonged to guys like Emory and me. That's what he meant when he said that I used to be like him. We did whatever we wanted. We said whatever we thought was funny with no regard to how our actions affected other people. We lived our lives thinking that everyone was exactly like us, and it was either be cruel or be somebody's fool."

"What changed?" I asked, already knowing the answer, but needing the confirmation.

"I met you," he said softly. "I met you, and you showed me that there are genuinely good people in the world. Emory says that having you as an Alpha has softened me. He doesn't understand. And I can't make him, not without telling him the truth. It's not your Alpha that tamed me. It's you, as a person. It's you as a woman. As the person who loves me. And I just want to be worthy of that love."

His words tore through me, leaving me silent as the love I felt for him raged war with the rational part of me that kept telling me that we had taken this too far.

I sighed in exasperation, drawing Daniel's attention. "What's wrong?"

I stared at him, so open and vulnerable, and a million thoughts rushed to my mind. I could tell him my fears, maybe he would understand. The way he watched me now, I thought he might.

"Do you think we've taken this too far? Do you think we're past the point of being able to end this when we should?"

I tensed, waiting for him to get angry. Instead, he regarded me levelly before wiping away a tear from my cheek; one that I didn't realize had escaped.

"Where is this coming from?"

I frowned. "From the start of this, we knew that eventually, it would have to end. I'd prepared myself for that, trying to protect myself, and you, so that when it did, we would be able to survive it. When you tell me that you can't live without me, and say such sweet things, I start to wonder if I'll be strong enough to let you go when I have to."

"I see," he stated, his face going blank. He pulled away from me, expression unreadable.

I stilled, waiting for his anger at my words to burst through the surface. Instead, he spoke. "Is that what you still want?"

An answer sprang to my lips before I could stop myself. "No." I winced and tried again. "I don't know. I don't know if my sense of duty to my pack can trump how I feel about you. I need time to think."

Daniel stared at me, thoughts turning behind his dark brown eyes. "Is that why you're sending me away?"

I blushed guiltily. "No." I paused before shaking my head in confusion. "And, yes. I really do feel you're the best choice to go there. But, I also need to sort my feelings."

"Christa, I don't think I'll ever be able to let you go. Not unless you send me away. But, I'm not going to force you to make any decisions today. If you need time, I'll give you time. Just don't make me wait forever."

My heart clenched in my chest, gratitude for his words and love for him overwhelming me. "Thank you, Daniel."

He smiled in return, inching closer to me.

I felt that we needed a change in conversation. "Do you

think I should be worried about Emory? Do you think that he's making all of this up because he's the threat?"

Daniel's defense came immediately. "No. He's loyal to a fault. If he was having problems with Lana, it's because he felt like she's quit protecting her pack. He's an asshole, not a traitor."

I bit my lip. "So, he's not dangerous?"

Daniel scoffed, "That's not what I said. Emory is definitely dangerous. You should stay away from him."

Something dark hung in the words he spoke. I wanted to ask more questions, but I had a feeling that whatever had happened between him and Emory, Daniel definitely didn't want to talk about it. Guiltily, I wondered if Emory would be willing to tell me.

I let the thought go, drifting into a peaceful sleep next to Daniel.

Sleep had gone a long way to refresh everyone. Consequently, the talk in the morning went relatively smoothly. Emory remained sarcastic, and I figured out pretty quickly that being snarky dominated his personality.

"You're not my Alpha. I don't owe you anything," he pointed out when we reconvened.

"She's your Alpha's Alpha. So, yes, actually she is your Alpha," Daniel promptly retorted.

One look at Emory's face and I could tell Daniel had struck a chord. "In case you forgot, I'm a rogue now, thanks to you. I don't have an Alpha."

"You're alive now, thanks to her," Daniel shot back, eyes narrowed.

I could feel the tension rising in all of us. Emory huffed, and Daniel glared at him, while I tried to find the words that would make my grand plan seem more appealing.

"Look, guys, I know none of this is ideal, but we need answers. Like I said before, this is the best way."

Emory's eyes flicked to my face, and he studied me for a moment. "What makes you think I won't kill you given the chance?"

Daniel stood quickly, murderous intent written all over his face. "Don't you dare threaten her!"

Emory rose, also, the expression on his face daring Daniel to make a move. I saw his hand twitch at his side, and I realized that if I didn't think fast, the two of them were going to tear each other apart.

I slammed my fist to the table, causing both of them to turn and stare at me. "I really don't care what problems you have between the two of you. Here's the deal. I *am* the Alpha. I call the shots, at least when it comes to you," I nodded my head toward Daniel. "You?" I nodded in the other direction at Emory. "Well, you're absolutely right. You don't owe me anything. I'm taking a chance on you, offering you an opportunity to rise above whatever Daniel thinks you are to prove that you're not just a louse, lounging around doing nothing while the world you live in turns to crap."

Emory stared at me, eyes flashing beneath narrow slits while he exhaled heavily. "I couldn't care less about what Daniel thinks about me. I don't really care what you think about me either, for that matter. But, I won't let our world go to shit, so I guess I'll help you." Emory didn't seem too thrilled, and in the back of my mind, I wondered why he decided to help at all. He was another mystery I was going to have to puzzle out, I supposed. At the very least, relief filled me when we all calmed down.

We sorted out the details. I would return to school the next day, Emory driving me to and from in the rental we'd acquired since my own car was in the shop getting repaired.

Daniel would leave immediately on the pretense that he needed to help with the research. He still wasn't happy about leaving me in Emory's care and urged me to be careful around him. I assured him that I had back up. I'd already called Des and filled her in on the general plan, and she'd promised me that if Emory was up to no good, she'd be there to help me stop him.

With nothing left to work out, we put our plan in motion. As soon as Daniel left, my heart floundered in a river of sadness, but I pushed through it, knowing that we all had to do what was necessary for us to succeed. After all, my pack depended on us to figure this whole mess out and keep them safe.

At first, the drive to school the next morning dragged on in silence. I watched Emory warily from the passenger seat, finding myself wondering what motivated him.

Without glancing over at me, he clicked his tongue. "See something you like, little Alpha?"

I rolled my eyes, annoyed that I'd been caught staring. "Nope. I'm just trying to figure you out."

Eyes still focused on the road ahead of us, he shifted uncomfortably in his seat. "Nothing to figure out. Like I told you, I am who I am."

His callousness grated against my nerves. "I think there's plenty to figure out. I've never met anyone like you."

Emory chuckled without humor. "Sure you have. You know Daniel."

Denial that the two were anything alike sprang to my lips, but I choked it back. Even Daniel had said that not so long ago he and Emory were alike. I wanted to pretend they were different, and maybe that held true now, but I could still remember the way Daniel could constantly make me feel inferior to him; how he'd toyed endlessly with me before I'd finally broke through his tough exterior.

Emory noticed my hesitation and pressed his advantage. "You broke him, you know? You broke him, and I don't know how, but as hard as you're trying to figure me out, Christa, I'm trying to figure you out."

"Nothing to figure out," I recycled his own words back at him. "I am who I am. An Alpha who wants to rule her kind with peace. I want to continue my mother's legacy. I don't want people to fear me like your pack fears Lana."

Emory winced at the mention of his old Alpha as he pulled up in front of the school and looked at me coolly. "Come on, little Alpha, we all know that your lot think fear is an effective tool."

I shook my head, waiting for Des to show up so she could come to collect me from Emory. "Not me. I think inciting fear is cowardly, a sign of weakness. If you show your pack love, they will love you in return."

Emory stared, assessing me in the same way he had the night I'd first told them my plan, no smugness or witty comments, just earnest interest.

I stared back, my eyes locked on his, not daring to look away. I focused so hard that I nearly fell out of the car when Des wrenched the door open peeking her head in. "Time to go."

"Well, damn, and we were having such stimulating conversation, too," Emory drawled, commanding Des's attention.

She looked at Emory, did a double take, and licked her lips. "Oh. Hello," she said, looking from him to me and raising her eyebrows. "Is this him?" she whispered.

I nodded. "Des, this is Emory. Emory, this is Des."

"Pleasure," he crooned; no sarcasm as he assessed her with appreciation.

"Taken," she shot back, the faintest hint of wistfulness coloring her words.

"Devastating," he answered, equally wistful.

What the hell? With me, he was all dark wit and mean comments, but with Des it was all pithy flirtations and appreciative looks. I groaned. Why did I even care? I had a boyfriend. Not that I was jealous of him flirting with Des, I just didn't understand why he was so nice to her and so rude to me.

I suppressed the urge to roll my eyes and reached back to grab my backpack. I'd just ducked out of the car when Emory grabbed me by the wrist. Alarm shot through me, and my eyes locked on his, relaxing instantly as I realized he meant no ill intent. His eyes sparkled with sincerity. "Karina wanted to rule with love, too. That sentiment got her killed. I really hope it doesn't get you killed, too."

His hand released my wrist, and I snatched it up to my chest while he reached down and closed the door. He rolled down the window, self-satisfied smile back in place, and waved a hand at me. "See ya at three-thirty, little Alpha," he offered before screeching out of the parking lot.

I stood staring after him, more confused than ever about him.

"What the hell?" Des asked from beside me, craning her head around so she peered in my face.

"What?" I grumbled.

"What? You didn't tell me that Emory was God-Incarnate."

I shrugged noncommittally. "Is he? I hadn't noticed."

I spun around, heading into the school with Destiny right beside me. "I call bullshit. Man, I can't figure out if you are the luckiest girl in the world or the most cursed. You are surrounded by hot dudes."

"Lucky, I guess."

Des leaned against a row of lockers next to me as I spun the combination on mine and started shoving stuff inside. She examined her fingernails, but I knew she had something on her mind. "Seriously, Christa. That guy is hot. You don't have a boyfriend. I don't even know why you called me. If I were you, I'd have no problem getting extra attention from him."

I rolled my eyes. "He's a jerk."

Des shrugged. "You spend all that time with Daniel, and he's a jerk, too."

I stopped and looked at Des in confusion. "No, he's not."

Des looked back with defiance. "Maybe not to you, but don't forget that to the rest of the world, and the people who aren't his Alpha or his pack, he's kind of a jerk."

I shook my head and headed into my first class, one that I

shared with Des, and took my seat next to hers.

She still rambled on as the rest of the students started filing in, many of them stopping to offer me best wishes and telling me that they were glad I was okay.

I turned to Des. "Yo. I know you're still over there fantasizing about Emory, but I have a legitimate question to ask you."

Des blinked in surprise and then gestured for me to continue. I took a deep breath, knowing that the last time we'd had this conversation, Des had shot me down immediately, telling me to leave it alone. But I really needed her support.

"I really, really need Casey's help."

Des shrugged casually. "Yeah, of course. He's your friend. He'll assist you with anything."

I nodded. "Great, I need him to talk to his-"

She cut me off before I could finish, shooting me a warning glare. "Except for that."

If either of us had more to say on the subject, it would have to wait. The bell rang to signal class was starting.

She spent the rest of the morning avoiding me. After our first class finished, she darted out before I could talk to her. At first break, I saw her and Casey together across the quad. I waved, and Casey gestured for me to join them. As soon as Des saw me, she grabbed his hand and led him to god-knows-where, and I didn't get to talk to them.

The bell rang to end the fourth period, and my stomach growled in relief. Lunchtime had started and I was starving. Also, I wasn't going to let Des avoid me again.

My phone rang as I headed into the cafeteria. I quickly darted off to the side to answer it.

"Hey." Daniel's soothing voice floated through the receiver, instantly lifting my spirits. "How are things going?"

"Not good. Des cut me off before I could even ask for Casey's help. She's been avoiding me ever since."

"You know, I really don't like the idea of you trying to go see Cooper Jones without me."

My fragile temper had already been wearing on me. Daniel's comments didn't do much in the way of helping to ease my frustration. "I know, and I don't care. That's the plan, and I'm sticking to it."

Daniel huffed, "I know, but you should stay away from him. Jones is dangerous." He paused. When he spoke again, his voice was softer. "And maybe Des is on to something. You do remember what happened last time you tried to force a family reunion, don't you? It almost got you killed."

I winced at the reminder. "Yeah, I remember."

"Not to mention, you don't want to push away your friends just to get what you want, do you? Trust Des's judgment. She's a pretty smart girl."

I rolled my eyes, annoyed that he would take her side. "She also thinks that since she doesn't know I have a boyfriend, I should make a move on Emory."

Daniel scoffed. "Forget what I said. Des is a moron."

I laughed at the tone in Daniel's voice. "Don't worry. I told her Emory wasn't my type. I prefer tall, dark, and brooding to blonde, tan, and insufferable."

He laughed, his sourness over Des's suggestion washing away. "Just be careful."

"I always am."

A long moment of silence met me, and for a second I thought he'd hung up or we'd lost the connection. "Daniel? Are you there?"

"Yeah." His voice seemed distant, and I realized that my bold declaration probably didn't offer much reassurance in light of recent events.

He didn't say anything else, and I decided not to push the Cooper Jones issue any further, for now. Instead, I wanted to know how things were progressing on his end.

"So, um, have you guys gotten any more info?"

Daniel exhaled. "As far as I can tell, Lana's pack seems content."

"What about the other thing?" I asked, voice low as my eyes darted around the cafeteria anxiously.

"They haven't figured out anything useful, just confirmed what we already suspected."

I nodded. "They used to be human."

Daniel's breath caught, and I knew he had something to add, but he was afraid of how I might react. I could practically see his cautious face in my mind's eye.

I waited for a minute before frustration took over. "Spit it out, D."

"Christa. These things. They didn't just used to be humans," he paused, and I felt my stomach knot with a tangle of nerves as I waited for him to continue. "They used to be werewolves."

I grimaced, thinking to myself that I just couldn't take any more surprises. "How?"

"I have no idea, but as soon as we figure it out, I'll let you know."

"I know. Listen, Daniel, I have to go. But, call me later, okay?"

"Okay. I love you."

"Love you, too." I hung up and stashed the phone, scanning the room for Casey and Des. I spotted them at a table in the far end of the cafeteria and picked my way through the crowd to where they sat, my face set with determination.

Des saw me as I went to sit and turned to Casey. "Can you get me a soda?" she asked.

Casey shot a look between us. "Sure," he looked over at me as he rose. "Do you want anything?"

"Nah, I'm good."

Casey nodded and headed off, leaving Des and me alone.

"I'm not letting you ask him," she said with no other preamble.

"I know, and for right now, I'll drop it because I have other, more important stuff to tell you guys, and I'm hoping that after you hear it, he will want to help."

Des watched me carefully. "What kind of stuff?"

I looked at my phone and realized lunch had rushed by me. "We don't have time right now. Just meet me out front after school. I'll tell you, Casey, and Emory all together."

Des shrugged. "Cool. We'll be there." She paused and fixed me with a sly smile. "Later, I'll stop by your apartment, and you can tell me all about Emory."

The bell rang as I stood up. "Can't wait," I told her, any animosity between us forgotten.

CHAPTER TEN

Des didn't want to leave me alone with Emory for any more time than necessary until she had felt him out. Casey didn't want to leave Des alone with Emory. So, despite the fact that it meant Casey had to leave his car at school and would need a ride back to get it later, Des and Casey met me in front of the school at three-thirty sharp. Emory was not there.

I don't know why I felt surprised, nothing about Emory made me think that he cared about punctuality. As the minutes ticked on, I got more and more frustrated.

Casey stood stock still, eyes darting around the perimeter as he assessed the area for threats.

Des bounced up and down on her toes, swinging her arms back and forth. "Where is this guy?"

I frowned, looking down at my phone. He was twenty minutes late. "Heck if I know."

I had just resigned myself to call Brock for a ride when Emory pulled up in a huge, lifted Dodge Ram. Definitely not the Kia Optima he had when he'd dropped me off this morning.

He rolled the window down and peered over at us, sunglasses hiding his eyes. I studied the truck in confusion.

"What happened to the Kia?" I asked.

He pulled a face, his distaste for the Kia obvious. "I took it back and got this thing. Get in."

"Why?"

"Uh, because you need a ride, and I'm your chauffeur."

I closed my eyes and rubbed the bridge of my nose. "No. I mean why did you get rid of the Kia?" I asked, pulling the door open and inclining my head toward Des and Casey, silently inviting them to get in.

"Because that car had no balls."

I groaned in disgust, wondering why in the world I had to

deal with this guy. "You're crass."

From the backseat, I heard Casey mumble to Des. "This guy is an asshole."

If Emory heard, he chose to ignore it. "I don't know what that means, little Alpha, but if it means devastatingly handsome and charming, then yes, I am."

I smiled without humor. "It doesn't"

He shrugged, unconcerned. "What's with the stowaways?" He turned and glanced at Des and Casey.

"Eyes on the road," Casey muttered.

Once again, Emory ignored him, and I got the feeling he did so on purpose. "Watch the road for me, little Alpha," he said as he drove with his knee and turned back to look at Casey and Des again. "So, uh, this thing takes a lot of gas. I don't want to point out the obvious, but no one rides for free. I take cash, ass, or grass."

"Oh my god," I muttered, punching Emory in the arm and turning back to look at my friends. Des ground her teeth, clutching Casey's shoulder for dear life. Casey began turning various shades of red, clearly trying not to lunge across the seat and hit Emory in the face.

Emory rubbed his arm and glared at me. "What the hell?"

I pursed my lips, trying hard not to scream in Emory's face. "This is Des and Casey. They're my friends. They're also members of the Lunata."

I couldn't be certain, but I swore I could see Emory pale slightly. He glanced sideways at me, no trace of cockiness as he narrowed his eyes. "Strange company you keep."

"No stranger than you. Anyway, they're here because I had something to tell them. Well, all of you, really."

Emory's focus remained on the road, finally, but I could still see that contemplative look on his face. "Well?"

I shook my head. "I'll tell you when we get to Les Loups-Garous."

Silence filled the car, no one knowing what to say to each

other. To the rest of my companions, the lack of conversation must have seemed tense, but to me, it was like a gift. It felt like it had been so long since I'd been able to just sit and think without any major pressing drama unfolding around me. Granted, I was dragging my friends to my house so that I could beg one of them to do something that he had already told me he didn't want to do, but still, the quiet provided a nice reprieve from the constant noise that filled my life.

I stared out the window, watching houses and cars flash by and wishing that I could have a simpler life, one without life-changing decisions and deadly threats lurking around every corner. Finding out I was a werewolf and, not just any werewolf but the Alpha of all Alphas, had been thrilling. It had made me feel special.

Now it just made my head hurt. I continuously put myself in danger, constantly having to put everyone's safety above my own happiness. I wanted to be able to live my life, be with whomever I wanted, and not have to worry about being savagely murdered because of it.

I shook the thoughts out of my head. I may not have chosen this destiny, but it was mine, and I would take care of my pack the way an Alpha should.

We pulled up to Les Loups-Garous and got out of the car, no one saying anything as a comfortable silence settled over us. The club had returned to normal for the most part, which made me sublimely happy. I hated that dark, lock down mode, and absentmindedly, I wondered how secure it really could be when locked down. I wondered how many people could comfortably fit if necessary.

I shook that thought off, too. Aside from all-out war, I couldn't think of an event that would warrant that.

I led the group to one of the booths lining the walls of the club floor. A few people milled about, preparing for us to reopen. All of the employees were pack, so I felt that it would be safe to talk to my group here.

We sat; Casey and Des on one side, and Emory and me on the other. All three of them looked at me, anticipation wearing heavily around them.

I frowned as I considered the best way to start the conversation. It just felt so cold to come right out and demand Casey help us, but it also felt weird to just blurt out Daniel's info without preamble.

I tapped my fingers on the table, waiting for inspiration to strike, and coming up blank.

"What exactly are you waiting for? A written invitation? Get on with it," Emory's voice broke through the silence.

As much as I wanted to scold him for his rudeness, a part of me was thankful that he spoke up.

"I talked to Daniel earlier. He had some info about those things that attacked me."

Emory chewed on his nail, completely uninterested. I got the impression that he wasn't even listening.

Des and Casey had more appropriate reactions, eyes widening as they leaned closer. "That's great! What is it?" Des asked, excitement lacing her words.

"Those things used to be human," I began before Emory cut in, tone obnoxious.

"Well, duh. It doesn't take a team of scientists to figure that shit out."

I rolled my eyes at him, but I couldn't deny the happiness that welled up inside me now that he seemed to finally be paying attention.

"Is that what you dragged us out here to tell us? Because, honestly, Christa, I love the hell out of you, but I've got better things to do. I need to be keeping a watch out for threats to my people," Casey stated.

I pursed my lips. "Nooo," I drew it out. "He also told me that those things used to be werewolves." My statement hung in the air as everyone inhaled in shock. Even Emory sat up a little straighter, attention snapping to me.

Casey leaned forward. "Are you saying your wolves are mutating?" he asked, voice sharp.

I resisted the urge to yell, trying to remind myself that this was just Casey. All business, all the time. I hoped that he hadn't meant to offend me by automatically assuming that these wolves were part of my pack, while also reminding myself that as far as the Lunata were concerned all werewolves belonged to the True Alpha. I understood the sentiment, especially since I did rule them all at the end of the day. His insinuation still irked me, though.

Emory, smart-ass that he was, spoke up, face deadpan as he stared at Casey in disbelief. "Yep. It's all the peace and love Christa's been putting into our water. We're just so full of love now that our bodies are bursting forth in the form of giant monsters. They're not dangerous. They're just misunderstood."

I snapped, my temper flaring as I slapped Emory on the back of his head.

He threw his hands up. "What the fuck, Christa?"

I glared at him. "You're not helping."

He crossed his arms over his chest and slouched down in the booth. "It was a stupid question. It deserved a stupid answer."

As much as it killed me to admit it, I didn't think Emory was wrong, but I couldn't give him the satisfaction of letting him know that. Instead, I looked back at Casey. "I don't know, but I don't think so. Daniel says the research team hasn't been able to figure out anything else."

"So, it wasn't really useful info. It just leaves us with even more questions about these things," Des observed.

I nodded, swallowing as dread filled me. "Yeah. The thing is that Daniel, Zee, Aidan, and a whole mess of scientists, well, they aren't having much luck with their experiments. I think it may be time to explore other options."

The guys didn't catch up to my subtext as quickly as Des, and her objection rang out clearly. "No."

I glanced over at her, eyes pleading. "We need answers fast. I think he has them."

Des didn't offer a response, shaking her head at me as her face set in angry determination.

"Uh, does someone want to clue us in on what the two of you are hissing about?" Emory asked, voice petulant as he glanced back and forth between us.

I ignored Emory, eyes locking on Casey. "Case, I-"

Des shot out of her seat, anger radiating as she stared down at me. "I said no, Christa," she spat furiously.

I shot up, too, my wolf bristling at the thought of someone looking down on me. "It's the only way!"

"Find another way!" Des screamed back, her voice shaking with desperation.

"Can someone tell me what the fuck is going on?" Emory shouted, his voice echoing through the empty bar.

Des spun, directing her anger at Emory. He didn't flinch under her icy glare. I found myself impressed, while also thinking that his refusal to look away demonstrated a huge character flaw. He carried too much pride, and my inner wolf told me he would be one to watch carefully.

"Christa wants to ask my boyfriend to help sneak us into a prison to talk to his dad," she paused, focusing that intense stare on me. "A dad he hasn't spoken to since he was a small, small child, and who he has already made clear he wants nothing to do with."

Recognition flashed on Emory's face as he, no doubt, recalled my plan from the night before, and he looked at Casey with narrow-eyed speculation. "Are you Cooper Jones's son?"

Casey, who had been staring at the table in silence, flicked his eyes to Emory. "Yes."

Faster than I could comprehend, Emory grabbed me around the middle and launched us out of the booth, not stopping, or letting me go, until we were in the middle of the room.

Eyes flashing with golden fire, Emory stepped in front of me, crouching down into a defensive pose.

Des and Casey shot out of the booth equally as fast, both producing guns from their hips and training them on Emory.

"Let her go, and we won't shoot," Des warned, voice soft but deadly.

"Don't speak for me," Casey muttered.

I understood Des and Casey's reactions, although I didn't feel afraid of Emory. They were missing what I had figured out. Somehow, Emory had perceived some sort of threat toward me, and his actions were a way to protect me. I took a step around him, arms up in a surrendering gesture and looked at Emory. "What are you doing?"

Emory kept his gaze locked on Casey. "I'm keeping you away from a murderer."

Shock coursed through me. "What?" I asked, disbelief dripping from my voice. My eyes darted to Des, who seemed every bit as taken aback as me. She lowered her gun a fraction of an inch.

"He's not a murderer," she hissed through clenched teeth.

"His father killed one of my kind in cold blood," Emory shot back.

Casey hadn't moved, that cool mask still in place. "That was my father. Not me. Don't make assumptions about people you don't know."

Emory didn't budge, either. "How do I know I can trust you? How do I know you won't hurt her the minute I'm out of the way?" he growled, inclining his head in my direction.

Casey's eyes flicked in my direction. "I don't need your trust, nor did I ask for it. I only need her to trust me, and she does. Don't you, Christa?"

I answered with no hesitation. "Of course."

Emory's head snapped to me. "His father killed Daniel's mother. His kind hunts ours."

I sighed, resisting the urge to roll my eyes at Emory's

misguided chivalry. "First, they don't hunt us unless we are threatening the humans they are sworn to protect. Second, as he already told you, his father killed Jamie Hawthorne, not him. And, in case you haven't figured this out yet, he wants nothing to do with his father because he's just as appalled as the rest of us at what his father did. Finally, he's my friend, and he'd never hurt me."

Emory's face hardened, and I recognized the look of someone who was about to argue. I didn't have time for it. "Enough. He's perfectly safe. Now, you can either stand up so we can get on with our day as a group, or you can go downstairs and wait until the grownups are done talking."

Emory stood, his usual indifference slipping into place, and looked around the room. "Are there grownups coming, or..."

"Don't be stubborn. You know what I meant."

Emory looked around for a moment, his eyes catching Des's before he slumped with defeat. "Whatever," he said slashing a hand through the air.

Des hesitated, and I waved my hand. She lowered her arm, clicking the safety into place on her gun as she stowed it away in the waistband of her jeans.

Casey, eyes still trained on Emory as he moved away from me, slid behind the bar and made himself a drink. He did not make any move to lower his own weapon.

I shot a panicked look at Des, silently pleading with her to do something. Her returning glare told me she was angry as hell with me. Mad or not, she slipped behind the bar and placed a hand on Casey's shoulder. He jumped slightly, turning his head to meet her gaze.

They stared at each for what felt like an eternity, silent messages passing between them. Finally, a visible calm washed over Casey, and he put his gun away.

Des's hand slid from Casey's shoulder, reaching down while Casey's fingers laced with hers.

Together, they turned, heading for the exit. "Hey," I yelled, voice desperate. They couldn't leave yet. I hadn't asked Casey to help me.

They paused, and still in that creepy synchronicity, turned. "It's time we headed out before a bad situation becomes worse," Des said, carefully.

I nodded, understanding why they needed to go, but still aching with the question burning inside me. "I know, but please, Casey, I need to talk to your dad. Or at the very least, if you could talk to him. It could mean the difference between life and death for my pack."

Casey pursed his lips thoughtfully. "I understand what this means to you, Christa," he started, and my heart filled with hope. He was going to help. I could feel it. He would come through for me.

"But, I can't help you. Find some other way." My hope shattered as Casey finished, letting go of Des's hand as he breezed through the door.

Des shook her head at me, meeting my shocked face with an exasperated sigh. "I'll call you later when we've all cooled down."

She didn't wait for my response, turning and heading after Casey.

I stared at the empty spot where they'd just been, disbelief coursing through me. How could they just say no? Didn't they see how important this was?

From across the bar, Emory spoke up, "Are your friends always so... friendly?" he asked, sarcasm dripping from every word.

I turned and looked at him, unable to formulate my own words as the hurt from my friend's rejection still resonated inside me.

Emory held up his glass. "Care for a drink? You look like you need one."

I rolled my eyes and shook my head in disgust before turning and stalking across the bar to the door that would lead me upstairs away from Emory and the bitterness forming in my heart.

I couldn't believe my so-called friends had let me down. I sat in the living room of my humble home, staring at the television but not really watching, as I stewed over my current situation.

Why couldn't Casey see that he had to help me? There was no other way! Even more frustrating, why hadn't Des, my supposed best friend, taken my side?

It had been hours since Des and Casey left and the sounds of the club downstairs echoed in the walls of the apartment, making it difficult for me to think through my troubled feelings.

I'd called Des a couple of times, but she kept forwarding my calls. I didn't like the answer I'd gotten from Casey, but even worse, I hated the way things had been left between Casey, Des, and I.

The sound of the phone ringing tore through my self-wallowing, and my spirits lifted slightly as Daniel's name flashed across my caller ID.

"Hello," I answered, excitement filling my voice.

"Did you really try to coerce Casey into sneaking you in to talk to his dad after I told you I wanted you to stay away from him?" Daniel's anger rang through the receiver, effectively killing my excitement.

"Not exactly." I offered glibly.

"Well, what exactly did happen? Because the story I got when Des called me, mad as hell, was that you tried to convince Casey to take you to talk to his father, and that was after Emory almost outright attacked him."

I frowned, biting my lower lip. "Eh. Well, okay, that's pretty close to what happened."

Daniel huffed, frustration so evident that I could practically see his raised eyebrows and this-can't-be-happening facial expression. "I told you to stay away from this," Daniel started.

I sighed, standing up to head to the kitchen as my stomach

growled. "I should have known you'd take their side."

Daniel stayed quiet for only a second before he started launching into a lecture about responsibility and friendship and blah blah blah. I knew I should really be paying attention, but I just couldn't. I rifled through the cupboards, found a bag of pretzels that looked appetizing, and began munching as Daniel droned on.

I crunched loudly, and Daniel paused. "Are you listening to me?"

I should have lied. I should have told him that of course, I was listening, but I just couldn't. Something inside me had snapped after all the disappointment of the day, and I couldn't find it in me to pretend like I saw his, or any of their, points of view.

"Kind of," I started, but reconsidered. "Not really. I tuned out about the time I realized you weren't on my side."

"Are you fucking kidding me?" His anger boomed through the phone, and if I wasn't currently emotionally dead inside, I would have flinched and begun apologizing all over myself.

"No. I am not. I don't want to be lectured. I've already had a crap day, and I don't want to hear you say 'I told you so,' or whatever other words of infinite wisdom you have to offer. What I want is for you to pretend to be my boyfriend for a minute and be outraged on my behalf because of the way my friends treated me."

"The way they treated you?" he asked in disbelief. "Do you know how selfish you sound right now?"

"Ugh," I groaned as someone knocked on the door. "No, I don't. Please set me straight." I retorted as I walked over to the door wrenching it open. I was making an already bad situation worse, and Daniel's sputtering response made that perfectly clear.

Emory stood in the hall, shifting from foot to foot. "What?" I asked, mouth full of pretzels.

"What, what?" Daniel cut in, thinking I spoke to him.

Emory eyed me up and down, taking in my messy bun, black leggings, and black spaghetti strap top, the bag of pretzels still clutched in my hand as I shoveled handfuls into my mouth unceremoniously. "Bad time?"

I addressed Daniel first, "Not you, D. Emory is here."

On the other end of the line, Daniel became scary quiet. "Why?" he asked suspiciously.

"I don't know, I'll ask." I pulled the receiver away from my mouth. "What do you want?" I asked Emory, tone hostile.

Emory's eyes darted around the hall, clearly confused by my attitude, before he held up a couple of bags of fast food. "I thought you might be hungry," he offered.

I put the receiver of the phone back up to my lips. "It appears he wants to feed me," I told Daniel as I waved Emory inside.

"Well, tell him to go away because you and I are in the middle of a conversation."

"Eh. Too late, I already let him in. And I'm bored with this conversation, so I'm going to go."

"Christa! Don't you dare fucking han-" I clicked the phone off, honestly trying to figure out where this indifferent boldness had come from and turned to Emory.

Emory watched me in amazement. "Did you just hang up on Daniel?"

I shrugged. "Yeah. What did you bring?" I asked, not waiting for him to answer as I tore into the fast food bag and produced a cheeseburger.

I unwrapped it and took a huge, unattractive bite, chewing loudly as the phone rang and Daniel's name flashed across the screen. I hit the screen to forward the call and reached into the bag again, grabbing a handful of French fries and stuffing those into my mouth, too.

My phone dinged, and I looked down to see a text message from Daniel. *Call me. NOW.*

Emory saw the message, too, face shining with humor as he

watched me stuff my face with food, huffing angrily. "Trouble in paradise?"

I narrowed my eyes at him, and snatched the drink he held in his hand. His eyes widened in surprise. "You don't want to," he started as I took a huge gulp, and then gagged. "Drink that," he finished.

I looked at the cup and then looked at him. "Is that straight vodka, or what?"

Emory shrugged. "I think there was some orange juice in there at one point."

I shrugged back at him and took another drink before handing it back. "What are you really doing here?" I asked, as my phone pinged again.

Christa, please. Call me. I'm sorry.

Once again, Emory looked at the phone. "Making your boyfriend jealous, apparently."

I scoffed, the denial already coming to my lips. "He's not my," I stopped and shook my head, not needing to explain myself to some guy I barely knew. "You know what? Never mind."

Emory reached over and plucked a fry from my fingers, popping it in his mouth while he stared at me curiously. The phone rang again; still Daniel.

Emory tossed me a lopsided grin. "You gonna answer that?"

"No. I'm still waiting for you to answer my question."

He shook his head. "After this afternoon, I thought maybe you could use some company. I expected to find you all sad and forlorn. Instead, I find you have shut off your emotions for the time being."

"What?" I asked.

"Your emotions? You've locked them away. It's amusing, but not something you should do for an extended period of time. Werewolves who keep it up for too long usually end up going feral."

I remembered that feeling of not caring anymore, of putting myself in a bubble, that I'd just experienced, and a small bit of relief washed through as I realized it was just a defense mechanism I'd snapped into place and not because I had suddenly become a major jerk.

The phone rang again, Emory's this time, not mine, and he looked at the phone, a small, amused smile forming as he licked his lips and answered.

"Yes." He started walking out of the living room and into the hall. I could hear someone frantically speaking into the receiver, but I couldn't decipher anything else.

"I see," Emory stated, his lips still stretched in that amused smile as he leaned against the wall and stared at me. "Hmm. Well, I can assure you that she is perfectly safe. She's just sort of shut off her emotions for the time being." He paused again, eyes dancing wickedly with humor as he clearly enjoyed himself. "Uh huh." His eyes flashed in surprise, before a hungry, dark, and undeniably sexy stare caught me and held my attention to his. "Scout's honor, Daniel. She's perfectly safe with me."

My eyes widened, partly surprised that he'd been talking to Daniel, although I had sort of guessed as much, and also at the way he stared at me, eyes smoldering.

Daniel said a few more things before Emory hung up the phone, and I watched, heart beating way too fast considering I had a boyfriend, as he slunk back into the room looking every bit like a jungle cat about to pounce on its prey.

He stood in front of where I sat on the couch, reached over and grabbed the fast food bag from next to me before he plopped down and leaned in.

Lips inches from my ear, he whispered. "Want to tell me again how nothing is going on between you and Daniel?"

I swallowed. "Nothing at all."

He shrugged and leaned away from me, that predatory air melting away from him as his usual indifference snapped into place. I felt myself breathe deeply, relieved to have the tension around us dissipate. "You got any video games?" he asked easily, as though he hadn't just tried to ratchet up the sex appeal in the apartment to a thousand.

I stared at him blankly, and he smiled at me earnestly. "Um, yeah. We have some sort of football game and a shoot-em-up war game."

"Which would you prefer?"

I cocked my head to the side, frowning as I considered; still not sure how to take Emory. "I suck at both."

"Football it is then."

We played the game for a while, my phone pinging with messages that I ignored as my frustration at continually losing the game took over.

We exchanged barbs with one another as we played, and I lost track of time. When he wasn't being a jerk, Emory was actually really easy to get along with.

"I never thanked you for saving my life. For not letting Lana kill me." Emory's sentiment broke into our easy conversing.

"Don't mention it," I answered, not looking away from the game.

Emory set his controller down, reached over, grabbed mine, and placed it next to his on the coffee table in front of us.

"Really though. I may be a supreme ass, but I know when I owe someone a debt."

"Er, really though. Don't mention it. I'm not in the right place right now to have heartfelt conversations."

I expected Emory to fight me on it, to try to draw me out and get me to talk to him, the same way Daniel would have. Instead, he smiled at me kindly and handed me back my controller. We resumed playing our game, but I could tell that Emory had something on his mind. I tried to ignore it, but it thickened the air between us until I felt like I couldn't breathe through the tension.

"Look, dude. Seriously, there is nothing to thank me for.

You deserved a chance. End of story."

He looked over at me and crooked me another grin. "Either way, I like to pay my debts. And I, uh, I think I know how I could pay you back."

I paused the game and gave him my undivided attention. He stared back at me, fire burning in his gaze.

He licked his lips. "I think I could probably get you into-" His words cut off as my phone rang, and he jumped. We both looked at the phone. It was Daniel, again.

Emory sprang up, running a hand through his hair. "Um, you should probably answer that before your boyfriend has a coronary," he said.

"He's not my boyfriend." I reaffirmed although the denial sounded flat even to my own ears.

Emory smiled, leaning over me to grab his keys from the side table next to me. "Keep telling yourself that, little Alpha," he whispered.

His face was so close to mine, and with traitorous guilt, my heart thundered in my chest while my boyfriend called on the phone.

He stared into my eyes, and I felt like he could see right through me. He closed his eyes, took a shaky breath, and straightened. "Let me know if you want to hear about how I could really make your day."

He left as I answered the phone, Daniel's voice tearing through me as he began apologizing for not taking my side, for calling me selfish, and for treating me like a child, again.

The whole time he spoke, I chewed on my bottom lip, guilt coursing through me as I realized I'd once again found myself in big trouble.

I couldn't possibly harbor a crush on Emory, could I? It was impossible. It had to be because otherwise, Daniel had been right about the way I'd been behaving. If I had feelings for Emory, I really was a terribly selfish person.

CHAPTER ELEVEN

I avoided Emory like the plague for the next week. He was complicated. My feelings about him were complicated, and avoiding complicated feelings was one of my skills.

I'd made amends with Casey and Destiny the day after the incident. They just walked up to me before school, told me that they wanted to put the whole ordeal behind them, then made me promise not to ask again. Considering the fact that I wanted to keep my distance from Emory, something they could assist with since they could get me to and from school in his place, I graciously accepted their terms and went on with life.

Daniel and I had been talking, but his team was no closer to finding answers. The lack of progress irked me, but at the same time, I felt relieved that I had more time to think about our relationship. With everything going on, I still hadn't puzzled out my troubled feelings for him. I desperately needed someone to talk to, but all my go-to people were out.

I couldn't talk to Daniel about it, especially since he was the focus of my distress. My confusion would just hurt him. I couldn't talk to Des about it. She didn't know about Daniel and me. To find out that I'd kept our relationship a secret from her for the last six months would devastate her.

My torn feelings churned within me. With no way to get them out, they'd begun eating away at me.

I sat at lunch picking at chicken nuggets and thinking about my situation, while Des droned on about something I had no interest in...prom.

"Yo! Christa! Are you listening?" she asked, her words slicing through my thoughts.

I shook my head, trying to clear out my distress. "Huh? Yeah. Prom. Yay." I responded without enthusiasm.

Des raised an eyebrow at me. "Something on your mind?"

I looked at my friend, eyes so curious as she stared back at me, and an idea came to me. "Have you ever met someone, and the way they made you feel, had you questioning your relationship with Casey?"

"Like, have I ever looked at other guys? Sure. I thought Emory was pretty cute. Until he opened his mouth, anyway."

I shook my head, trying not to wince at the mention of Emory. "No. I mean, like, have you ever thought that maybe Casey wasn't the right one for you, then met someone who was able to make you feel something for them, thus perpetuating that maybe your relationship has run its course?" I paused and took in Des's very confused face. "Hypothetically, of course. I'm just asking for a friend," I added.

"I'm pretty sure I'm your only friend, so, um, where is this coming from?"

I pouted. "I have other friends. Brock is my friend," I answered, interjecting Brock's name out of pure desperation.

"Uh huh. And is Brock the one having relationship troubles?"

I pursed my lips and shook my head before popping a chicken nugget into my mouth. "It's just a hypothetical question," I reaffirmed.

"Okay, good. Because, I'll be honest, I don't know much about their relationship, but I think that's because Brock and Rowan choose to keep it pretty private. Either way, I don't see Brock coming to you for advice especially since your one experience with a boyfriend didn't go so well."

My jaw dropped a little as I tried to ignore her subtle reference to my very short-lived romance with Brendan. Instead, I focused on her totally off-base assumption about Brock and Rowan. "What are you talking about? What relationship between Brock and Rowan?"

Des looked at me like I was crazy. "Well, I mean, they're like a couple. Have been for years."

"No. You're wrong."

Des smiled with amusement. "Nope," she started, placing her hand on her chest. "Hand to heart, it's the truth."

I couldn't believe it. "How on earth would you know that?"

She shrugged. "We have dossiers on all the major werewolves and their connections, romantic or otherwise. Some of the minor ones too."

I found it so ironic, how proud she felt that they had all this top-secret info about my pack, but had no idea how the Alpha and the Omega, two very major players, were connected.

I wouldn't be enlightening her. Also, I wasn't going to argue with her about Brock and Rowan. I made a mental note to ask Brock about it later and pressed on with my question. "Seriously, Des. Have you ever had a feeling like what I was saying when it came to you and Casey?"

Des shrugged. "Not really. I mean, if we're fighting or something, I'll sometimes second guess our relationship, but the truth is, Casey and I just make sense. I know that he's the one I'm meant to be with."

I nodded, letting the subject go, mostly because her answer offered no insight to my current problems.

Des watched me curiously, and I could tell she wanted to say something, but the bell rang, mercifully saving me from finishing this awkward conversation. She wouldn't be able to ask me about what was on her mind until later. Suddenly, I didn't feel so well.

We started walking out of the cafeteria. Des turned left in the direction of the classrooms, as I split to go right out of the front of the school. Des paused. "Aren't you coming?"

I shook my head. "Nah, I'm going home. My stomach's rolling over itself."

She frowned with sympathy. "Oh, man. That sucks. Don't you need a ride though?"

"I'll just start heading out, and once I'm free of the school, I'll call a cab or something."

"I don't think so, buttercup. Not with those things out there."

I grimaced. I'd completely forgotten about those guys.

"Well, damn. I guess I'll try to soldier up and stay at school then."

"I can take you home," she offered.

I definitely didn't want to spend any more time with Des. I desperately feared she'd start pestering me about my questions, and I was in no way ready to tell her what had really been going on these last few months. "Nah. I don't want to make you ditch."

She grinned. "Probably for the best. I do have a calculus test right now. We can call Emory. He's a bum. I'm sure he's just slumming around Les Loups-Garous anyway."

"No," I choked out, shaking my head as my voice cracked, betraying my feelings about him.

She stared back at me blankly. "Okay. I can call Brock."

I frowned. "I don't want to bother Brock. He was up all night working at the club. I really can walk."

Des's returning glare told me she thought I'd lost my mind. "Yeah. I'm pretty sure Brock would rather be bothered than find out that you didn't call him after you've been torn apart by some crazy-ass monsters."

She pulled out her phone and started typing away. I grabbed for her phone, but she spun away from me. "Please, Des. Don't bother him. I'll just stay at school. Please don't call him."

She tucked her phone back into her pocket and looked at me smugly. "Too late. He says he'll be here in fifteen," she paused, looking around as the tardy bell rang. "I've got to get to class. I'll call you later. Love you! Bye!" She ran off with a little wave in my direction.

I watched her for a minute before I turned and headed out of the school.

I felt conspicuous just standing in front of the school, so I started sneaking toward the middle of the parking lot. Despite Brock's claims that he would be here in fifteen minutes, I knew that in good traffic Les Loups-Garous was about twenty minutes away, and I didn't think I had that long before some faculty member or another came out and found me loitering in the parking lot. Even though I thought that Des's warning seemed wise, I needed to get the heck out of Dodge, so I strolled right through the gates of the parking lot and started making my way up the road.

The weather had begun warming up around Kennington. Graduation loomed just a few weeks away, and from there I didn't really know what life had in store for me. A year ago, I'd just been another plain, ordinary seventeen-year-old girl. Now I was the True Alpha of every werewolf in the world, and a war could be starting for my kind at any time. My stomach somersaulted again at the thought. Maybe my sudden tummy-ache was a side effect of anxiety.

I walked down the street far enough that I could no longer see the school. Just the road to my right and the giant forest to my left, and I thought about the same thing that had been occupying my mind for the last few weeks. What if Daniel and I had outgrown each other? The thought made my heart hurt.

The crunch of leaves behind me alerted me that something followed, and I tensed, reaching around me for pack magic as I prepared to shift if I needed to. Whoever was behind me had tensed also. I could feel the stillness that settled stagnantly between us.

I spun, bringing my arm around so that I could throw a wicked right hook at whoever was stalking me and froze, my punch halting just inches from my follower.

"James?" I asked in bewilderment as I stared at the gangly, sallow-looking werewolf in front of me.

James and I weren't fond of each other, and his returning scowl told me that my last few months as his Alpha hadn't changed his opinion of me much. "You should announce yourself next time. I almost knocked your head off," I told him, lowering my punch and crossing my arms in front of my chest.

His scowl didn't change. "Doubtful."

I stood waiting impatiently for him to say something else, but he just stared back at me. I darted a glance at the road expecting to see Brock's sleek '72 Chevelle at any moment, but alas, he was nowhere in sight.

I looked back at James and returned his scowl with one of my own. "What do you want?"

He looked around like he wanted to make sure no one watched and then reached into his pocket, producing a sealed white envelope with creases all over it from being in his pocket. "I'm going back to where I belong. I have a message for you from an ally. If you want answers, this information can help you get what you need."

I stared at him in disbelief. "What are you talking about?" I asked, making no move to take the envelope. Clearly, this kid was way weirder than I'd given him credit for.

The sound of classic rock over the roar of a beefed up engine rang through the wilderness, and I knew without having to look that Brock was pulling up. James glanced over at the oncoming car then reached forward to push the envelope into my folded arms. "You'll know when it's time to open that. When you're ready to get the information you need, I'll see you again."

He darted one last glance over at Brock who had pulled up next to us before he took off running into the forest. I stared after him for a moment, shock briefly immobilizing me before I turned and jumped into Brock's car.

He looked off into the direction where James had just gone. "What was that about, boss?" he asked.

"I don't know. He gave me an envelope and told me he was going back to where he belonged. Has he always been so weird?"

Brock shrugged. "Hell if I know. He only showed up about a month before you did. Wouldn't give us any details about himself except that his name was James, and he needed a pack. You going to open the envelope?"

I looked down at the envelope that I'd crumpled in my hand

when I got into the car. Curiosity prickled at me, but I wasn't in the mood for any mysteries at the moment. I shoved the note into the back pocket of my jeans. "Maybe later. I just want to go home and get some sleep right now."

Brock sighed. "Look, boss, I don't know how to tell you this, but..."

As he trailed off, I felt my stomach roll again as anxiety took over. Yep, my stomach issues were definitely stress related. "What?" I asked, trying and failing to sound calm.

"Emory's been hitting the booze all day and is currently making a big scene about how he refuses to be ignored by the Alpha any longer. He says that as soon as you get home, he's going to march right upstairs and make you talk to him. I don't know what's going on between the two of you, but he's in a right state."

I rolled my eyes. "Nothing is going on between us. He just annoys the hell out of me, so I've been avoiding him as much as I can."

Brock glanced over at me, sympathy written all over his face. "He's waiting for you, so I don't think you'll be ignoring him today."

"Well, damn." I blew out a resigned sigh and slumped into the seat. I couldn't deal with sober Emory, how on Earth was I going to handle belligerent Emory?

I needed an escape plan, stat. It was Friday, most of my friends were still at school, and I just wanted to be alone with my thoughts.

Inspiration striking, I sat up. "Take me to my grandparents' house. I'm going to spend the weekend with my family catching up."

Brock nodded and turned left towards my family's home. I was grateful for his easy-going nature, and the fact that he never asked many questions. We could have made the trip in comfortable silence, but Des's insinuation from a little bit ago nagged at me. I am a curious little creature, so I had to ask.

"Brock, can I ask you something personal?"

He shrugged nonchalantly. "Sure."

I spoke slowly, trying to choose my words carefully so that I didn't sound like an offensive bigot. "Are you and Rowan together?"

Brock continued staring straight ahead as he answered. "Most of the time."

I sighed, not wanting to pry, but just so damned nosy. "No. I mean, are you guys a couple?"

Brock chuckled. "I knew what you meant. Yeah. We're together most of the time. We have our arguments, we break up, and then we realize there's so much love between us, and we get back together."

"Wow," I murmured, amazed that Des had made such an astute observation that I hadn't especially since my ability to read people and situations appropriately had always been a source of pride for me. "I never would have guessed," I admitted, slightly begrudgingly.

This time Brock looked at me and furrowed his brows with an accompanying frown. "Why not?"

I shrugged and chewed on my fingernail thoughtfully. "You just don't fit the stereotype. I mean you guys ride Harleys and seem like such manly-men."

He laughed again. "Well, that's a bullshit stereotype if I've ever heard one."

His tone remained light, but his words still shamed me. "I'm sorry, and you're right. Like I said, I never would have guessed. Does everyone know but me?"

Brock shook his head. "No. Most people don't know. It makes me wonder how you know. You must have really honed in on your Alpha magic if you're starting to see how people connect to each other in your pack."

I grinned sheepishly. "Hardly. But that adds something for me to look forward to practicing. Honestly? Des told me."

"I figured she might know. The Lunata knows about the

majority of our interpersonal relationships."

I froze, his words causing me to wonder if they knew about me and Daniel. I shook that away just as quickly. We were so secretive that hardly anyone knew, including Des. "Is it a secret? Your relationship with Rowan?"

"Not really. We just don't feel the need to put it out in the open. If people know, they know. It's still a weird thing. Most of the pack wouldn't understand, and we don't want to feel uncomfortable."

"Well, your secret is safe with me," I vowed.

"I know, boss. You're not a gossiper." He fixed me with a level stare as we turned into my grandparents' driveway. "But like I said, it's not a secret. It's just nobody else's business."

He paused as I got out of the car and spoke again as I closed the door. "Kind of like whatever is really going on with you and Daniel."

My jaw dropped, and Brock winked. So much for him being an oblivious teddy bear.

"Don't worry, Christa," he said with a kind smile. "Your secret is safe with me, too. Have a good weekend."

I could only manage a small half-wave through my shock. He knew. But, how could he know? And if he knew, how many other people did?

He started to pull away, but I waved at him to stop. I had half-a-mind to try to slip a lie past him, but I decided against it. He'd been honest with me, I felt that I owed it to him to return the favor.

"How did you know? Is it that obvious?"

He shook his head, a sly smirk still tugging at his lips. "It's not obvious at all. But when you're so used to keeping your own relationship quiet, it gets easy to notice when others are doing the same."

My returning smile was small, my mental exhaustion taking hold. "Thank you for the ride, Brock. And, thank you for keeping mine and Daniel's secret. You're a good friend. I'll see you Sunday night."

"No problem, Boss. I'll see you later." He paused, and I watched his face as indecision warred with the need to say something. After a few seconds, the latter won out. "Hopefully, you can work out whatever is going on between you and Emory before Sunday, too. Or at the very least, before Daniel gets home. Otherwise, you are in for a very awkward situation."

I sighed. "Do you know everything?"

He just shrugged again in response.

"For the record, there really isn't anything going on with Emory. Anyway, I'm working on it. I'll talk to you later," I told him, turning and jogging to the front door.

I fished my keys out of my backpack as I reached the entrance, unlocking the door and then locking it again once I got inside.

I took the stairs three at a time as I headed up to my old room bursting through the door and bee-lining straight for the bed. I flopped down and fell asleep as soon as my head hit the pillow.

I didn't know how long I'd slept, but when I awoke, the sky had grown much darker as the sun had begun its descent.

I stretched, yawning as I shook away my nap, and I glanced at the alarm clock. The red numbers glowed alerting me that it was a few minutes past six.

Just in time for dinner, I thought to myself as my stomach growled in agreement. I still wore jeans and a plain white t-shirt, but since I hadn't had the foresight to bring a change of clothes, my grandmother was going to have to deal with my casual dinner attire.

I made my way downstairs not surprised that my family already chatted it up at the dinner table and wondering why no one had bothered to wake me.

Stepping into the dining room, I cleared my throat. "Sorry I'm late, guys. I fell asleep, and no one woke me." I tried and failed to keep the accusation from lacing my words.

As one, my entire family froze, clearly surprised to see me. My grandmother recovered first. "That was because no one knew you were here, Christianna," she offered with a purse of her lips.

I thought about it and nodded. It made sense. I hadn't told any of them I was here. How silly of me to think they'd just know.

"Er, yeah. I'm home for the weekend. Just needed a little quiet time."

My family, stoic as they are, did not probe or ask any further questions, instead, just ignoring my statement. The only indication that anyone had heard me was my grandmother tsking before she clapped her hands. "Eloise, you need to set another place for Christianna," she called out. To me, she waved her hand. "Sit."

I sat, not wanting to cause any more of a spectacle as Eloise started bringing me food.

My grandmother eyed me suspiciously. "Why are you here?" she asked before taking a sip of her wine. I felt fairly certain she wasn't trying to make me feel unwelcome on purpose, but her abrupt bluntness still had me feeling like I shouldn't have been there.

"I wasn't feeling well. I was just super tired and needed a break from my apartment."

My grandmother shook her head. "You don't look like you've been sleeping well. You look awful. And that terrible accident you were in! You should have come home so we could take care of you properly. For all we know, you have some sort of infection from mediocre care." She paused and stared accusingly at my Dad. "I told you, Ivan. I told you that letting her live in that apartment above that bar was a bad idea."

My dad opened his mouth to respond, but I beat him to it, unceremoniously interrupting. "It's not the bar. I can't even hear the noise downstairs when I'm home. I've just been overwhelmed with work and school and trying to piece together a personal life."

My grandmother looked slightly taken aback by my interruption and regarded me coolly for a few moments before speaking again. "Well, since your work is doing bookkeeping for that bar, and your friends are hooligans, it would behoove you to drop both of those efforts and just focus on school."

I nodded, knowing better than to correct her. After all, it's not like I expected her to understand that the job I referred to was actually as the non-paid leader of the werewolf nation, and that the personal life I referred to actually meant the guy who she already thought I was too young to be friends with, let alone secretly dating. "Something to consider," I offered with a tight smile.

If my grandmother noticed my irritation with her speculations, she gave no indication, instead bulldozing forward with her misinformed opinions. "Really, Christianna, I know that you wanted to be out on your own and all that, but you really should just move home. Your lucky to be alive after the accident, and clearly whatever else is going on in your life is taking its toll on you. There is no shame in admitting that you weren't ready and just finishing out the next couple of months here before heading off to college. And that's another thing, have you even thought about where you are going to go? I haven't seen one acceptance letter, or well, any letters, from colleges. What is your plan for the future?"

Well, this conversation had taken an unexpected turn. I couldn't tell her my plan for the future, because I didn't have one. I lived in a constant state of now. My life a continual repeat of how do I handle the current crisis? It was maddeningly hard to be proactive about the future when I always had to be reactive in the present.

I opened and closed my mouth returning my grandmother's expectant gaze with wide-eyed puzzlement. My current plan for the future? Stay alive. After that? I didn't have a clue.

With each passing second, my grandmother grew more agitated with my lack of an answer. "Well?" she pressed.

"Umm... I don't know. I was thinking that I would just work at the bar and take community college classes until I figured out what I wanted to do with my life." I offered, as close to an honest answer as I could come up with.

It was decidedly the wrong answer.

My grandmother shot up from her seat, all signs of that calm and collected woman I knew disappearing as a look of animal rage akin to one of my wolves going feral slipped into place.

Her clenched fists hit the table, and she glared down at me. She may have been two people over from me, but the effect was the same. I shied away from her anger. "My granddaughter will not slum around Les Loups-Garous, never leaving this town, and spending all of her time with those God-damned Hawthorne boys! You will not repeat Karina's mistakes!"

I flinched as though she had slapped me, the reference to my mom almost more than I could take. I could feel the rage, the need to tell my grandmother off, washing over me. I made to stand, no longer wanting to allow her vitriol to go unchecked.

My father's hand flew to my shoulder, shoving me back into my seat as he, himself, stood. "That's enough, Mother."

His voice didn't rise, but the bite of his tone caused my grandmother to step back.

My grandmother glared at my dad. "Excuse me?"

My dad met her angered gaze with a hard look of his own. "That's enough. You will not tell Christa how to live her life. You will not dictate her path to her, and I swear to God, Mother, you will never disrespect my wife in my presence and definitely not in her children's presence."

My grandmother's shock lasted only a few seconds before she rose up even higher on her toes to try to intimidate my dad. Her hand flew up from the table, her pointer finger at the ready as she no doubt prepared herself to unleash on him.

She was once again interrupted by the most unexpected person. My grandfather generally kept to himself, not speaking for or against anything my grandmother had to say. I guess after so many years of marriage, he had just learned how to choose his battles. I'd also never heard him take a stern word with her or anyone for that matter, which was why it surprised me so much when he spoke up.

"It's enough, both you," he barked, not bothering to get up from his seat. He didn't need that power-play, the tone of his voice enough to cow even the most stubborn of Alphas, and I wondered if maybe there wasn't a little wolf in him.

My grandmother and father turned slowly to look at him, shock coloring both of their faces before shame took hold.

He returned their looks calmly as he ran his tongue over his teeth. "This conversation is done," he started before pushing his seat back and standing in one graceful motion. "This whole meal is done." He turned and looked at me and smiled apologetically. "You should go home, Christa. You're not going to find the rest you're looking for here."

I nodded trying not to feel hurt by the dismissal. I knew my grandfather didn't want to make me feel unwelcome, but I could also hear the truth in his words. On top of everything going on in my Alpha life and my romantic entanglements, my family now teetered on the verge of battling one another.

My grandmother shot me one last simpering look, no doubt still fuming at my callousness for my future, and stormed out of the dining room.

My dad reached into his pockets and fished out his keys tossing them to Jackson. "Drive your sister home," he mumbled before he, too, stormed out of the room.

My grandfather eyes darted back and forth between Jackson and me. "Things'll cool down here," he said, that apologetic smile still on his face as he followed the other two out of the room.

Jackson looked at my dad's car keys then glanced at me

scratching his head in amazement as he addressed me. "So, uh, do you need to grab anything from upstairs or are we good to head out?"

I shrugged. "My back pack is upstairs. Let me go grab it, and I'll meet you at the front door."

Jackson's only response was a quick nod. I ran upstairs, hastily making my bed before bending down and grabbing my backpack by the nightstand. I slung the pack over one shoulder and gave the room a quick once over making sure I hadn't left anything behind.

I had. My phone lay on the nightstand. I picked it up, checking it for messages as I did. I grimaced. There were a ton of them. Some from Brock. Some from Des and about twenty missed calls and texts from Daniel and even more from Emory. All of the messages had the same general content: *Call me now.*

I rolled my eyes. These people were so damned needy. They could wait. All of them. I stuffed the phone in my back pocket not bothering to listen to any of the voicemails or open any of the texts messages. I would be back at Les Loups-Garous soon enough, and I would deal with them all then.

I rushed down the stairs with my phone ringing in my back pocket. I reached back and slid the phone into my hand, glancing briefly at the caller ID before I grimaced and stuffed it back. It was Daniel, and I was no closer to being able to deal with that emotional roller coaster than I had been a few hours earlier.

I met Jackson at the door right as his phone began to ring. He took a look at it and looked up at me. "Dude, your friends have been calling me all night. Earlier I told them you weren't here because I didn't know that you were, but Daniel is calling me for the like the hundredth time. Do you want me to answer?"

I rubbed my hands over my face in annoyance. "Oh, my God! These people are killing me. No. Don't answer it. I'll deal with it in half an hour when I get back to Les Loups-Garous."

Jackson's phone rang again, and he looked down outrage for me evident when he looked at me and spoke, "It's Des. Man, these people can't let you be for like ten seconds!"

I sighed. "I know, right?" I told him before pulling the front door open. "Let's get me back before one of them strokes out."

Jackson chuckled and followed me to my Dad's car.

We began our drive in silence, but I could tell that he had something he wanted to say. I tried to ignore it, not wanting to rehash the blow out from our not-so-stellar family home evening, but his unspoken words hung heavy between us.

"What?" I finally blurted far more harshly than I had intended.

Growing up in our family, Jackson was exceptionally adept at ignoring brashness, so he answered me jovially although his words were touched with concern.

"So what's really going on? Why are you dodging your friends and avoiding your apartment? Troubles in paradise?" he asked.

I toyed with the idea of just brushing him off before I remembered that he knew about me and Daniel, and while he might be my younger brother, he, at least, provided an ear I could bend about my problems.

I sighed. "You could say that," I started before Jackson shot me an alarmed look and cut in.

"Daniel's not hurting you, is he? I'll kill him!"

I suppressed a laugh, imagining my brother trying to fight Daniel's three hundred pound wolf. Jackson may have been a scrappy little fighter, but he couldn't hold his own against a werewolf.

"Hardly."

Jackson's face morphed from protectiveness to disgust. "You... You're not... You know..." Jackson sputtered, unable to vocalize his thoughts.

"I'm not what?" I asked, slightly annoyed by his stuttering.

"Pregnant!" he blurted, his eyes wide.

My lip curled as I responded. "No! We haven't even-"

Before I could finish, Jackson cut in. "Stop. I don't need any more details!" He shouted in desperation.

Jackson took a moment to compose himself before he spoke again. "So what is it? You guys just aren't getting along? I mean, I thought he was off in Pennsylvania."

My shoulders slumped as I responded. "He is. But you know he's there with *Lana*," I started, not liking the jealousy that dripped from her name.

"So?"

"So? She's his ex, who I'm not one-hundred-percent certain he actually bothered to officially end things with."

Jackson laughed. "Oh come on, Christa. Daniel is crazy about you. He loves the hell out of you. He would never do anything with Lana. He would never do anything to hurt you."

I only took a moment to evaluate the irony of the fact that five minutes before, Jackson had asked if Daniel was hurting me, and now he wanted to tell me that Daniel would never hurt me. I had too much to get off my chest and having a person to vent to was cathartic.

"Yeah, well I know that, but it's more complicated. You know we have to hide our relationship from the entire world. Des keeps trying to hook me up with random guys, and Daniel constantly treats me like I'm a child. We're not allowed to be together, so of course, I'm questioning if we should even keep going or if we should end this before someone gets hurt..." I trailed off, the last part hurting my heart to even admit. "And there's this other guy, Emory. He's a complete asshole. But, he treats me like an equal and not some sort of porcelain doll. It's really making me question my relationship with Daniel."

I knew that I had rambled, but Jackson seemed to have caught every word. "Wow," he started. "That is quite the laundry list of issues." He ran a hand through his hair, obviously gathering his thoughts because he spoke again a few seconds later. "Look. I don't have that much experience with all of this, but I'll tell you what I think. You and Daniel are great together. There's so much love between you that it's hard to imagine you guys not finding a way to make this work. But honestly? You're eighteen. Like, you don't have to choose your life partner right now. Do you love the guy? Yeah. But that doesn't mean that you have to be with him forever. People come into our lives, and sometimes they have a purpose. Sometimes that purpose runs its course, and then you move on. On the flip side, if you feel so strongly for him then screw what the rest of the world thinks and get your man," he paused and shrugged.

"As for this Emory guy, I don't know him. But I also know that people who are confused will latch onto anything new and exciting, so I wouldn't rush into that guy's arms if things don't work out."

This time, it was my turn to be surprised. "Wow, Jackson. When did you get so wise?" I asked, not taking my eyes off of him.

He shrugged. "Sometime while you were off Alpha-ing," he answered.

"Well, maybe you should be an Alpha yourself," I started, but trailed off as I caught sight of his face.

With no warning, his features had shifted from carefree to terrified. The look on his face caused shivers to roll up my spine. Something had changed, gone wrong, in the few seconds that had passed while we were talking. "Christa, you need to look," he whispered, his voice cracking with desperation and sadness.

His face and tone left me no room to question and I turned away from him, facing forward, my breath catching as I absorbed the sight before me.

Red flames licked everything in front of us, smoke billowing from the trees as the lights of the fire trucks flashed before us. I saw, but I couldn't process the scene around me. My wolves stood outside Les Loups-Garous, blankets wrapped around them as they stared mesmerized at the club.

In my mind, a persistent voice kept repeating, *This isn't*

happening.'

Jackson pulled the car to the side of the road, and I slid out on autopilot, still unable to reconcile what I saw.

This isn't happening, the voice echoed.

My phone rang. I answered, already knowing who it was without looking.

"Christa! Are you okay? Where are you? We've been trying to get hold of you. Do you even know what's going on?" Daniel's panicked voice rang through loud and clear on my phone.

My whole world went numb. This was why they had been calling me, and I had been too selfish to answer.

Still, I couldn't bring myself to acknowledge the facts. *This isn't happening!*

Despite the voice in my head vehemently expressing its denial, I whispered the words Daniel expected to hear, my tone expressionless as I gazed at the flames before me. "Les Loups-Garous is on fire."

"I know," Daniel choked back, his voice catching with desolation. His defeated intonation did me in, and I fell to my knees.

This was happening. In front of me, fire and smoke billowed out of my home. In my mind, the voice in my head switched its mantra.

Les Loups-Garous is on fire.

CHAPTER TWELVE

Ash rained down around me, the sound of breaking glass piercing the air as I stood outside the smoking building. The fire department worked diligently to put the fire out. I'll give them credit, they worked quickly, for I which I had immense gratitude.

Brock stood next to me on one side, Jackson on the other, neither of them saying anything as they stared blankly at what I imagined was the skeleton of the club. I couldn't look. Emory's arms surrounded me, sheltering me from the horror surrounding us. Giant, gut-wrenching sobs wracked my body. Fear and anger consumed me. Someone had set fire to my home. I knew with certainty that this had not been a random coincidence. Whoever was behind this had come to destroy us.

The Alpha inside me begged to be set free. I reminded her that I would let her out when the time came. I promised her that the person responsible would pay with blood, and I'd be sure to let my wolf deliver the killing blow.

Emory's voice broke through my internal monologue. "One of the firefighters needs to talk to you."

I took a deep breath and Emory squeezed me softly. "It's okay, Christa. The fire is out. The building is still standing. You can look."

I nodded against his chest and turned to face the man in front of me. He was attractive, for an older guy, with salt-and-pepper hair and kind emerald eyes.

"Christianna Ellsworth?" he asked me.

I gave him one curt nodded and stared at him expectantly. In turn, he offered me a small smile.

"We've got the fire out. Luckily, the damage is mild, mostly contained to the outside of the building and the main floor of the bar. Thanks to the quick response from your staff, we were able to get here before it reached the upstairs. Your insurance company will have its work cut out, but with some new paint and some new windows, the club should be up and running again in a few weeks. My men are inside right now, boarding up the windows. You'll need a crew to come in and clean the ash, but you guys are able to go in. The foundation is stable. You've got yourself a sturdy building there."

Relief flooded through me, washing away the adrenaline that kept me standing and making my knees weak. The ability to speak escaped me.

I had so many questions, but I couldn't find the words to express my gratitude, let alone pose my inquiries.

Emory, keen as ever, somehow knew what to ask. "Do you know how this fire started?"

The firefighter frowned, face serious. "We surveyed the area, and it looks like someone threw a crudely fashioned explosive through one of the windows in the back. That's where the fire started, and where most of the damage took place. It's a good thing it hadn't started near the bar. With all that liquor, the fire could have spread much more quickly."

"So, definitely arson?"

"Without a doubt."

The firefighter promised that the police would work hard to apprehend the culprit. In my furious state, I prayed they found him before I did. I had murder on my mind, and I felt pretty certain that the Kennington Police Department would be a lot more lenient than me.

After he left, I turned to Emory. "The rogue did this."

Emory nodded once. "Yeah. I think so, too."

I sighed. "We need a plan. Get everyone together."

I called an emergency pack meeting, inviting Des and Casey to represent the Lunata, and we came up with a plan. The bar would be closed indefinitely even after the repairs were finished. I had to do what was right for the pack, and so I'd made the decision to put the club into emergency lockdown mode. Ironic, since I had fought so hard to get it out of lockdown mode not too long ago.

The pack formed teams doubling up security around the perimeter. Des and Casey assured us that they would add their own people to reinforce our numbers.

Lunata and pack agreed, they needed to keep me as sequestered and protected as they could, which irked me to no end because I knew that I needed to be on the front lines.

"They're trying to make sure that their leader is kept safe," Daniel told me on the phone as I sat on the couch in our apartment fuming over the decision to cut me out.

"Yeah, well, I'm not some weak little pup! I can help."

Daniel sighed in exasperation. "I know you think that you can help, but honestly, if the pack is too worried about watching out for you, they aren't going to be focused on catching this damned rogue."

I blew out my own sigh. "Emory thinks I can help. He treats me like an Alpha and not some sort of liability."

I could practically hear Daniel's eye roll over the phone. "Emory is a moron. And no one thinks that you're a liability. They just want you to live so that you can rise to your potential. You're a beacon of hope for most of the pack. Karina's bloodline returned to reestablish peace. And why are you mentioning Emory again? Is there something going on there that I should know about?" Daniel's tone changed noticeably from consoling to jealous.

Shit. Had I mentioned Emory too much? I tried backpedaling. "No. Of course not. I'm just saying that he treats me like an equal."

Daniel didn't say anything for a long stretch, and when he finally did, I could tell that he tried hard to sound neutral, although he couldn't quite swallow back his suspicions. "I've said this before, and I'll say it again. Stay away from Emory."

I fought the urge to argue, realizing that Daniel's irritation stemmed from insecurity about our relationship; something I could sympathize with considering that I still fumed over the fact that he was off gallivanting around Lana's compound. Never mind the fact that I'd sent him there this time.

Instead, I changed the subject. "Are you guys close?"

Daniel breathed deeply, not needing me to elaborate. He knew that I was really wondering when he would be home.

"No. We can't crack these things, can't figure out how they got to be this way, or how they operate. But it doesn't matter because I'm coming home. Next week. I have to wrap some things up here, but I'll be back Saturday."

A week? Daniel would be home in a week. Emotions warred inside me, the elation I felt at being reunited with him conflicting with the fact that I still didn't know what to do about our relationship.

The former won out, and I squealed with delight. "Really? Oh my gosh, I miss you so much, and I'm so excited to hear that."

Daniel chuckled, the sound so light it lifted my spirits considerably. "Well, I figure that gets me back in time to declare to the world that I don't care what they think and take you to that damned prom."

Despite the fact that I knew his words were so dangerous, I felt my lips part as my stomach did a not-unpleasant somersault. "Really?" I repeated, this one much more sultry than the former.

"Yeah. This time apart has made me realize that I don't care what the world thinks. Fuck them. We're meant to be together, I can feel it in my whole being. And you and I, we can fight the whole world if we want to. If it means we can be together."

My heart beat thunderously in my chest. His words were downright traitorous. And sexy as hell. "Daniel," I started, flinching with guilt as a knock on the door interrupted us. I sighed, trying to release some of that built up tension. "Someone is at the door."

Daniel's throaty laugh told me that this conversation was just as dizzying for him as it was for me. "Answer it. I've got to go anyway. But just remember, Christa. I love you, and I'll see you Saturday."

"I love you too," I told him.

Another knock at the door reminded me that we really needed to wrap this up.

"Oh, and Christa?" Daniel intoned.

"Yeah?"

"Pick a sexy dress." A goofy smile danced across my face as I heard the click letting me know he'd hung up. I tried hard to wipe it off my face as I made my way over to answer the door.

The scene that awaited me when I answered was enough to kill my good mood. Des stood before me, rocking on her heels and chewing her thumbnail as Emory, of all people, leaned casually in the doorway, looking every bit as sexy as he ever did.

"Little Alpha," he started, his voice a purr. "Have I got a proposition for you."

I gulped as the smile slid from my face.

"What is it?" I asked, gesturing for the two of them to come in. They complied, following me to the living area and flopping down on the couch in unison.

Needing to not focus on Emory, I turned my attention to Des.

"Where's Casey?" I asked, wondering why I found her hanging with Emory since she seemed to dislike him so much.

"Casey can't know I'm here," she said, leaning forward and resting her elbows on her knees.

"Why?" I asked.

She swallowed and looked at Emory, who just grinned like the cat who had caught the mouse and nodded. She turned back to me. "Umm... because he would hate me forever for this, but it needs to be done."

"What?" I asked still not catching on.

Des went to answer, but Emory spoke first, his silky voice

thick with excitement. "Because we need to see Cooper Jones. Casey doesn't want us to, and Des and I can get us in to see him without Casey."

I stared between them in disbelief. "How?"

Des found her voice, cutting in before Emory could explain. "Emory has seen the layout of the prison-" she started before I interrupted, eyes cutting back to Emory.

"How?" My question of the hour, apparently.

Emory shrugged. "Lana's dad designed it. The blueprints are down in the lab. Most lesser wolves aren't allowed down there, but I'm her Beta." Emory paused, an unnamed emotion flitting across his features. He cleared his throat and continued, "I was her Beta."

I licked my lips, this new information sending the gears in my head turning. "Okay. So, what? Are you thinking you'll sneak us into a heavily guarded Lunata compound?"

"Yes," he answered simply.

"And then what? Even if we can sneak in and find Cooper, what makes you think you can get him to talk?"

Des joined the conversation again. "I think I can offer him something that he won't refuse."

I swallowed and rubbed my face, the impossibility of what they were suggesting warring with my need to find out what those things were and how to fight them.

I slumped down on the coffee table in front of the couch, pulling my legs up so I was sitting Indian style, and placed my hand on my chin pensively. "Why now? Why are you guys suggesting this now? What has changed? What do you think you can offer Cooper Jones that no one else could? Freedom? Do you think we're going to launch a daring prison escape on top of sneaking in?"

My queries were aimed at Des and she answered in kind, firing off her answers as quickly as I had shot off the questions. "Things have changed. The threat has made an active attack on a heavily secured Alpha den. We need fast answers, and Cooper

Jones has them."

I narrowed my eyes at her. "I've been saying that since the beginning."

"I know, but I'd hoped Daniel and his team could find answers before it came to this. Time has run out. It's time to move to a new plan. Emory will sneak us in, and we will get the answers we need from the one person we know for sure can give them to us."

"Okay. But that still doesn't explain how you're going get Cooper to talk. What do you think you can offer him?"

Des, usually so sure of herself, shied from my questioning glare and stared at her folded hands. "I'm going to offer him what he wants. The chance to reconcile with Casey," she whispered.

I cocked my head. "You think you can convince Casey to talk to his father?"

Des squeezed her eyes shut, obviously pained, but the answer once again came from Emory.

He leaned forward catching my eyes with his, no playfulness burning in the golden fire of his pupils. "No, Christa. She doesn't. She's going to lie."

I shook my head, not believing that Des, who prided herself on being honest, would be willing to stoop to that level to get answers. "That's cruel!" I gasped indignantly.

Emory sat back into the couch and gave a half-shrug. "This is war, little Alpha. Nothing is cruel; things are neither fair nor unfair. This is about survival, and our kind will find a way to survive. We will find a way to win."

I stared at Emory for a long moment, wanting so badly to scream at him, to tell him that he was wrong, but knowing that he wasn't. And hey, maybe later on down the road Des could convince Casey to see Cooper, and it wouldn't be a lie at all. I knew it was a slim chance, but I had to tell myself that to keep from feeling the guilt of what they were proposing.

"I don't know, guys. Daniel was pretty adamant that I stay

away from this."

Emory scoffed. "You afraid to piss off your boyfriend?" he barked. I shot him a shut-the-hell-up stare.

Des laughed, thankfully not taking Emory seriously. "Daniel? Christa's boyfriend? That's a funny one. There's a better chance he'd date his own cousin. No offense, Christa."

"None taken," I told her, internally sighing with relief that she didn't suspect anything and fuming that Emory still thought he knew what went on between Daniel and me. Never mind the fact he was actually right.

"Anyway," I continued. "He's my right-hand man, so I take his advice very seriously. Let me run it by him, and I'll keep you posted."

Des nodded, standing up and heading towards the door. "That sounds reasonable. Just don't wait too long to decide. Time is running out for us to crack this case."

I nodded in understanding, standing to follow as Des and Emory headed for the door aiming to lock it behind them.

Emory waved Des off, telling her he just needed to follow up with me on a private matter and he would catch up to her. She went on, either ignoring my pleading eyes or too preoccupied with the betrayal she was planning to notice.

Emory stood in my doorway, staring at me as though I were a puzzle he couldn't figure out. "You hang on every word he says. You let him treat you as though he's your Alpha, all because you what? You love him? Don't miss your chance to do something important here, Christa. Don't let the fear of losing whatever it is you have with him keep you from defying him if you, as the True Alpha, feel it's the best thing for the pack."

I had expected some sort of cajoling, partially flirtatious interaction. I definitely hadn't expected him to sound so damned reasonable. I couldn't find the words to respond, which didn't seem to bother him. He gave me a small half smile and reached for the doorknob, catching my eyes again as he made to close the front door.

"Just think about it, Christa. Really think about it."

He closed the door, leaving me standing in front of it with reeling thoughts.

He was right. I was the True Alpha, and I didn't have to bow down to Daniel. He was also right that I constantly did because I feared that if I made him angry he would leave me forever.

Whether Emory was right or not, it felt wrong to just agree to do it without at least seeking Daniel's counsel. I sighed, and picked up the phone, dialing his number in a blur. He answered on the first ring, for which I felt grateful.

"Hey. Miss me already?" he asked, sounding sleepy.

"No." I started and then realizing how insensitive that sounded I backtracked. "Well, yes. But that's not why I'm calling. You know how Cooper Jones claims he knows what those things are, but he won't talk unless Casey comes, but Casey won't do it?" I rambled.

"Yeah," he answered, voice careful.

"Emory thinks that he can get Cooper Jones to talk..." I trailed off, not knowing how Daniel was going to react to hearing Cooper's name, let alone Emory's, again.

The other end of the line remained damnably silent, not even the sound of Daniel's breathing evident.

"Daniel?" I whispered. "Are you still there?" My heart beat loudly to my own ears as I waited for Daniel's anger to break through the silence.

Instead, he sounded deadly quiet. "What did you just say?" The softness seemed somehow worse. If he had yelled, I might have at least defended what I had to say. Instead, I found myself cringing as I responded.

"It's just that you guys don't seem to be getting any closer to figuring out what those things are, and Casey isn't interested in helping us get the information from his Dad, so Emory suggested that maybe we didn't need to send Casey at all."

"I told you to stay away from him." Daniel's voice was still too calm, the anger boiling just under the surface.

I blew out a sigh. "I know, and I wanted to. I really did. But, I tried to plead with Casey, and he just won't help. I need to do *something* to help, so I figured that Des, Emory, and I could go. I know that you don't want us to interrogate him, but maybe it's the best way to get the info we need."

Daniel scoffed. "I'm not talking about Cooper Jones."

I felt my lips pull into a confused frown. "Who are you talking about then?"

"Emory." Daniel began, the name coming out flatly.

"Emory? What's your problem with Emory?"

"He's dangerous, and he's cocky, and I don't trust him." The words tumbled out of Daniel's mouth, and while he did his best to hide it, I could once again detect the hint of jealousy.

After the tenseness of the last few weeks, we were just starting to get along, so I decided not to point out that I suspected Daniel's only problem with Emory was that he was jealous. Instead, I just pleaded my case.

"Well, I trust him, and he's going to help me get Cooper Jones to talk."

Daniel's tone continued to stay annoyingly even. "No, he's not. And, while we're on the subject, there's no way in this world or the fucking next one that I am going to let you near Cooper Jones."

I was trying so hard to keep calm. I was trying so hard not to fight with him. But, I was getting tired of him treating me like a child. Anger coursed through me, and I laughed out defiantly.

"No offense, Daniel, but there is no way in this world or the next that you're going to stop me."

Daniel's silence stretched for the space of the second before he hissed out a reply. "Don't test me, Christa. What makes you think I couldn't stop you? Hell, scratch that. What makes you think Jones will talk to you?"

"I'm the True Alpha. I'll figure something out." No way would I admit that our master plan involved my best friend bold-faced lying to her boyfriend's dad.

"Stay away from this, Christa. I'm telling you."

I wasn't going to fight with him. He didn't see my point of view, and he wasn't ever going to. Best to just agree. "Fine."

"Great," he answered back. "Now get some rest, and I'll talk to you tomorrow."

"Fine," I answered again before hanging up.

It was not fine. And I wasn't going to just sit around and let Daniel treat me as though I was incapable of making decisions.

I opened the front door fully intending on running down to the basement and waking Emory up only to find him standing on the other side, hand poised to knock.

"Oh. Hey. Good timing," he said, arm dropping to his side.

"I was just about to come find you."

"Oh?" he grinned. "Were you feeling lonely?"

I glared at him. "No. We're going to break into the Lunata prison."

"So I guess Daniel signed off on it?"

I shook my head. "No. Which is why we have to do it next Saturday before he gets home in the evening and tries to stop us."

Emory looked at me in surprise before his lips split into a huge grin. "Secretive and backhanded. My kind of deception. It's a date," he told me with a wink.

"Don't get ahead of yourself," I retorted, shutting the door in his face as the guilt I felt began making a home in the pit of my stomach.

Over the next week, Des, Emory, and I worked out a plan. Emory had drawn out a map, one that pointed out all the entrances and exits to the prison.

It wouldn't be easy to get in, not with all the security that The Lunata would undoubtedly have guarding the place.

"This isn't going to work," I told them, frowning at the map while we ate pizza in my living room. "There is no way that we're going to be able to slip in through any of these entrances undetected."

Des nodded her agreement while Emory chewed thoughtfully on his food. "Who says we have to sneak in?" he asked.

I glared at his denseness. "How else are we supposed to get in? It's not like we can just stroll right through the front door."

"Why not?"

"Because it's a prison. And we're civilians," I answered, waving a hand around us.

Emory shook his head, unconcerned. "Not really. Des is a member of their group, and you're the True Alpha. It's not exactly like we're a bunch of low levels."

I opened my mouth to argue, but Des put up her hand and nodded. "He's right. We're looking at this wrong. No one ever said we couldn't go visit the prison. They just said that we couldn't see Cooper, mostly because there was no point. He won't talk."

"Okay," I said slowly. "So you think we can just walk right in and ask to see Cooper?"

She shook her head. "Not at all. But I think that we could just walk right in. Like Emory said, I'm one of them. It makes sense that I would want to tour the facility, familiarize myself with it. And it makes sense that you would want to see it, too. You're the Alpha of all Alphas, and this facility poses a threat to your security."

I frowned at her. "How so?"

She grinned back. "It's a facility full of werewolf hunters not playing by our rules. Every one of them is a danger to you."

I considered that for a second and then darted a glance to Emory. "If it's going to be that easy, what the heck do we need him for?"

Emory started in on what had to be his tenth piece of pizza. He shot me a grin, mouth full of food. "Muscle."

I pulled a face, disgusted at his rudeness. Talking with his mouth full! My grandmother would have kicked him out of her dining room. "Gross, Emory."

He smiled again and took another wolfish bite.

Des rolled her eyes. "He's the tour guide once we get in. He's seen the blueprints, he knows where the cells are, and we need the guards to believe that we know our way around so that they don't try to go with us."

I sighed deeply, processing this plan as well as I could. "We're just going to outright tell them Emory has seen the layout and can show us around?" Somehow, I didn't think that The Lunata were going to like hearing that a werewolf knew the ins and outs of their prison.

Then again, Lana's dad had built it, so maybe it wouldn't surprise them all that much.

"This is the plan? We're just going to march right through the door and ask to take a lap through their facility?"

Des and Emory both nodded at me. I shook my head in disbelief. This plan was possibly the flimsiest thing I'd ever heard, but it was all we had, so I would go along with it.

With the plan set, Des and Emory left and I went to bed. Tomorrow, we would try to get our much-needed info from a man who could best be described as a cold-blooded killer. Tonight, I would try to get some sleep. This last week of lying to Daniel weighed heavily on me, and planning a covert op with Des and Emory tonight had been draining.

I just had to get through the interrogation. If I got what we needed from Cooper Jones, then there was no way that Daniel could be angry with me, right?

I kept trying to convince myself of that as I drifted off to sleep.

CHAPTER THIRTEEN

I t would be a couple of hours before we would be heading over to the prison, but I woke up the next morning knowing that I had a whole other mission to complete.

Assuming that my upcoming stunt didn't anger Daniel enough that he changed his mind, I would be attending the prom later on in the evening.

I needed a dress. A *sexy* dress, to be specific.

I just had one problem. I didn't know the first thing about being sexy, and I hadn't brought Des along for my shopping trip. Not that I hadn't thought about asking her to come, I just didn't feel like it was the right time to tell her that I would be attending prom after all.

With Daniel, who felt this was the right time to tell the world we'd been in a relationship for months.

A relationship so secret, that Des had no clue. Nope, I was not ready to have that conversation with her.

So, instead of shopping with my best friend since kindergarten, I currently browsed through racks of gowns with Emory. It was a living nightmare. This man could not take a damn thing seriously, and this proved to be no exception.

"How about this little number? You'd be sure to knock them dead in this one," he told me, holding up a dress.

Well, dress was an overstatement. I doubted that the bright pink strip of fabric covered enough to be considered a shirt. I frowned at him. "No. And I don't need your help picking anything out. I need you to tell me which one looks best once I've tried them on."

Emory shrugged and hung it back up. "After you, then."

I made my way to the dressing room with about fifteen items, trying them on and modeling them for Emory.

I'll give the guy some credit. He gave honest feedback each time I came out. I just didn't like his feedback. According to him, none of the stunning dresses that I had picked made me look beautiful.

"This is useless!" I huffed, flopping down next to him on a chair outside the fitting room in the final dress I had picked out. One that he said made me look like a giant cupcake.

Emory watched me for a moment, and I feared that a snarky comment would be springing to his lips at any moment. He frowned thoughtfully before standing and beginning to browse through the racks behind me. "Who are you going with anyway?" he asked, his voice betraying no emotion.

"It's a surprise."

He nodded. "Ah. So... Alone."

I rolled my eyes, shooting up and spinning around to face him as he shoved a piece of silky black fabric into my hands. "Try this one."

I held it out and looked it over skeptically. It had more fabric than the last one he'd suggested, but I could tell it would still be pretty short. I opened my mouth in protest, but he cut me off before I had the chance.

"Just trust me," he whispered.

I sighed and took the dress into the fitting room.

It was as short as I'd thought, barely swirling against my mid thigh. The material had a silky feel. It had halter-top straps, and the top hugged my chest and torso nicely before loosening up at my hips. I didn't glance in the mirror to see how it looked, too afraid that I would be disappointed.

Turns out, I didn't need a mirror. I stepped out of the fitting area and searched around for Emory. His back was turned as he browsed through a few more dresses, and I cleared my throat and tapped him on the shoulder to get his attention. "So, um, what do you think?"

Emory turned around, and his jaw dropped, his eyes glued to my face. "Stunning," he whispered, the word falling away from his lips like a prayer. My stomach did the little swoop thing that it usually reserved for Daniel.

He stepped closer, a feat that seemed impossible considering that we were already so close, his eyes burning like golden lava.

"Who are you going with?" he asked again, no hint of a joke in his tone.

My mouth went dry. I licked my lips and tried to regain my senses. This was bad. This was very, very bad. Because at this moment, I wanted nothing more than for Emory to kiss me.

His head tilted. My eyes closed.

"Daniel," I whispered.

Emory leaned back surprised. "What?"

I took a shaky breath, finally able to regain my composure. "Daniel is taking me."

His face went blank, and he stood up taller. "I see." He took a step back and nodded, "So I was right about you guys," he muttered more to himself than to me.

"It's complicated," I whispered, while the wolf inside told me that I shouldn't be trying to explain myself to Emory. She was right, of course, but I still felt like I needed to set things straight.

"Yeah," he answered dryly. "I bet."

I opened my mouth to respond but drew a blank. I didn't know what to say. He had been right the whole time, and at this point, with Daniel and I so close to telling the world, I couldn't figure out why I felt the need to convince Emory that he was wrong.

The she-wolf hissed her answer in my mind. *Because you have feelings for him.*

I shook her away. Her suspicions were impossible. I loved Daniel, end of story.

Even still, I needed to make things right for Emory. "Emory, listen," I started, but he shook his head and meeting my gaze, offered me a small, sad smile.

"Daniel is a lucky guy. I hope he knows that."

I stared, waiting for him to say anything more about the subject. Instead, he checked his watch and waved his hand at the dressing room. "You better go change," he paused and shot me a roguish smile. "We're going to be late for *our* date."

My stomach plummeted, and not because I felt any disappointment at his subject change.

We were going to finally talk to Cooper Jones.

The tires of Emory's rented truck crunched on the gravel road as we made our way toward The Lunata prison camp.

Despite the fact that lumps had formed in my stomach from the tension in the car, I found myself trying to suppress a smile. I knew that we were all nervous about what we were about to do. How could we not be? Our plan was downright asinine.

We were going to walk right through the front door as though we had every right to be there, and yet all of us had chosen to dress like spies. Black tee shirts, black pants, black boots. When we'd met outside of Les Loups-Garous, we'd all stared around at each other in amusement though none of us commented on our attire.

The humor of the inadvertent wardrobe matching kept us in high spirits as we drove toward our destination. Coming up on the building, I could feel the shift as we all became anxious.

I really hoped this would work because I had been dodging calls from Daniel all morning, afraid that if I talked to him, I would give away our plan. With how guilty I felt about what we were doing, I didn't doubt for a minute that with a little cajoling on his part, I'd have sung like a bird.

Emory parked the truck on the side of the road where we could see the front of the prison, but with any luck, any personnel they had couldn't see us. We shuffled out of the vehicle meeting each other at the tailgate and staring at the building before us.

It wasn't fancy. The whole building had a clerical feel, at least from the outside, and I expected that the inside would prove to be more of the same. Plain tan, rectangular. A huge, miles-wide rectangle, but a rectangle nonetheless.

Around the perimeter, miles and miles of razor-wire fencing surrounded the building. The only break in the fence was a guard stand where a man stood diligent watch.

The same man controlled a gate right next to him, and occasionally we would see a car pull up. He would talk to the driver for a moment, and then, assuming that the person had clearance to go in, he would open the gate to allow them access.

Des frowned and glanced over at Emory. "Did you bring the binoculars?" she asked holding out her hand.

"Yeah," he answered, reaching into the bed of his truck and rifling around in a toolbox. He produced the binoculars and handed them over to Des.

She peered through them and pulled a face. "Shit. It's Carl."

"Okay. So, you know him, then?" I asked.

"Yeah. He's in love with me."

"And that's a problem how?" Emory interjected.

Des groaned and rolled her eyes. "It's good and bad. I'll probably be able to sweet talk him through the gate, so that's good. He's just so damned annoying."

"Well, good thing he's stuck at the gate; that way you'll only be inconvenienced for a moment." Emory gave Des a toothy grin, and she rolled her eyes again.

Taking a deep breath, I shook out my arms. "Let's do this," I stated, blessedly sounding more confident than I felt.

After a moment of Des and Emory arguing about who would drive, we piled back into the truck. Des ended up driving because as she had pointed out, it made sense that if we were banking on her flirting our way through the gate, she should be the first person the Carl guy saw.

She pulled us right up to the guard post, rolled down the window, and flashed her most dazzling smile. "What's up, Carl?"

"Des? What a nice surprise," a voice answered. The face followed as he peered into the car.

Carl wasn't a bad-looking guy with bronze hair flopping into his hazel eyes and a nice strong jaw. The way he looked at Des made him seem even sweeter. He stared at her as though she was the most beautiful person on the planet. If it weren't for the fact I loved Casey, I would have thought the two a good match.

He glanced around the car, eyes scanning right over Emory as though he wasn't there and resting on me. "What brings you out here with a packless Beta and the True Alpha?" I flinched. This guy was pretty observant and seemed up to date about everyone in the werewolf community.

Des shrugged, unconcerned. "I'm interested in taking a look around, checking out the facility, and Christa thought it was a good idea to see what kind of security we have to make sure that none of the crazies get out and come after her pack." Her tone made it sound like she was mocking me, and I resisted the urge to tell her off. When Carl responded, I understood why she had been so offensive.

"Gotcha. Just like a werewolf to think we can't do our job," he frowned and shook his head sympathetically at Des before shifting his gaze to Emory. "What about you, big guy? What brings you out here?"

Emory afforded Carl a tight-lipped smile. "I'm over-protective."

Carl jerked his head toward me. "She's an Alpha. I doubt she needs your protection."

Emory's jaw clenched, and I noticed his hand clench into a fist. Des needed to hurry this along before Emory bashed Carl's head into a wall.

I elbowed her as subtly as I could and jerked my head slightly toward Emory so that she could see what I already had.

She grinned at Carl and placed a hand on the arm that rested against the window. "He's her boyfriend," she shrugged.

Emory snickered while my face went white as I glared at Des.

"Gotcha," Carl repeated. "Well, I don't see why you guys

can't go in. I--" he paused as another person joined him in the booth.

He turned back to us and smiled, "I was just gonna say, I'm off the clock. My replacement is here, so I'll take you guys on a tour."

We all stilled. "That won't be necessary," Des started, as politely as she could. "We don't want to keep you after you just got off work."

Carl waved off her comments with a laugh. "No problem. I'd love a chance to show you guys around." He paused and then narrowed his eyes. "Unless there's a reason you don't want me to come."

The she-wolf in me bristled, silently reminding me that if we didn't navigate this carefully enough, this guy could stop us in our tracks.

Des opened her mouth, probably to try to decline his offer again, and I made a split-second decision, guided by the wolf. "It's not a problem. He's more than welcome."

Both Des and Emory shot me puzzled looks while Carl grinned like he'd just won the lottery.

"Great. I'll buzz you guys in, and then I'll meet you in the lobby."

"Great!" I repeated, smiling as he turned and hit the button to slide the gate open.

As we drove through, Emory turned to me and asked, "What was that?"

I shrugged. "He wasn't going to take no for an answer."

"Well, I hope you have a plan," Des added.

I shrugged again. "We lose him once we're in."

It seemed solid, but once we were inside, losing Carl proved harder than I'd anticipated. He followed us like a hawk, not letting us out of his sight for a moment; the whole time he rambled on about the features of the prison, and how they had top-notch security.

After about twenty minutes of listening to him drone on, I

understood why Des couldn't stand him.

He pushed forward, and Emory grabbed my arm holding me back. "We're coming up on the detention center. We need to ditch chatty Cathy over there."

"I know," I hissed back, louder than I'd meant to because it caught Carl's attention.

"Everything okay back there?" Suspicion laced his voice as he addressed us.

More quick thinking was in order. "Yeah. We were just wondering if you could show us what's behind those doors?" I tried to keep my tone sweet and clueless as I inclined my head toward the entrance to the cells.

Carl grimaced. "What d'ya wanna go in there for? Those are just prisoners. Nothing you need to concern yourself with." Carl turned to start walking forward again, and I made another split-second decision. I had a feeling our tour was wrapping up, and several missed calls from Daniel told me that I'd already run out of time on that front.

I sighed and decided that honesty was the best policy. Otherwise, I was going to have to knock the poor kid out.

"Look, Carl, we haven't exactly been honest with our intentions here. We need to get information from someone. Someone who happens to be locked up in one of those cells."

Carl eyed me carefully for a moment. "Like, you need to interrogate someone?"

"Yeah."

He was silent for a heartbeat, then his eyes lit up with excitement. "Oh, that's so cool! Can I come, too? I promise I won't get in the way."

I blinked, surprised that he'd be so quick to let us in there, but then reconsidered. I supposed if your only job in life amounted to sitting in a guard shack for hours at a time, something like this would seem pretty glamorous.

I took a deep breath. "Sure."

That received more confused stares from Des and Emory.

If I wasn't more careful, I'd end up shocking them to death.

I gave Carl a quick run through of who we were there to see. After making him promise, again, not to get in the way, we made our way to where Cooper was being held.

There were no bars outside his cell or any of the cells for that matter. Each one we'd passed had been enclosed, like a bedroom. Each had a steel door with a window, and when we paused in front of Cooper's cell, I peered through the window.

I got only a glimpse of a shapeless lump lying on the bed before Carl used a key card to open the cell, and we filed in.

Carl cleared his throat, puffing up his chest, as he strolled over to Cooper's bed and ripped the sheets down exposing a middle-aged man. Nothing but skin and bones, with long brownish-red hair and a beard long enough that he could have been the long-lost member of ZZ-Top.

He faced the wall, lying on his side, and wore what looked like blue pajama bottoms and a white tee shirt

"You've got visitors, so you better sit up and be on your best behavior." Carl huffed, trying for all the world to sound intimidating and failing on so many levels.

Cooper groaned and rolled over, popping open one eye at Carl. "Shut the fuck up, Carl."

His tone alone shut Carl up, and Emory snorted. "Well, he's got style," he whispered.

Cooper sat up and stretched his arms into the air, looking around at my friends. "What have you brought, Carl?" he asked as his eyes flicked around the room. "Michael's daughter," he started, and Des winced at the mention of a father who had abandoned her.

He glared at Emory. "The broken Beta," he added before his eyes rested on me, and he grinned without humor. "And the True Alpha. Interesting."

"They're here because they have some--" Carl started, but halted when Cooper shot him a cold look.

"No one told you to talk."

Surprised by the amount of influence this man seemed to have over Carl, I realized it was a good thing Emory had insisted on coming after all because it had become apparent that Cooper terrified Carl.

Truth be told, he was scary, looking every bit the part of the deranged prisoner. Even his eyes held a dissociative quality, as though he was there, but not really checked into reality. I had some other concerns about Cooper. I wanted to know how a man who'd spent the last seventeen years in prison knew about all of us.

Not one to shy away from bluntness, I asked. "How do you know so much about us?"

He stared at us for a long time not saying anything, but I could see the thoughts working from behind his clouded eyes. When he spoke, it became clear that he was much more astute than I'd given him credit for.

"I'm a prisoner, but I still interact with the people here. They tell me the gossip. They keep me informed. When that fails, I am very observant."

"So, you know why we're here?" I asked.

"Christianna Ellsworth, daughter of Karina. True Alpha. I can't say for sure that I know, but I can probably guess why you are here. You have finally encountered the *others*." He paused, another humorless smile forming around that last word.

He remained silent, staring at me as he waited for a response.

I obliged. "Yes. With an unknown rogue leader threatening to usurp power, the last thing we need is to waste time trying to figure out what they are."

Cooper laughed, the sound harsh and too loud for the small room. "Unknown? I know who your rogue is. And I know what those things are. But, I can't help you."

I clenched my jaw. I knew he wasn't going to be forthcoming from the beginning, but still, I found his refusal infuriating. Choking back the desire to strangle him into submission, I tried tact and politeness.

"With all respect, Mr. Jones. You can't help or you won't? Because those are two very different things."

He waved my comments off. "Call me Cooper, please. And you're right, they are different things. So, I guess the answer to your question is that I won't help you."

"You will if you know what's good for you," Emory growled from my side.

Cooper's eyes flicked to Emory, clearly not seeing any danger. "I may be a prisoner here, boy, but you'll do best to remember that you're still a packless Beta inside of a facility run by a group that has dedicated their lives to making sure that your kind aren't a threat." He paused again as he assessed Emory, and I started to become suspicious that Cooper wasn't funny in the head at all. Instead, I began entertaining the belief that he just chose to silently observe things, evaluating them and filing the information away so that he could use it to his advantage at a later time. If anything, he seemed cunning.

"Why are you here, Travis? Got tired of chasing after the Hawthorne boy's leftovers? Got tired of living in his shadow? I hear all the gossip, I know about how the two of you used to run around like you owned the world." His eyes flicked back to me, briefly, before he turned on Emory again. "She'll never love you like she loves him. No matter how hard you try to win her over. The True Alpha belongs to the Omega. It's prophecy, after all."

"Shut up," Emory growled.

"You'll always be second best."

Emory snapped, lunging at Cooper. He would have reached him, too, if Carl and Des hadn't been so quick to tackle him to the ground. He fought against them, bucking hard from where they sat on top of him.

"You don't get to talk about him! Not after what you did to his family! Not after what you did to Jamie!" Emory screamed.

"I didn't mean to kill her!" Cooper yelled back, losing his composure in return. "I would have done anything for her! I loved her!"

"Enough!" I shouted. I spun around to glare down at Cooper. "Will you tell me what I want to know if I offer you something you want in return?"

Cooper turned from the scene at the floor before him to watch me carefully. "What do you think you can offer me that I want? Freedom? No thanks, I'm safer living my life in this cell than I am out there, especially with the knowledge I have about your rogue and his monster army. No, I only want one thing, and you can't give that to me."

"You want to see your son. To have the chance to explain yourself. I can give that to you."

He inclined his head, surprise and intrigue all over his face. "How?"

I jerked my chin in the direction of Des, who still sat on top of Emory, although Emory had stopped fighting. "She's Casey's girlfriend. She can convince him to see you if you tell us what you know."

He eyed me carefully, considering my offer before he sighed and gestured for me to sit. I did so, sliding down to the floor and sitting cross-legged.

"You can really deliver on your side of the bargain?" he asked hope and skepticism lacing his words.

Des shot me a guarded look and jerked her head toward Cooper. "Yes."

He nodded to himself before he turned to me. "I tried to warn your mother. I told her that she was in danger. I know that she didn't believe me. But she put precautions in place anyway, just in case."

"Precautions against the rogue? If you knew who it was, without a doubt, why wouldn't she believe you?"

Cooper's eyes took on a haunted look as he remembered something from long ago. "I loved Jamie. I didn't want to hurt her. I was trying to rescue her from the evil she swore lived in her house. When I went there that night, she was supposed to be at work. I didn't know that she had switched shifts with her husband."

I didn't see what any of this had to do with what I needed to know, and I informed Cooper that I didn't care to take his stroll down memory lane. "Get on with it. I don't care about some unrequited love you had for Daniel's mom. It's irrelevant."

"Is it?" he asked, not waiting for me to answer. "I went there and accidentally shot Jamie when she came down the stairs because I thought she was her husband."

"Why did you want to kill Aidan? Jealous and just trying to get him out of the way?"

My comments were rewarded with a cold glare. "No. I was trying to save her. I was trying to save all of you. Aidan is the rogue, and he is going to use those monsters to start a new kind of pack."

My friends and I froze; the shock of what he'd said leaving us speechless. His claims were absurd. Aidan may be a jerk, but I knew for certain that he wasn't a traitor.

"No." The only protest that I could bring myself to utter.

Cooper stared at me, expression betraying nothing. "No? Your mother thought I was wrong, too. And she paid with her life."

I shook my head. "Brendan killed my mother. He tried to kill me, too."

"Brendan was a pawn." An inexplicable sadness filled Cooper's features, and given his statements about his love for Jamie, a theory started poking at my consciousness.

"He's dead," I stated, fixing Cooper with a steely stare. The flash of anguish that crossed Cooper's face affirmed everything I had started to suspect.

"What's the matter, Jones? Just sorry that you didn't get to kill Brendan yourself? I know how you want to end the whole Hawthorne family. Enough so that you would slander Aidan," Emory goaded from where he sat on the floor next to Des.

Cooper, eyes wild, glared at Emory. "He wasn't a

Hawthorne! He wasn't a Hawthorne, and Aidan used him to punish us!"

Emory rolled his eyes. "What the fuck are you talking about?"

I ignored Emory. "Aidan knew?"

"He suspected." Cooper stared at me, his sadness breaking my heart. "You understand, don't you?" he begged.

I nodded.

I understood.

"I'm so sorry."

I turned away, trying to fight the tears that my revelation had caused and opened my mouth to speak.

Des beat me to it, shooting away from her seat next to Emory to kneel in front of Cooper.

She grabbed his hands in hers gently forcing him to look her directly in the eyes. She wasn't trying to hide her tears. She'd made the same conclusion I had.

"This is what you wanted to see Casey about, isn't it? You don't want to explain yourself. You wanted Casey to help him? You wanted Casey to save him?"

Cooper nodded and began to shake, all semblance of cockiness gone as he allowed himself to feel his sorrow.

Des cried harder and pulled Cooper to her in an embrace. "I'm so sorry," she whispered. "I'll make sure he comes. It may be too late to save him. But you can still tell Casey the truth. I swear to you, Cooper, we will make this right."

I choked back the sobs that had started wracking my body as Emory stood to put an arm around my shoulders as he tried to comfort me. "What the hell is going on?"

I stared at Cooper a moment longer before I turned and looked Emory in the eyes. "Aidan Hawthorne isn't Brendan's father. Cooper is."

CHAPTER FOURTEEN

“ **I** don't buy it,” Emory mumbled as we made our way back to the car. “Jamie was a saint. She'd never cheat on Aidan. And Aidan might be a dick, but he'd never betray the pack.”

I agreed with him about Aidan. I hated the guy, but he did everything in the best interest of our pack.

When it came to Jamie, and more specifically Brendan, I one hundred percent believed it. No one reacted to news about a complete stranger the way that Cooper did. And more importantly, it was because I knew Aidan to be such a jerk that I could easily see how Jamie may have strayed in her marriage. When you feel under-appreciated, or like you aren't as important to someone as they are to you, dangerous thoughts start to form. I knew first hand. My current relationship with Daniel, and the subsequent feelings I could no longer deny that I had for Emory, were proof that when something is starting to break, people seek approval elsewhere.

Of course, given that I wasn't ready to admit to the king of the jerks that he was absolutely right about Daniel and me, let alone that he'd somehow managed to wedge himself into my heart, there was no way that I would tell him my thoughts on Jamie Hawthorne.

Instead, I opted to change that subject. “Whatever the truth is, we need to all agree on something.” I paused and darted serious looks at Des and Emory. “Until we can find out more. Until we can confirm or deny Cooper's allegations, we can't tell Daniel or Casey what we heard today.”

Des nodded her agreement, but Emory stared at me, amazement and secrecy hiding in the glint of his golden eyes.

“What?” I snapped when I couldn't stand his impish glare any longer.

“Nothing.” He shrugged before smiling. “I just don't think your boyfriend will like it when he finds out you've been keeping secrets from him."

"He's not my boyfriend," I spat from behind clenched teeth. It was futile, even I could hear the lie in my voice.

Des, thankfully, stayed oblivious, laughing as she turned to stare at Emory incredulously. "You sound as crazy as Cooper back there with his whole 'the true alpha belongs to the omega'! Everyone knows that Daniel doesn't think of Christa as anything more than his little sister. He's overprotective, sure. But honestly, there's a better chance that hell would freeze over before Daniel and Christa ever dated."

Des climbed into the driver side of the truck while Emory and I walked around to the other side.

"Really?" I whispered furiously at him.

Emory shrugged and opened the passenger door for me. I rolled my eyes and stepped around him.

With a quickness that surprised me, his lips were at my ear. I froze, the closeness keeping me from moving forward.

"Hell must be pretty cold tonight, huh?" he whispered before stepping away and allowing me to climb into the truck.

I swallowed, less because of his punny quip, and more because of the way my heart rate had notched up considerably at his closeness.

We drove back into town in silence, no one saying anything until we dropped Des off at her home. After she hopped out of the truck, Emory slid into the driver seat.

"Will I see you tonight?" Des asked me. I knew she was referring to prom, and since she still didn't know that Daniel was going to take me, I just shrugged.

"Maybe."

Emory choked on a laugh. "Chances are good that she'll get there one way or another," he told her, slamming the door shut.

I waved bye to Des as Emory drove us away.

Alone in the car, tension began to settle between us. I recognized the feeling. Before Daniel and I had given in to our attraction, our interactions had been similarly fueled.

Emory cleared his throat. "So you're pretty good at keeping secrets, aren't you?"

I glared at him. "Well, considering that I'm a werewolf, yeah, I'd say keeping secrets is one of my skills."

"Some people might call you a liar," he mused.

I stared heavenward, silently asking whoever was up there why I constantly found myself attracted to arrogant jerks.

"Some people..." I started, spitting those first two words venomously. "...will never understand what it's like to be in my position. Call me a liar. Call me whatever, but I do what I must to protect myself and my pack."

"So, you tell lies to protect the people you love?"

I grimaced, hating the fact that he kept using the word *lies*. "I keep things confidential until they become important."

Emory grinned, knowing that he had frazzled me. "Chill, little Alpha. I'm just trying to figure you out."

I had a snarky retort on my lips, but words failed me as we pulled up to Les Loups-Garous. Daniel was home, standing out front, and glaring at our approach.

I swallowed, two things running through my mind:

Daniel was more beautiful than my imagination gave him credit for being. Staring at him now, the way my heart beat in my chest, I couldn't believe that I'd ever doubted my love for him. Time and distance tricked me, but with him so close, I realized that what we had together trumped any stupid crush I thought I had developed.

The second thing running through my mind was that Daniel seemed angry.

I mentally kicked myself. I should have texted or called him so that he knew I was okay. Or, at the very least, so that I could hide what I'd been doing.

Emory glanced at me. "What are you going to tell him?"

I sighed. "I'll tell him we went dress shopping," I answered, reaching behind us to where I'd stowed my purchases from earlier.

He frowned at me. "You really are the Queen of deceit." The way he spoke held none of his usual playfulness. He almost sounded disappointed.

I didn't have time to respond to him. Daniel headed our way and judging by the look on his face, he demanded answers.

I scrambled out of the car and approached Daniel cautiously. His eyes kept darting between me and the truck where Emory took his time getting out.

We stood face to face now. "Hey," I offered, my voice small.

His eyes flicked away from glaring at Emory and settled on me. He assessed me coolly, and I resisted the urge to flinch.

"What's going on here?" The quietness of his voice grated against my nerves in much the same way it would have if he'd just outright yelled.

"Nothing. I just needed a ride to the store." I held up my bag hoping that it would be enough.

Daniel glanced down at the bag with disinterest before meeting my gaze again.

"You went dress shopping with him instead of with Des?" He didn't believe me, and his tone made it clear.

Considering that I wasn't lying about that part, his distrust offended me although only slightly since I was keeping secrets from him.

I lowered my voice. "I needed a ride, and he happened to be available. I didn't want to have to explain to Des why I needed a dress at the last minute, especially since she doesn't know about us. Em doesn't ask questions."

Daniel pulled a face and groaned, "Ugh, you have a nickname for him."

I just stared, unable to formulate anything in response to that level of pettiness. It didn't matter anyway because Daniel wasn't done talking.

"You don't think that she's going to figure out what's going on between us when we show up there together?"

I shrugged. "I figured we could come up with something

when we got there. Honestly, there are a million reasons why you'd go with me that don't have to be romantic."

Daniel's eyes flashed with anger. "And I told you I was done coming up with something. I don't care who knows about us anymore."

I shuffled from one foot to the other and bit my lip. "I know what you said, but it's not that easy. What's going on between us could be dangerous for the pack. It could get one, or both of us killed. You know that."

Daniel's stare remained hard, but I met his eyes without flinching, hoping to make him see my point.

His eyes had just begun to soften when Emory chose that moment to speak up from where he'd hovered to the side of us. "She's right, and you know it."

I saw any progress I'd made in calming him down fall to pieces as his hard mask slipped back into place.

"Stay out of this, Travis," he spat.

Emory shrugged. "I'm just saying. If you loved her as much as you think you do, you'd listen to her."

"This is none of your fucking business," Daniel responded, stepping around me so that he stood between Emory and me.

Emory took a step toward Daniel. "If the two of you do something stupid, say, like out your forbidden relationship, it will have disastrous consequences for the pack. Then, it will be everybody's business."

Daniel moved again, closing the gap between them even more. "You're not pack. So, again, it's not your business."

Emory growled. "She's the True Alpha. What concerns her, concerns all of us. And, if she gets hurt because of your carelessness, I'll kill you."

Daniel's eyes twitched toward me before he set his steely gaze back on Emory. "Is that a threat?"

Emory took a step around Daniel and chuckled. "Chill, D," he began, walking toward the door of Les Loups-Garous, pausing only after he wrenched it open. He tossed another glance over at Daniel. "It's not a threat. It's a god-damned promise."

He slid into the bar, and I swallowed nervously when I turned back to Daniel. His fury set his face ablaze. "You can't tell Destiny, but he knows?"

I swallowed again. "He guessed," I offered weakly.

Daniel sighed, running his hands through his hair in frustration. "I asked you to stay away from him."

I frowned. "No. You demanded that I stay away from him, and you know I don't take direction well."

"He's dangerous, Christa." Daniel grabbed my shoulders, his voice pleading as he begged me to understand.

I'd spent quite a bit of time with Emory over the past few weeks, and while I thought that he was an inconsiderate jerk, I couldn't see how he was dangerous.

"Why?" I asked.

Daniel's fingers bit into my shoulders more urgently. "He just is."

I shrugged myself out from under his painful grip. "No. He's a cocky, rude, insensitive person who only cares about himself. But he's not dangerous."

Daniel sagged forward, his gaze averted to the ground as he avoided my eyes. I shook my head and turned to walk away.

This definitely hadn't been the reunion I'd been hoping for, and I needed to get away before the urge to cry overwhelmed me, and I broke down.

His voice, small and broken, gave me pause. "You're wrong about him."

I took a deep breath. I wasn't going to waste my time defending Emory, and it disappointed me that Daniel wouldn't drop this and hold me like I wanted him to.

"Okay. Well, I'm going to get ready now. Pick me up at seven downstairs." I slashed my hand through the air. "Or don't. I really don't care anymore."

Daniel's arm shot out, and he grabbed my arm, spinning me

back around to face him.

My heart froze as I took in his face. I'd never seen him look so lost, and it broke through my disappointment like a brick shattering a window.

"You're wrong about him only caring about himself. He cares about you. And I think you care about him, too."

I could see how hurt he felt at just the idea that I cared about another man. I found myself keeping so many secrets from Daniel, but I knew that in this instance, I had to be honest with him. "I do care about him," I whispered, stepping forward and wrapping my arms around his neck.

I could feel him shaking, could feel how my words had torn him apart. I pressed my forehead against his. "I care about him, Daniel. He's been a good friend. But, I only *love* you. It would take the end of the world to change that. You're the only person that I want to be with."

Daniel drew in a shaky breath, his dark eyes locking on mine and holding me hostage.

I stared back, taking in how beautiful what we shared really was before I brushed my lips against his softly. With that small invitation, a dam broke, and he kissed me back with an intensity that weakened my knees. All of the anger, all of the resentment I'd felt over the last few weeks melted away, and I finally felt at peace. I felt like I had finally come home.

I pulled away first, sliding my hand down his arm and into his waiting palm, tugging him gently toward the entrance as our fingers intertwined.

"What are you doing?"

I smiled, secretly relieved that I didn't need to come up with any more excuses about where I'd been. "I have to go get ready."

"So... We're still going?" His voice held hope, and it just made my smile deeper.

"If you'll still take me."

He frowned. "I thought that you didn't want people to know

about us."

I shrugged. "I'm more in the train of thought that we just do what we do, and if people know they know. Other than that what we do is our business."

He answered with a lop-sided grin. "That's very wise of you."

"I stole it from a friend," I answered, thinking of Brock. "One day, when we're safe, and this rogue threat has been neutralized, that's when we can throw caution to the wind and tell the world about us."

"We could be waiting for a long time for that."

I turned, capturing him in an embrace. "Well, I guess it's a good thing that I'd wait for you forever, Daniel Hawthorne."

Daniel held me tightly. "You'll never have to wait for me again. I have you now, and I am never letting you go."

My heart swelled in my chest. With Daniel by my side, I could handle anything coming my way.

Even a Rogue war.

CHAPTER FIFTEEN

A while later, I stepped away from my mirror to assess myself. I had swept my hair into an up-do, with little curly ringlets hanging down, and I'd spent a lot more time putting on my make-up.

If I'd planned it better, I would have gone and got my hair, nails, and make-up professionally done, but considering my time crunch and the impromptu field trip I'd taken to visit Cooper Jones, a trip that had taken up a considerable portion of my day, that hadn't been an option. At any rate, I hoped that what I'd accomplished myself would be enough to take Daniel's breath away.

Trying to keep up with the tradition of being picked up by your date on Prom night, Daniel had gotten ready down in the basement/training room while I got ready in the apartment.

After sliding the dress on carefully over my head and stepping into a pair of black high heels, I chanced another glance in the mirror and smiled. My training and all the exercise from being a werewolf did wonders for my body. Whereas I had been a naturally thin teenager, there had never been any muscle behind it. I was very trim and muscular now, and it looked damned good. Seeing myself at this moment, I felt as beautiful as my mother, something that I'd never imagined I would be able to accomplish without her guidance.

I grinned at my reflection and then slipped out the front door of the apartment, taking the steps down into the bar carefully. I paused when I reached the bottom. Daniel's back was to me as he made a drink behind the bar and spoke to the person sitting there, Emory.

"You wanted a double, Travis?" Daniel asked, all professionalism as he took care of his customer.

"Yep," Emory huffed, tossing some cash onto the counter.

Daniel spun gracefully, setting the cocktail in front of

Emory and cocking an eye at the money. "I told you, it's on me."

Emory shook his head. "I don't want your charity. I just want to know what this is about."

Being naturally curious, I stepped back into the shadows and eavesdropped. I wanted to know what was going on, too.

Daniel's lips pursed as he regarded Emory levelly. "I just thought we could talk."

I couldn't see Emory's face, but by the tone of his voice, I imagined he glared daggers at Daniel. "About what?"

"Christa," Daniel whispered my name, and I leaned forward, even more interested now that I knew I was the subject they were discussing.

"What about her?" Emory kept his voice mostly neutral, but I detected the faintest hint of irritation at hearing Daniel say my name.

"I feel like she's keeping secrets from me. Secrets that, for whatever reason, she feels that she can share with you."

I watched as Daniel stopped pacing around the bar and stared intently at Emory.

Emory cocked his head to the side, and I really wished I could see what his face looked like. "Everyone's entitled to their secrets, Daniel. You, of all people, should understand that."

"Christa and I don't keep secrets from one another." I winced at his words. I'd clearly underestimated the level of honesty in our relationship. I'd always assumed that Daniel kept secrets from me, too. If possible, I felt even worse about keeping my visit to Cooper, and the life-altering things we'd learned, a secret.

Emory huffed in response. "You're not going to honestly try to sit here and tell me you don't keep secrets from her. I know that you do, D. I know that you have. I know how you are."

Daniel shook his head. "Any secrets we had are in the open, at least on my end. When it comes to her, I've vowed to be different. I have to be because she's worth it."

Emory sighed, and I don't know what look sat on his face, but I could see remorse on Daniel's. "Why her, Daniel? Our friendship, as much rivalry as there is in it, could have survived almost anything."

Daniel closed his eyes, gripping the bar as he thought over Emory's question. "Anything but her," he laughed bitterly, finishing Emory's sentiment.

Emory shrugged in agreement. "Why her?" he repeated.

Daniel sighed. "It's always been her. I've known it since we were kids. I fought what I felt for her for a long time, but somehow, I always knew my life would start with her, and it would end with her."

Emory leaned forward. "If I were an honorable man, I'd leave. I'd let you be, and forget about her. But I'm not an honorable man because I'm not going anywhere. I'm going to wait around, wait until you make a mistake because I know you will, and then I can rush in and sweep her off her feet."

I expected Daniel to get angry, to yell at Emory and kick him out of Les Loups-Garous. Instead, he crooked him a lop-sided grin although it didn't quite wipe the sadness off his face. "Do what you want, Travis. But don't hold your breath."

I heard the humor in Emory's voice as he leaned over the bar and slapped Daniel on the shoulder. "Something tells me I won't have to hold my breath too long."

Daniel shook his head. "You never answered my question. What secrets are the two of you keeping?"

Daniel's question was my cue to make an appearance. I couldn't listen to this anymore, and I couldn't sit in the shadows and let Emory reveal our secret even though I wasn't sure that he would.

Any response Emory had was cut off as I stepped into the bar, my heels clicking against the floor in a soft staccato.

Emory turned, catching my eyes with his liquid gold stare. He gave me an appreciative once-over, the corner of his lips curving into a seductive half-smile. "Beautiful," he whispered.

Daniel had been watching Emory, but he looked up as I approached the bar. His eyes flicked to me, and I saw him go still. He swallowed, and his mouth opened slightly as he pinned me with his dark gaze, the heat in his eyes making me blush.

Daniel stepped out of the bar, stopping once he stood in front of me, and we stared at each other for a long time. The tension thickened around us as I assessed him just as much as he appraised me.

He wore a tuxedo well. He had slicked his dark hair back into a low pony-tail, but some pieces escaped and hung like shadows around his face. His tongue darted around behind his partially open lips, hunger dancing in the features of his face. For the first time since we started dating each other, he made me nervous in an altogether pleasant way.

Ever since realizing I was an Alpha werewolf, I'd made it a point to try not to look away from someone. Tonight, the nerves got to me, and I looked away from his gaze. "Do you like the dress?" I asked, peeking up at him.

"Very much," he whispered, the heat in his voice doing strange things to my heartbeat.

Emory glanced back and forth between us, eyebrows drawn and a disgusted look on his face. "Yeah, I'm not watching this," he muttered, scooting out of his chair and sidestepping around where Daniel and I stood.

Daniel's eyes flicked to Emory, and that smile on his face widened even deeper, a wicked slant reflecting. "Bye, Emory. Great talk, Emory. Wish you could stay." His tone was taunting, and although I should have told him to stop, especially since Emory was my friend and he couldn't help how he felt about me, the she-wolf in me relished the way Daniel marked his territory.

"No thanks, I don't want to be here when the two of you start ripping each other's clothes off."

Daniel's eyes flicked back to me, that hunger still

transforming his face into something too dangerous to look at, and he licked his lips. "Better hurry, then," he growled back.

I swallowed, my knees turning to jelly as Daniel's hand snaked around to the back of my neck, and his lips crashed against mine. He pushed into me, backing me up against the bar as his tongue danced against mine, and his hand slid my dress up my thigh, claiming me as his own.

Clothes didn't get ripped off, something that both relieved and disappointed me all at once. Ever the gentleman, at least when it came to me, Daniel backed off after a moment of one of the most mind-blowing kisses we'd ever shared. I tried to pull him back to me, but he so gently reminded me that we were in the middle of a public place, and that we had a date.

"We wouldn't want that dress to go to waste on the floor," he purred in my ear.

I took solace in the fact that, at least, this time, he hadn't pushed me away telling me that I wasn't ready. Maybe later, we could continue where we'd left off.

We pulled into the parking lot of the town hall. Most of my high school dances were held at the high school gym, and since the last time I had gone to a dance I'd almost been murdered, I was glad that the school had decided to dig deep into their budget to rent out the hall for Prom. The last thing I wanted on my first public date with Daniel was a repeat of the excitement from Homecoming.

I had been to one previous dance at the town hall back when I'd first moved back to Kennington. Every year, the City Council put on an end of summer sock hop. I smiled to myself thinking of that night. It had been the first night that I'd seen Daniel since I'd moved back, and while, for whatever reason, the memories of our shared childhood had been hidden from me at that time, I knew even then that Daniel would claim my heart.

And claim it, he had.

He placed his hand on the small of my back as he led me

through the crowd of students filling the room, and I wasn't surprised to see the jealous stares from many of my classmates.

Daniel was a God to these girls, even the ones who didn't know him as our local Omega werewolf. Everyone knew him, and every girl I knew had fantasized about him. I tried not to look *too* smug as I ignored their glares.

I sat down at one of the round tables that had been set up around the perimeter of the dance floor, and Daniel went off to grab drinks. I didn't usually like to be the center of attention, but I knew that my choice of date had made me the talk of the school.

Suspicions were confirmed when I watched as my sort-of friend, Bree, a notorious gossip, broke away from her group of friends, including her on-again, off-again boyfriend, Brad. She rushed over and sat down next to me at the table staring at me expectantly but not saying anything.

I turned to her and fixed a pleasant smile on my face, even though I wanted to tell her to kick rocks. "Can I help you?" I asked sweetly.

Bree folded her arms and inclined her head toward the punch bowl. "Dish."

I glanced up and saw that Daniel had paused in his drink pouring and watched Bree and me with amusement before I turned back to Bree and shrugged. "Nothing to dish. I asked him to take me, and he said yes, as a favor to me, so that I didn't have to go alone."

She looked over at Daniel and then back at me. "He doesn't look at you like he considers you just a friend. He looks at you like he thinks the sun shines just for you."

I tried to keep my composure even though I knew she was right. Daniel watched me in a way that would make it obvious to anyone in a one hundred mile radius that we were in love with each other, but as Brock would say, it wasn't any of their business.

I shrugged again and decided to change the subject. "You

look beautiful, Bree. I love your dress."

Bree picked up the subtext, and understanding that the subject was closed, she pursed her lips before smiling at me kindly. "You look dazzling. You're honestly probably the most beautiful person here," she started before she leaned forward to whisper in my ear. "But it looks like your *friendly* date pulled your hair loose in the back. Come with me to the bathroom, and we'll fix it before people start talking. Last thing you need is people whispering about your illicit affair with the local bar owner."

I reached back to touch my hair, blushing as I realized that Bree was right. I smiled at her sheepishly. "Thanks," I said standing to follow her to the bathroom.

Daniel reached us then eyeing Bree warily. She shot him a thousand-watt smile, one that he barely even noticed as he turned to me. "Where are you going?" he whispered.

I made to answer, but Bree beat me to it. "You pulled her hair out. I'm going to go fix it for her before people start talking."

Daniel's eyes flicked to my face, and he bit his lip, trying and failing, to look as innocent as possible. "I don't know what you're talking about."

Bree rolled her eyes. "Uh huh," she answered, pulling me with her to the ladies' room.

She fixed my hair quickly, honestly making it look even better than it did before. "I thought you and Des would have come together," she told me as we made our way back to the table where Daniel had been joined by the rest of Bree's flock.

He met my gaze from across the room, and I took pity on him. He'd left high school a long time ago, and I could tell by the look on his face that he did not enjoy the stroll down memory lane.

"Earth to Christa. Quit staring at tall, dark, and delicious over there." Bree's voice cut into my head, and I turned to face her.

"Huh?"

"I asked you where Des was. I thought the two of you were inseparable."

I frowned. "She's not here?"

Bree shook her head. "No. Was she supposed to be here already?"

I thought over the question. I didn't really know what Des had planned since I hadn't discussed prom with her. I knew the night was still young, especially since Prom had only started an hour or so ago, but considering that she had been practically salivating over the night for the last couple of months, I found it strange that she hadn't arrived yet.

"I don't know. We didn't have any formal plans set up." I told her as I sat back down next to Daniel and reached into my little clutch purse.

Bree's groupies surrounded her as soon as we'd returned and the whole lot of squealy girls left their dates with Daniel and me while they scampered off, probably to interrogate Bree on what she'd uncovered about my date.

I pulled out my phone and looked down at Daniel, inclining my head toward a back door. He cocked an eyebrow in confusion but stood to follow me, nonetheless. We slipped out the door, and Daniel, mistaking my sneaking off as a way to cuddle with him, put his arms around me and leaned his chin on the top of my head. "I still want to actually dance with you. I didn't ask to take you to the prom so that we could stand in a dark alley and make out, although that idea does have its own appeal."

I tapped Des's number into my phone, ignoring the way my insides went mushy as Daniel pressed against me. "Des isn't here yet, and I haven't heard from her since earlier."

Daniel shrugged. "I'm sure she'll get here when she gets here."

"I know, I just want to call her to make sure she's on her way."

I couldn't shake the feeling that something was wrong, and maybe it had something to do with my paranoia over school dances being cursed for me, but I needed to hear Des tell me she was okay.

The phone rang twice and went to voice mail, and I hung up without leaving a message, my mouth forming a frown.

Daniel bent down, trailing kisses down my jawline all the way to my shoulder and I shivered. "Relax, Christa," he whispered, reaching into his jacket and producing a flask. He took a pull and offered it to me.

I eyed it warily. "So you've got to get drunk to take me on a date?" I asked, mostly playfully.

"Not at all. I just thought if we were going to spend a night, pretending to be a normal couple at prom, we ought to do what normal couples at prom do."

I turned around to face him, swiping the flask in a surprisingly graceful move. "And normal couples get drunk at prom?" I asked.

He nodded, a naughty gleam in his eye. "You haven't had the punch yet, but I did, and I can promise you someone out there has already spiked it."

I rolled my eyes and giggled. "Bottoms up, then, I guess." I took a drink and resisted the urge to spit it back up. Straight whiskey, no mixer for Daniel.

We passed the flask back and forth for a little while, and I found myself actually understanding what Daniel meant. Our lives didn't allow for little moments like this, and even though I knew we were being silly, I relished the small sense of normalcy we had managed to find on this night.

When the flask was pretty much empty, we slipped back into the building, giggling like two fools. We stood at the edge of the dance, watching as the other attendees danced to an atrocious pop song, and I felt content. Nothing could shatter this night for me.

Daniel's arm slid around my waist, and he brushed his lips

against my ear. "I love you, Christa. And for whatever reason, you love me, too. I promise you, I'm going to spend the rest of my life proving to you that I deserve your love."

I smiled, "The rest of your life is an awfully long time."

He didn't get a chance to respond, as Bree, and her group of friends, reached us and pulled me away from Daniel. "Come dance with us!"

I groaned. "Have you seen Des yet?"

She shook her head. "No. But don't worry about her. She's a big girl, she'll get here when she feels like it. You smell like booze by the way."

I wrinkled my nose. "So do you."

She chuckled, "Brad spiked the punch."

I laughed. "So I've heard."

I danced with the group of completely normal teenage girls while Daniel sat back drinking spiked punch with the guys and no doubt talking about barbaric manly things. I had fun, and the world didn't end. The night had very much turned out to be just a normal high school experience. No one pressured me with questions about Daniel, my date didn't try to lure me to my death, and for a good hour or so I forgot that I needed to be worried about where Des was at that moment since she still hadn't shown.

When a slow song came on, Daniel came and swept me into his arms. I leaned into him, breathing in the scent of whiskey and cologne he carried around him. We didn't have to make small conversation; we were so comfortable with one another. As he held me, and we made slow circles on the dance floor, a part of me wished that this moment didn't have to end. It had been the most perfect night, and this was the highlight.

Of course, I should have known that it wouldn't stay perfect. I felt Daniel tense, and I looked up from where I leaned against his chest. His narrowed eyes glared behind me, and I turned to face Emory.

"What are you doing here?" Daniel growled.

Emory's eyes barely passed over Daniel as he met my gaze. "I need you to come outside with me."

I leaned back in confusion. "Um, no."

Emory closed his eyes and gestured toward the door. "Please. I don't want there to be a scene here."

Daniel snorted. "You're unbelievable, Travis."

Emory ignored him, instead deciding to plead with me. "I'm not here to try to ruin your night. It's about Des."

I stilled, not liking the feeling crawling up my spine. "What about Des?" I asked, trying to keep my voice level.

"She's out front. And she's not okay."

I didn't stay to listen to anymore. I'd understood enough. Something had happened to Des, and she needed me. I tore across the room, slamming through the doors like they weren't even there and skidded to a stop next to where she sat in flannel plaid pajama bottoms and a black tank top, mascara tracks running down her cheeks and a bottle of cheap vodka hanging from her hand.

"What the hell?" I asked.

She hopped up and threw herself into my arms, sobbing uncontrollably and mumbling unintelligibly.

I stepped back a little and put my hands on her shoulders, frowning at her as I tried to figure out what had happened. "Are you drunk?"

Des took a swig off her vodka bottle. "Yes," she offered, nodding somberly before she hiccupped. She leaned forward and sniffed at me suspiciously. "Are you?"

I shook my head. "No." I wasn't even lying. Thinking that your best friend had been hurt had a surprisingly sobering effect. "What's going on?"

Des sniffled. "I tried to go to your apartment, but Emory said you weren't there, and that you had gotten Daniel to take you to the prom as a favor to make me happy. So we drank for a few hours and then I decided I needed to come rescue you. The only reason you dragged yourself out here was to make me happy, and I'm not even going now that..." She trailed off as she began to sob again.

I shook her slightly. "Stay with me, Des. What's happened."

I heard the doors behind us open and slam closed, and I assumed that Daniel and Emory had joined us out on the steps, but I couldn't acknowledge either of them at the moment since I was trying to get to the bottom of Des's melt down.

"Fucking, Carl!" Des wailed, and I felt myself stiffen. I chanced a glance at Emory who grimaced and nodded. I knew where this was going, and I needed to get Des out of here before she ruined my night.

"Come on, I'm taking you home."

Des dug her flip-flopped heels into the ground. "No! I wanna dance. And Emory is going to dance with me." Des shot Emory a glare. "You owe me, don't you, Em? None of this would have happened if you hadn't cooked up that wild plan!"

My heart pounded wildly in my chest as I tugged on Des with all the strength I could without ripping her arm out of its socket.

"Please, Des. Let's just go to the bar. I'll buy you more drinks."

"I don't want more drinks! I want Casey, and he just broke up with me because he ran into Carl, and Carl happened to mention that the three of us stopped in and interrogated Cooper Jones this afternoon!"

I winced. I froze. And then Daniel spoke, his voice steely, and my heart stopped.

"What the fuck is she talking about?"

CHAPTER SIXTEEN

"**H**uh?" I asked, but the she-wolf was right there in my mind, telling me that even that sad excuse for a response had spoken volumes. *Too shrill. Too guilty.*

Daniel came down the steps, hands at his side as he glared down at me. "I didn't fucking stutter. What is she talking about? Did you go see Cooper Jones after I specifically told you not to?"

I knew he could see the answer written all over my face, but I also knew Daniel, and he wouldn't let this go until I either confirmed or denied it.

Of course, denying it wasn't an option. Des had inadvertently seen to that. "Yes."

Daniel spun around, facing Emory dead on. "And you knew. You went with them? That's the secret you were keeping from me." Daniel shouted now, more angry than I'd ever seen him before.

"Don't drag me into the middle of this. This is between you and your girlfriend."

I winced again and shot a look at Des. She wasn't paying attention, seeing as she had gone back to chugging her vodka. Even still, I needed to say something to keep her from getting suspicious.

I sighed. "I've told you, Emory, he's not my-"

Daniel spun back around to face me, eyes flashing. "Don't you dare fucking finish that statement. I'm sick of walking around on egg shells for these people, and I've already told you that."

I took a step back, my heel slipping on the edge of the step behind me. I barely managed to catch my balance in time to keep from falling down the stairs. Daniel glared down at me, anger morphing his face into one that I didn't recognize, or like. In fact, he terrified me at that moment. I shot a panicked look at

Emory, who stared at the scene in front of him in dumb founded shock. Apparently, he'd never seen Daniel so angry before, either.

He took a tentative step toward Daniel, arms in the air in a surrendering gesture. "Easy, Omega."

Daniel whipped back around and pointed at Emory. "You stay out of this. It's none of your god-damned business. This," he paused and pointed at me. "This is between her and me."

Travis cracked his neck. "That's probably true, Daniel. But I need you to look at her. Really look at her, because at this moment, *she's fucking scared of you.*"

Daniel and Emory stared at each other for several seconds before Daniel blinked and looked back at me. I cowered, and my she-wolf growled. I ignored her because, for the first time, this actually had nothing to do with being a werewolf.

I had lied to someone I loved, and he responded with very human anger. Daniel's face, which still held so much fury, softened a little as looked back at me. I knew I looked pathetic. I had crossed my arms around me protectively, and I shook from the adrenaline of all of this.

For all my waxing poetic about this being a very human argument, I couldn't help the way I instinctively took another step back, crouching into a defensive stance when Daniel stepped forward. I was still a werewolf, after all.

Daniel winced, and I internally groaned realizing that my small movement had added even more salt to the wound I'd ripped into his heart.

He stared at me, expressionless for a long moment before shaking his head and meeting me at the bottom of the steps. He grabbed my bicep, not roughly, but deliberately.

"You don't need to worry about your excuses anymore. Now when you tell them I'm not your boyfriend, you won't be lying."

My mouth dropped open, and I could feel tears. Daniel stared down at me, and I could see the regret on his face mixed with something else. He was waiting. Waiting for me, I supposed to do something. Beg him not to do this, maybe? I didn't know, but I wouldn't give him the satisfaction. So we just stood there locked in a silent battle of wills staring each other down.

At that moment, for as much as I loved him, I felt that old resentment rise up. The hostility I'd felt when I'd first remembered him and realized that I had been in love with him my whole life. The bitterness I'd felt when he had tried, and succeeded, to make me feel like he didn't return the feeling.

The more I thought about it, the longer we stared daggers at one another, the more I realized that this feeling inside me was mutating to something worse than resentment.

There's a thin line between love and hate, and when I finally broke the silence between us, I meant every vile word that spewed forth from my mouth.

"I hate you."

Of course, as soon as the words left my mouth, I realized I didn't mean them, but the damage was done. Daniel blinked at me in shock, and it became clear that those words had done exactly what I'd intended them to do. He'd gone off and broken up with me and whether he had meant it or not, had been irrelevant. It had hurt, and I'd responded in kind.

Daniel didn't answer, he frowned and nodded once, then turned and walked away. His retreating back seemed to kick my mind back into gear, and I realized that I had to stop him. This was wrong. It couldn't end like this.

"Daniel," I shouted, but he didn't slow, and I just stood there frozen, unable to move through the numbness of it all.

Emory stepped down, putting a hand on my arm. I turned slowly to look at him. He rolled his eyes and ran his free hand through his blonde hair. "Go," he whispered, inclining his head toward the parking lot.

I nodded and turned toward the parking lot just in time to see Daniel peel out onto the street.

"Fuck," I muttered, running my hand over my face.

Des stumbled forward then, clutching my dress in her hands, as she looked up at me in drunken confusion. "I'm going to be sick," she muttered before leaning down and puking on my shoes.

I groaned and looked at Emory. "You got your truck?"

Emory nodded. "Yeah. You're not going after Daniel?"

I sighed. "Let's take her home, and then you can help me find Daniel."

Emory didn't answer, but he dug his keys out of his pocket and motioned for me to follow him. He bent down and picked up Des, threw her over his shoulder, and marched off to the parking lot.

I followed, plucking Des's shoes off her feet. "What are you doing?" she slurred at me.

"You puked on my shoes, so I'm borrowing yours."

We dropped Des off and then went to the first and only place I could think of to look for Daniel, Les Loups-Garous. Unsurprisingly, he wasn't there.

Emory had suggested that maybe he went back to the prom to apologize. He hadn't been there either. We drove around for another hour before I finally gave up and told Emory to take me home.

When we pulled back into the parking lot, I jumped out of the truck before Emory had even put it in park. I walked into the bar, grabbed a bottle of whiskey, and went back outside before Emory could even make it into the building.

Stalking off towards the edge of the forest, I tossed a glance over my shoulder. "Are you coming?"

Emory looked surprised. "Where are you going?"

I help up the bottle. "I'm going to get drunk."

Emory shook his head and jogged up to me. We picked our way through the forest until we came into the clearing where my Alpha's throne sat. I climbed up and drew my knees into myself, staring off into the sky as I took a swig off the bottle.

Emory came and sat next to me, putting his arm around me and letting me lean into him as I fought hard to keep my tears from spilling over. "This is such a mess."

Emory pulled me closer, taking the bottle from me and bringing it to his lips. "Daniel is my best friend. Even now, I still think of him that way. But you're right; this is a mess."

"What does that have to do with me and Daniel?"

Emory sighed. "Everything. But you don't need to concern yourself about it. Despite how I feel, at the end of the night, I'm going to do the right thing."

I glanced sideways at Emory, knowing that I shouldn't pry, but their conversation from earlier played back in my mind. "Are you in love with me?" I blurted.

Emory stilled and looked away from me. "Don't. Please. Don't ask me that."

I stared at him, willing him to look in my direction. "Why?"

He looked down at me then. "Because you don't want to know the answer."

I met his gaze unflinchingly. "Answer the question, Travis."

Emory closed his eyes and took a deep breath. When he opened them again, his eyes were like fire. "You never call me by my name," he whispered.

"You didn't answer my question."

He leaned in, his lips brushing against mine. "Yes."

My heart stilled, and for the briefest of moments, I considered letting him kiss me. I wanted him to.

But reason stopped me. I may have feelings for Emory, and I felt pretty certain that Emory wasn't lying when he told me that he loved me, but I didn't love Emory.

I loved Daniel, and nothing in this world could change that.

I sprang away from Emory so fast that I almost lost my balance. "I'm so sorry. I'm so sorry, Emory. I can't do this. I care about you so much, but I-"

Emory held up his hand and afforded me a small, sad smile. "You love Daniel. And despite that passionate break-up I just witnessed, you're not ready to give up on him yet."

I shook my head. "No. But if I kiss you, that's the end. He'll probably forgive that I lied to him. He won't forgive me if I let myself fall for you."

Emory hopped down and put an arm over my shoulder, and we made our way back to Les Loups-Garous. Neither of us broke the silence until we reached the edge of the clearing, and Emory turned me to face him. "I understand that you're going to go in there, you guys will probably make-up, and everything will go back to normal for you. But I need you to understand something for me. I'm not leaving. I'm going to be here for you, in whatever capacity you will let me."

I smiled and squeezed Emory's hand. "In another life, I would have chosen you."

Emory shook his head. "No," he whispered. "I don't think you would have."

I offered him one last smile before I took off at a jog across the parking lot. I made quick work getting through the bar and up the stairs to the apartment, but I froze when I stood right outside the door. I knew Daniel was home, I'd seen his Jeep in the parking lot. I knew that I wanted to make things right with him, but words failed me.

I couldn't take back what I'd said, I could only do my best to convince him that I didn't mean it, but I navigated uncharted waters. I'd never been in a relationship before, I had no idea how any of this worked.

I knew I couldn't be a coward. I had to face him, no matter the consequences, so I turned the knob and slid into our apartment.

Daniel sat on the couch, staring at the wall. He looked up at me when I entered, but his face stayed blank.

"Hey," I offered tentatively.

"Hey."

"Can we talk?"

Daniel eyed me warily, and for a moment I feared he was

going to tell me to get out. Instead, he motioned for me to sit down. I took a seat next to him on the couch and stared, trying to figure out something, anything to say. "Where did you go?"

Daniel looked at me coolly. "What does it matter? You *hate* me. Remember?"

I licked my lips before catching my bottom one with my teeth. "You know I didn't mean that." Daniel stared at me, not adding anything further to the conversation, so I spoke again. "Where did you go, Daniel?"

"For a run. I went wild for a little while, let the wolf take control. Where have you been?"

"With Emory." I felt Daniel stiffen at my answer, and I knew I needed to explain. "You left me at the prom with no ride home after you dumped me. He took Des home and then drove me around while I tried to find you. When that failed, he sat with me while I cried."

"And that's all that happened?" His voice was too calm, and I didn't like it one bit.

"No."

He groaned, and I saw his eyes flash. "You've been lying to me all day, and you choose this moment to be honest?"

I ignored his lying jab and told him what happened. "He almost kissed me. I told him no."

"Why? I broke up with you, right? You hate me, right? You're free to do whatever you want."

"Is that what you want? Do you want us to be over? Do you want me to do whatever I want?"

Daniel stared at me, not saying anything. I stared back waiting for my answer. He wouldn't meet my eyes, and he wouldn't answer. I felt my heart break into a million pieces because at that moment, I realized that maybe what happened tonight wasn't fixable.

I swallowed a couple of times, blinking back tears and nodded. "Right." I didn't know what to say, I just knew I needed to get out of this room before I lost it.

I stood and turned in the direction of my bedroom, wondering what the hell I was going to do now. I lived here, and our current situation as a pack meant that I couldn't go home.

"No." Daniel's voice cut through the silence. I stopped and turned to glance at him.

"What?" I choked. I needed to get out of here, I could feel the tears, and I wasn't going to let him see me cry.

Faster than my mind could reconcile, Daniel shot out of his seat and to me. I backed against the wall, more a reaction from how quickly he moved than anything else. He put his hand against the wall, boxing me in. "I said no. I don't want us to be over. I don't want you to go anywhere." He leaned his forehead against mine and sighed deeply. "This isn't just about me, Christa. You have to make choices, too. You have to decide what you want."

I reached up to touch Daniel's face, our gazes locking. "I want you. I've always wanted you."

The world around us went still. Daniel closed his eyes, and it felt as though he were on the edge of a decision so monumental, a decision that I didn't know how to help him make.

My heart hammered in my chest as I waited for him to do something, anything.

And then he did.

He pressed against me, his lips crashing against mine with such force that I had to wrap my arms around his neck to keep from sliding down the wall.

His hand came around to the back of my head, and he pulled me even closer as he grabbed my hair tie and ripped it out, allowing my curled hair to fall freely down my back and around my face. His lips pulled away from mine, and he trailed kisses down my neck and to my shoulder like he had earlier in the night, but with more urgency. I wrapped my legs around him, and he spun me away from the wall, carrying me down the hall and through his bedroom door before he pinned me beneath him on the bed.

He paused, leaning back to look at me questioningly, but didn't say anything. I sat up and stared back, biting my lip as I really thought about where this was going. I could tell him no, and he would back away. We'd fall asleep, and everything could go back to the way it had been before.

The innocent part of me screamed at me to tell him no.

But the part that loved him, the part that belonged to him, didn't want to.

I licked my lips and pulled my dress over my head. Daniel let out a breath I didn't realize he was holding. "Oh, Christa," he whispered before his lips found mine again.

More clothes came off, and he looked down at me again, taking me in. I thought that I would be self-conscious but, instead, the appreciation and love on his face just reinforced that I made the right decision.

He met my eyes questioningly one last time. I nodded. He leaned down, his lips brushing against my neck.

"I love you," I whispered.

"I love you, Christa," he whispered, saying my name like a prayer.

He continued to pray to me while he took what I could have never offered to anyone else.

After we finished, I laid against his chest, sheets wrapped around us, and felt content. I'd always thought that life would instantly change after I'd slept with someone, and it surprised me that I felt no different about myself than I had before. Maybe it came down to the fact that for me it had happened with someone that I love so much, or maybe the reality of what had just taken place hadn't quite set in.

I knew one thing for certain; we couldn't go back to hiding our relationship now. There was no way that I would ever be able to lie about what was happening between us.

I leaned up and kissed Daniel. He brushed my hair out of my face and left his palm on my cheek. "Are you okay?"

I smiled and nuzzled into his chest. "Mmm. Better than."

Daniel started to speak, but a knock on the door interrupted. "What the hell?" He mumbled as the knocking quickly escalated to full on banging. He sat up and then reached down to grab a pair of shorts from the floor, slipping them on before heading toward the bedroom door.

I pouted, "Don't go."

Daniel crooked me a grin, full of promises of things to come. "Wait here, I'll get rid of whoever it is and be right back."

He pulled the door open, not closing it all the way, and I heard his steps as he crossed the hall and pulled the front door open.

The voice that answered from the other side started my heart in a completely different way.

"Where is Christa? I need to see her now." Des's demand rang clear throughout the apartment. I pulled the sheets up higher on my body, praying that Daniel could get her to leave. I may not be hiding my relationship with him anymore, but I definitely didn't want Des to find out like this.

"She's not here."

"Bull shit. I need to see her now. It's important," I heard as she pushed her way through the door and past Daniel, passing his room and into mine. Of course, I wasn't in there, and I hoped that she would see that and just assume I really wasn't home.

"Where is she?" I could hear her frustration, and I really felt for her, but now was not the time for me to worry about what bothered her.

I could hear Daniel behind her, trying to explain that he would tell me to call her when I got home.

"Cut the crap, Hawthorne. I know she's here. I saw Emory downstairs, and he said she came home hours ago." She paused, and I could see her and Daniel standing right outside through the crack in the door. She looked at Daniel and then looked at the door. "Why are you all sweaty?"

Daniel glanced sideways at the door. "It's hot in here?"

Des shook her head, and then pushed the bedroom door open. She looked in, and her eyes widened. She glanced back and forth between Daniel and me several times, her mouth opening and closing, but her mind unable to find words.

When she finally settled on a response, I had to admit that it was an appropriate one. "What the fuck?"

I flinched. "Des, I can explain."

She held up a hand, sneered at Daniel one more time, and then glared at me. "No time. Get up. Get dressed. We have to go."

"Go where?" I asked. I didn't want to go anywhere. Daniel had plans, some of which he had shared with me, and I wanted to get back to those.

"Zee has been kidnapped, and Casey has gone to rescue him. We have to go help him. He's going to get himself killed."

I sat up, making sure to keep the sheet wrapped around me. "What are you talking about? Zee is in Pennsylvania with Aidan and Lana," I paused and glanced at Daniel. "Right?"

Daniel nodded. "Where are you getting your intel, Des?"

"From Casey. He sent me a text stating he needed back-up because he had gotten a call from a blocked number. He said that the person on the phone told him that they had Zee, and that they were holding him hostage. He told him to go to the Alpha's Throne," Des paused and stared at me somberly. "You understand what this means, right?"

I nodded, the truth dawning on me, but it was Daniel who put words to my thoughts. "The rogue is making his move. If he has Zee, my dad could be in danger, too."

"Unless your dad is the rogue," Des offered, clearly without thinking.

Daniel spun on her. "Why would you say something like that? Where would you even get a crazy idea like that? My dad is loyal to our pack! He would never betray us, and in the last few weeks, I think he's come to regard Zee as a friend."

Des met Daniel's anger unflinchingly. "Don't be so naive, Daniel. If Aidan hasn't let you know that there has been a security breach, and he was supposed to be with Zee, then the logical conclusion is that your dad is behind it."

"Unless he's in danger, too," Daniel reaffirmed, his jaw clenching as he fought against the urge to scream at Des. "Where is this coming from, Destiny?" Calling Des by her real name was a no-no. She hated it, stating that it always made her feel like she was in trouble, which was why Daniel had done it, I'm sure.

The gears were turning in my head, and I hoped that I was wrong, but either way, I knew that we needed to tell Daniel what we knew. "Cooper Jones," I whispered.

Daniel and Des turned away from each other to stare over at me. "What?" Daniel spat.

"That's where she got the idea." I sighed, knowing that there wouldn't be an easy way to do this. "Cooper says that Brendan was never the rogue; he was a pawn. A pawn used to punish him specifically. Your dad hated Brendan, and he used Brendan to orchestrate my mother's murder from the shadows."

Daniel huffed. "Why the hell would he do that? Brendan was his son. Cooper Jones is crazy."

Des looked over at Daniel in pity. "Daniel, Brendan wasn't Aidan's son. He was Cooper's. And Aidan wanted to make sure that Cooper paid for the affair he'd had with your mom."

Daniel shook his head. "Cooper Jones lied to you."

Des looked like she wanted to say more, to try to convince Daniel that Cooper had told the truth, but I shook my head at her.

"He's right, Des. For all we know, Cooper is lying, and we're feeding right into it. Aidan has always looked out for the pack, and until we know otherwise, we shouldn't be slandering him."

Daniel fixed Des with a triumphant glare before grabbing a

t-shirt and a pair of jeans and heading into the bathroom. Des darted into my room, grabbing me some clothes and tossing them onto the bed for me. "We're going to need to talk about this, later," she warned, gesturing toward the crumpled bed sheets.

I rolled my eyes. "Yeah, one thing at a time. Let's go confront a rogue and save the world, and then I'll tell you all the details of my secret relationship with Daniel."

"How long?" she asked. I shot her an exasperated look, and she threw her hands up. "Just answer that one, and I'll leave it alone. For now."

"Since my birthday."

"Since your birthday! That's seven, nearly eight months!"

I sighed. "Later, Des."

She pursed her lips but didn't pry further about me and Daniel. She had other more pressing questions on her mind. "Do you really think that Cooper lied and this is all a big coincidence?"

I sighed, again. I didn't really want to discuss this one either, because the truth was, I didn't know what to believe. "I don't know, Des. But I hope for Daniel's sake, and the pack's sake, that it is."

Melancholy settled over us as Daniel stepped back into the bedroom and we all made our way downstairs.

No matter what we discovered, or what happened, I knew one thing with absolute certainty.

The rogue was here. The war had come.

CHAPTER SEVENTEEN

We weren't exactly working against the clock. We hurried down the stairs, but we had yet to come up with a concrete plan and, judging by the stream of text messages between Des and Casey, we hadn't missed much.

In fact, we hadn't missed anything. Casey's most recent communication indicated that he currently hid out in the woods, but hadn't seen a single creature, werewolf or otherwise.

The bar was empty, still not open after the fire, but I knew that we were going to need reinforcements, and I also knew that there happened to be at least three people downstairs in the basement, so I headed down, leaving Des and Daniel to come up with a plan on their own.

Just as I expected, Brock, Rowan, and Emory were sitting on the dingy couch in front of a small television screen, beers and pizza boxes surrounding them.

Brock looked up at my approach. "What's happening, Boss?"

"Apparently Zee has been kidnapped, and Casey has gone off to rescue him. We're going to help."

Rowan turned off the TV and met my eyes. "What do you need from us?" he asked, his deep voice booming loudly against the walls of the basement.

"Call the pack. Tell them to meet us at the Alpha's Throne in an hour. We're going to help."

Emory scoffed. "Sounds like a Lunata problem. I don't see why we need to be involved."

I glared at him. "We're involved because our rogue is the kidnapper. This isn't about the Lunata. This is about drawing me out."

"So, by going, aren't you just playing into whatever scheme this guy has laid out for you?" Emory shot back.

I shrugged, tring to look nonchalant even though my thunderous heartbeat betrayed me. "Probably. But I figure it's better to meet the enemy head-on than to keep hiding from him."

Emory stared at me, brows furrowed as he considered my words. "I'm going with you."

I shook my head. "No, I need you guys to gather my pack. We're going to need a show of force if we're going to defeat the rogue."

Emory rolled his eyes and stood. "These guys can handle that. I'm going with you."

"Em, this is a pack problem-"

"No," Emory cut me off. "This is a werewolf problem, and I'm not letting you face it alone."

"I'm not going alone. Des and Daniel are coming, too. And we're meeting Casey out there."

Emory scoffed. "Sounds like you've assembled a crack team, Chief," he stated sarcastically.

I rolled my eyes. I didn't have time to argue with him, so in the end, I let him come with me.

Daniel glared at Emory as we stepped back onto the main floor, and Emory had the good grace not to look directly at him, which I was supremely thankful for. The last thing we needed was for the two of them to get into a fight.

Emory glanced over at Des, who was busy tapping away at her phone. "You sobered up quickly," he told her.

Des didn't look from the screen as she answered. "Yeah, that'll happen when you find yourself in the middle of an emergency."

"So, I take it you and Casey made up?"

Her eyes flicked up, and she fixed Emory with a blank stare. "No. But I'm still his partner, so here we are, trying to do our jobs without letting our personal problems get in the way."

She'd kept her voice even, but I could tell that she still felt upset over the current state of her relationship with Casey.

"Don't worry, Des. Once this is over, I'm sure you guys will work this out," I offered.

She coughed, clearly uncomfortable, and stuck her phone into her pocket. She turned to Daniel. "Did you bring your car keys?"

Daniel frowned. "I thought we were going to Alpha's Throne. We don't need a car to get there."

Des shook her head. "We need to stop by my place first."

"Why?" I asked, wondering what could possibly be so important at this moment.

Des grinned mischievously. "We need to grab some supplies."

Des's supplies turned out to be weapons. Daniel, Emory, and I stood in Des's living room watching as she flipped couches, and turned secret panels, and opened safes full of arsenals.

And not just any run of the mill stuff either. Des had an entire armory's worth of military-grade weaponry.

She flitted around the room, grabbing things and tossing them at us. I just barely managed to catch some C-4 that she threw at me when she grabbed something that looked strangely like a bazooka and threw it to Emory.

Emory's face lit up like it was Christmas morning. "Is this is a fucking rocket launcher?"

Des's only answer was a small smile.

Me, personally? I couldn't figure out why we would need military grade C-4 or rocket launchers. "Uh, Des, I appreciate the merchandise, but what exactly are we supposed to do with this stuff?"

Des paused in her mad dash to collect her toys and glanced at me. "Oh. That's C-4."

"Yeah. I know what it is. I just don't know why you grabbed it. Not to mention, should you just be tossing this around so carelessly? It's an explosive, right? Doesn't that mean it's likely to, you know... explode?"

She shrugged. "It doesn't just explode. It needs heat and

pressure. And I gave it to you because you never know when you're going to need to blow something up."

I glanced at Daniel, who smiled like a kid in a candy store as he turned over some sort of giant rifle in his hands. "You can't fault that logic."

Actually, I could. There was no way in hell I would ever need any of this stuff, but I decided not to voice my concerns.

Once we finally made it to the edge of the forest, we were laden down with a duffle bag each, full of an assortment of weapons that I felt fairly certain we didn't need.

The extra weight didn't make for a pleasant hike, and by the time we finally caught up to where Casey sat crouched in the forest, a light sheen of sweat peppered my forehead. He had chosen a pretty decent spot about 200 yards from the clearing where my Alpha's throne sat. We were hidden by thick foliage, and the place we sat offered us a good vantage point, one where we could see people coming into and out of the clearing, but they couldn't really see us.

Casey looked over at our approach, and his eyes widened. "Jesus, Des. I said to bring the binoculars and the 50 cal rifle. Not the entire stock pile."

Des shrugged and inclined her head toward us. "Blame the werewolves."

I narrowed my eyes at her, and she grinned, clearly finding herself funnier than I did. She swung her own duffle around and lowered herself to her knees, digging around and pulling out a bunch of metal pieces. She handed the pieces to Casey, and then dug the binoculars out of her bag, bringing them to her eyes and scanning the perimeter.

Casey grunted in frustration from where he crouched, clicking the pieces together methodically. "You couldn't have assembled it before you came here?"

Des lowered the binoculars and stared at Casey. "No time. I thought that you were seconds from being ambushed. Clearly, I was wrong because no one is here."

He'd finished assembling the rifle. It looked like a machine gun, black and long, but it looked light, so I found it odd when he positioned it onto two stands in the ground and laid on his belly to aim it. He shook his head. "They're coming, Des. I know it. And with this bad boy already aimed to kill, Zee's extraction should be easy peasy."

"Isn't it going to be hard to aim at the dude's head if you're lying down like that?" Emory asked.

"I don't need to shoot him in the head. I just need to hit him. Pretty much anyone this bullet tears through is a goner."

I swallowed, not at ease with the casual way that Casey talked about blasting holes through a werewolf, even if said werewolf was a rogue. I pushed that feeling back and instead focused on Des, who had begun busying herself by rifling through the rest of the bags and haphazardly divvying up supplies.

"Here," she said, pushing the C-4 in to my pocket. She handed me what looked like long pin needles with cords attached to them. "What are these?" I hoped they were something useful because the C-4 wouldn't be leaving my pocket.

"Blasting caps."

"Huh?"

She paused and stared at me like I was the dumbest person on the planet. "You stick the part that looks like a giant needle into the soft part of the C-4, light the fuse at the end, and run like hell."

I grimaced. "Oh. Can I have something useful?"

Des ignored me, instead, turning to Emory and Daniel. She handed each one of them a handgun, which they both tried to refuse. She held up her hand, silencing them. "I know you guys are your own weapons, but honestly, if just aiming and shooting is the most efficient, the way that gets us in and out, and ends this tonight, then it's better to be prepared."

Neither one of them had a response, and I watched them

both tuck the guns into the waistbands of their jeans.

Des turned on me. "I need to pee. Will you walk with me?"

I glanced through the trees into the clearing, which was still empty, and nodded. Something laid heavily on her mind as we walked, and I could tell she needed to talk.

"What's up?" I asked.

Des turned to me, pulling me into a tight hug. "Whatever happens tonight, don't be afraid to fight," she started. I opened my mouth to tell her that of course, I would fight, but the concerned look on her face halted me, and she continued. "More importantly, Christa, don't be afraid to run."

I blinked at her, confused. "What do you mean?"

She closed her eyes and took a deep breath. "I love Zee like a dad. You know that. But what's taking place tonight isn't really about him. The person behind this knows that the people you love are your weakness, and he's used Zee to draw us out. But Zee isn't his aim. You are. And I need you to remember this: your life is the only one that has to be protected tonight."

"Des, I'm not going to let the rogue win, even if it means losing my life."

She shook her head, hands on my shoulders as she jostled me slightly. "Christa, the rogue can never take true power as long as you're alive. He may be able to divide the packs, and he may be able to start a war, but until the last True Alpha has been killed, he will never have total control. Please understand me. The magic doesn't belong to some title. It doesn't belong to that throne, or even to Moon Bay Cliff, even though that's where it's usually stored. It belongs to you. It's in your blood. Moon Bay Cliff, the throne, they could be destroyed, and the only thing that would happen is that the magic would settle inside you."

"How do you know this?"

Des bit her lip. "My real Dad, Michael. He delivered the Rogue War prophecy to your mom."

Betrayal, hot and deep, sang through me. "You know what

the prophecy says, and you never told me?"

"No. I only knew that part because my Dad told me that I would need that knowledge some day. That was the last thing he said to me before he disappeared."

I was still angry that she had kept even that part from me, but I let it go, realizing that now was not the time to start an argument with her.

Des stared at me expectantly, but I didn't know why. "What?" I asked her, my voice unkind.

She winced but held her ground, fingers biting into my shoulders as she stared at me levelly. "If it looks like we're losing, if we fail tonight, promise me, Christa. Promise me that you will run."

I wanted to tell her I would make no such promises. I wanted to tell her that I was not a coward, and I would stand by my friends until the end, but her earlier words halted me. If I died tonight, this would be the end. The rogue would win, and the world as we knew it would be doomed.

Slowly, I nodded. "Fine. If it seems like it's going to hell, I'll do it."

My answer wasn't good enough for Des. "Do what, Christa?"

I snorted, angry at Des for pushing me, and angry at fate for putting me in this position. "I'll run, Destiny!" I shouted at her.

She smiled thinly. "Good."

The anger I felt still bubbled up in me as we made our way back to the group. We'd apparently missed a lot in the fifteen minutes we'd been gone though, because when we reached them, they were all crouched low, staring off into the clearing.

Easing myself down, I followed their line of sight and saw that the werewolves had finally arrived.

Not just any werewolves either. I recognized many of them as Alphas and Betas, and I wondered who could have possibly gathered them all here. They all mumbled to one another, just as confused about why they were here as I was.

A loud howl tore through the night, an announcement of arrival as opposed to a battle cry. The wolves in the clearing came to attention, glancing around them as they waited for the source of the howl to come forward.

Slowly, but with purpose, a line of people filed into the clearing from the opposite side of where my crowd and I hid.

I watched as they marched across the clearing, their anonymity protected by the dark blue hooded cloaks that they wore. I did a quick head count. The line consisted of about six cloaked figures at the beginning, followed by three prisoners, each one with a black canvas bag shoved over their heads, and shackles binding their wrists and ankles. Bringing up the rear, six more hooded figures walked.

They stopped at the base of the Alpha's Throne, and the first person in line stepped to the side, holding out his hand as he helped the next person climb up and onto the rock. I felt my she-wolf stir, growling at the intrusion to our territory.

The three prisoners were lined up in front of the throne and forced to their knees, and I watched as the werewolves in the crowd exchanged glances.

"What's the meaning of this?" one person called.

"Where is the True Alpha?" shouted another.

The person standing on the rock laughed, and shock coursed through me at the sound. That laugh belonged to someone decidedly female, and I knew who she was before she flung off the hood.

Lana.

Of course, her dramatic entrance still had the desired effect on the crowd, even if I found it just a little too theatrical.

Either way, she had made herself known.

At that moment, I felt relief that Lana turned out to be the rogue and not Aidan, although I still wasn't sure how considering that she would have just been a kid, but I figured maybe her Dad had been the original and upon his passing she had just picked up his mantle.

I also felt pissed off. This girl just kept causing me trouble, and I wanted nothing more than to tear her limb from limb.

Finally, I felt fear as she bent down and tore the masks off her hostages. That fear pounded against my chest, made even worse as I registered who they were.

Zee, of course. And Aidan, which explained why Daniel hadn't heard from him.

I wanted to save each of them, but it was the last hostage, the one she currently sat behind, effectively making sure that if Casey were to take his shot, he'd have to hit the prisoner, too. This was the hostage that made my heart stop.

That hostage was *my* Dad.

We stayed hidden, too shocked to move. We'd expected to see Zee, but to see my Dad and Aidan on their knees in front of Lana rocked me to my core. I didn't understand her aim. Why parade her prisoners to a group of Alphas and Betas she was trying to convince to join her?

Luckily, I wasn't the only person who wanted answers. From out in the crowd, one of the wolves spoke up. "What is the meaning of this, Lana?"

Lana smiled and addressed the crowd. "These three people you see before you are relics of an ancient time," she paused and looked down at Zee. "The oppressor, the leader of the group who patrols and hunts us against our will, all because our True Alpha, and those that came before her, allowed it. The Beta, the man who should have put an end to her line years ago, but continually failed."

"Why the human?" someone asked when she didn't add anything about my dad.

Her grin widened. "Oh, this one is for fun. This is the Alpha's father. I'm hoping that I can use him to draw her out, to make sure she complies with my plans."

"And what exactly is your plan, Lana?" This question was

asked by a deep, booming baritone from the edge of the clearing. I glanced over and saw Rowan, followed by the rest of my pack, stepping into the clearing, murderous intent written on all of their faces.

"Where is your Alpha?"

Rowan shook his head, his anger crackling through the air as he glared at Lana. "She's safe, hidden away from whatever nefarious plan you've cooked up. And I ask again, what do you think you are doing?"

Lana stood, and I saw Casey stir as he positioned himself and took aim to end her with one of his lethal bullets. "I'm taking the Alpha's Throne, and you can either join me or die."

She extracted a gun from her hip and trained the barrel at the back of my dad's head.

I didn't think. I saw red, and I reacted, springing forward and rushing into the clearing, hitting the butt of Casey's rifle and directing it off course as Casey pulled the trigger.

The shot went wide, lodging somewhere in the tree line, but the sound of the bullet temporarily distracted Lana, who looked up to see me rushing toward her like a locomotive.

The rifle abandoned, my friends tore off after me through the clearing, screaming at me to get back. A little voice reminded me that I'd promised Des I wouldn't risk myself to save someone else, but I had also made that promise before I'd known my dad was in danger, so I had an all-bets-are-off attitude about it.

From across the clearing, my pack rushed forward, pushing through the crowd of confused werewolves as they moved to aid me.

I was so close to my dad that if I reached out my fingertips would brush him. From somewhere next to me, Lana had recovered from the shock of my appearance and laughed triumphantly as she trained her gun on me.

I slammed into my dad, the force knocking us both to the ground and looked up just in time to realize that Lana aimed to shoot me.

Time stilled around me, and I watched in slow motion, not afraid, just knowing that things would be okay. Rowan sailed through the air, already in wolf form and torpedoed into Lana, sending her gun flying as he threw the two of them off of the Alpha's Throne.

Brock ran to my side, grabbing my father and rushing him out of the clearing.

Des reached Zee, pushing him off towards the tree line, while he shouted unintelligibly and tried to rush toward Aidan.

I watched as Daniel paused halfway through the clearing, wide-eyed as he stared to the person next to me. "Dad?" I heard him yell, hurt and confusion dripping from his words.

Finally, I turned and saw Aidan, who had somehow freed himself of his shackles, and now stood with a cool and triumphant look on his face.

Through the stillness, Zee's words rang through the forest. "It's a trap."

Casey had rushed to Aidan to free him. I saw only the faintest confusion as he paused and assessed that Aidan was already loose.

The world stopped completely as I watched Aidan pull Casey towards him, and with one swift movement, he snapped Casey's neck.

CHAPTER EIGHTEEN

Des screamed, her agony tearing through the night as Casey's body fell to the ground in front of Aidan. Zee tried to pull her away, but I saw her strain against him, as she tried to reach Casey.

I ran my hands over my face, unable to process anything. I couldn't look down. I couldn't acknowledge that my friend lay dead at Aidan's feet. Just the thought of it made my chest constrict.

Instead, I had to force myself not to name it. That lifeless body wasn't Casey, it was just a body. It had to be. At least for now, because we weren't done here. There would be time to mourn later. Around me, my friends and pack battled with Lana and her pack, all, of course, who had betrayed me to serve her and Aidan.

"Stop!" I screamed, and the clearing went still as all eyes turned to Aidan and me, standing side by side in front of the Alpha's throne. I met Aidan's dark gaze, the indifference on his face causing the contents of my stomach to churn. Everything else disappeared as the world shifted to just the two of us, staring at each other, discussing the end of our world as we knew it. "Why?" I choked out, my voice a hoarse whisper.

His voice was cold as he spoke, the chill of it sending shivers up my spine. "Your mother was weak. You are weak. You follow her example, allowing us to be governed by what is acceptable to The Lunata and for the lowly humans. She wanted to tell the world what we were, but she wanted to do so in a way that made them feel safe. She didn't want them to be scared of us. I do. I want them to know that they are inferior to us."

"You're insane. You had your son kill my mother so that you could unleash a rebellion against humans?"

Aidan smiled darkly, "You know as well as I do that

Brendan was not mine."

I resisted the urge to flinch, instead focusing on keeping my face blank. "You have to get them to pledge their allegiance to you," I whispered, inclining my head toward the crowd.

That damned smile never left his face. "Do I?" He whispered, turning to the crowd. "Didn't you hear dear old Hannity tell you this was a trap?"

At his unspoken command about a quarter of the crowd stepped forward, coming to stand on the other side of an invisible line I hadn't realized had been drawn until now.

This time I smiled, the first real emotion I'd had since watching Casey's body hit the ground coursing through me. "Looks like my crowd is bigger than yours."

"You could keep them all. I have something better." Aidan slashed his hand through the air, and the clearing filled with his monsters. The people around us erupted into panic, but the creatures did not attack. He leaned forward, victory written all over his face. "I always liked you, Christa. I even tried to hide the wolf from you, in hopes that maybe the wolf inside you would die off, and you could live a normal human life."

Understanding flooded through me, and I realized that I'd known all along that Aidan was the rogue. I'd always lamented on how familiar his voice sounded, and as he spoke, the words he'd uttered on that night so many years ago slammed into my consciousness.

"Dormir toujours, petite louve," I whispered.

Aidan nodded. "To sleep always, little she-wolf." He frowned, something akin to sympathy washing over his features. "She should have listened. You could have lived." He paused and held his palms in the air. "Now, you have a choice. Relinquish your birthright to me, or I take it. Either way, it will be mine before the night ends."

Cautiously, I shifted my eyes around the clearing, doing my best to assess the situation around me without losing focus on Aidan. Des sprawled on the ground, her head on Casey as heavy sobs wracked her body, and Zee tried to pull her out of harm's way. Daniel stood in the center still rooted to the spot as he watched his father betray him. My pack, and the wolves who hadn't joined Aidan's efforts, stood scattered around Daniel, boxed in by the monsters that surrounded them. I allowed myself a moment to mentally berate myself for not asking Cooper Jones what those creatures were when I'd had the opportunity.

Well, I had the opportunity now, and I knew enough about myself that I wouldn't let Aidan have what belonged to me without a fight. First, though, I had to figure out what we would be fighting against when I declared war against him.

"What are they?" I asked, and Aidan cocked his head, surprise evident in the set of his mouth.

"Lycans. The most basic form of the werewolf. They are what happens when there is no humanity left inside one of us. I have spent many years building an army from them, and while they may not be human any longer, they are tremendously loyal to me. I feed them and provide them with basic comforts, and they do my bidding."

I raised an eyebrow. "So, they're your pets?"

Aidan pursed his lips. "I've grown tired of this, girl. Give me what I ask for."

I sighed and bit my lip. "Yeah. I'm not gonna do that. You want it, you're gonna have to fight me for it," I paused and stood up taller, rolling my shoulders and cracking my neck as I did. "And it's going to be a fight to the death."

"Oh, Christa. I'm going to k-" Aidan started.

I felt pretty certain that he had been about to tell me that he was going to kill me, but at that moment, Daniel found his feet. He plowed right into Aidan, knocking them both to the ground as he threw punch after punch against Aidan's face while yelling "traitor," over and over again.

Daniel's action spurred everyone else, including Aidan's lycans, and without much more ado the entire clearing erupted into chaos as fighting broke out.

"No one touches her! I must be the one to kill her," Aidan screamed from his compromised position before I heard the crunch that indicated that Daniel had landed another punch to his face.

Lana lunged at me from the left, but I spun away right as Rowan caught her around the middle. "I don't think so, bitch," he growled as he wrestled her to the ground.

I took the opportunity to fling myself into Des, grabbing her around the waist and spinning us both around before heading for the edge of the forest. Her protests came fast as she begged me to let her stay with Casey. Considering that I was pretty sure the Rogue War had just begun, there was no way in hell I would be doing that, so I just ignored her pleas.

Zee followed us, surprisingly agile for an old guy. We crouched low as we reached our bags of stuff, and I started digging through them. I tossed a gun to Zee, along with Casey's cell phone, which he'd left sitting on top of one of the duffle bags.

"Call your men! Get them here, now! My pack is outnumbered. We can hold them for a minute, but there's too many."

Zee nodded and went right to work, and I spun around to assess the battle. Brock had returned, and I allowed myself just a moment to hope that he'd stowed my dad somewhere safe before I yelled at him to watch out for the lycan that closed in on him.

Aidan had somehow gotten free of Daniel, and the two now stood, circling each other, each one waiting for the other to make a move. I looked at Des, who seemed to notice nothing but the body lying 200 yards away from us.

I bent down. "Des, we need to go. Now."

She looked at me, eyes empty. "He's gone."

I licked my lips. "I know, but if we don't move, Aidan is going to kill me."

She looked at me, then. Really looked at me, as though I was the first thing she'd seen in a long time. "He can't kill you. If he kills you, then all of this was for nothing."

I grimaced at her as I stood and tugged at her arm. "We don't have time for this. We are losing. You need to run."

Instead of getting up, she nodded emphatically. "Exactly! We need to run! I told you to run!"

I shook my head. "Des. No, I have to end this. I can't let anyone else die for me. I don't..." I trailed off as her words from not more than an hour ago slammed into me.

Aidan thought that I either had to relinquish power willfully or die to make him the True Alpha. He was right about that last part. My brother didn't have the werewolf gene, and I had no other family on my mom's side with it, either. If I died, the power would transfer to my Beta. I was willing to bet he had no idea that I couldn't just give him my birthright because the magic was a part of me.

I was also willing to bet that he solidly believed that the magic belonged to Moon Bay Cliff and the Alpha's Throne.

From the back of my mind, my she-wolf snarled. I know what you're thinking, and I don't like it.

I ignored her, instead, reaching into Des's pocket and grabbing her lighter. I turned to Zee. "Keep her here, until I get back."

He looked surprised but didn't ask me what I had planned. He just nodded in agreement.

I tore off back toward the Alpha's Throne, heart pounding in my chest as I worked out a plan.

Gunshots rang out around me, and I smiled. The Lunata had arrived, and it pained me that I couldn't stop to admire their work.

I briefly glanced back to watch as one of their ranks took aim at one of the Lycans. His bullet had aimed true, but it didn't stop the beast from swiping the man across the belly. Both hit the ground, and I winced.

The huge rock sat just ahead of me, and I allowed myself a moment to scan my surroundings. Bodies, lycan and werewolf alike, scattered the field. I felt tears spring to my eyes. These were my people, and too many of them had already been lost tonight. I needed to end this now.

To my left, Emory faced off with two of Lana's pack. To my right, I met Daniel's eyes. He'd shifted into wolf form and fought with a large lycan, but he seemed to have the advantage. His eyes widened in fear, and I couldn't puzzle out why. I could tell that he tried to communicate with me, but I figured out his message a split-second too late.

Daniel fought a lycan, which meant he no longer battled Aidan. This fact became excruciatingly clear as I felt his fist connect with the back of my head.

I stumbled forward, landing hard on my hands and knees as the world shimmered from the force of the hit, but I willed myself to keep my eyes open. Aidan reached down, grabbing a fist full of my hair and lifting me off the ground.

"I'm really getting tired of you," he growled, his eyes glowing as he contemplated shifting into his wolf form.

I looked around desperately. Daniel had ended the fight with his lycan and made his way across the clearing, trying to get to me, but I could tell he wouldn't make it before Aidan made the switch.

I grimaced, knowing my only option was to change, too, but realizing that it was going to hurt, a lot, since Aidan still clutched a large chunk of my hair in his fist.

I steeled myself, gathering the magic I would need to shift, right as more gunshots rang out.

Aidan screamed in pain and dropped me, and I turned to see who had rescued me. Des walked through the clearing, tears streaming down her face as she continued to shoot the gun, without aiming, at Aidan.

I rolled off to the side, reached into my pocket and grabbed the C-4. I wedged the brick into a little groove under the Alpha's

Throne and lit the fuse.

Springing quickly to my feet, I tore off towards Des, grabbing her hand before turning to look over my shoulder.

"Everybody better run!" I screamed.

Something in my voice must have been enough warning for both sides, because, like animals in a stampede, the whole clearing stopped their fighting and sprinted off into various directions.

From next to the Alpha's Throne, Aidan called out to me. "Running like a coward, Alpha?" he jeered.

I paused and spun around to face him. "If I were you I'd run, too."

Aidan laughed. "Oh?"

"Yeah. I just planted enough C-4 to send this whole cliff into the ravine. That fucking rock is about to blow."

I had the satisfaction of watching his face contort into a mask of rage before I spun around and sprinted like a bat out of hell.

As I ran, I couldn't stop thinking of how stupid I'd been. I'd made two major mistakes tonight. I'd rushed into the clearing to save my father when Casey had the shot that would have taken Lana out. That mistake had ultimately resulted in his death.

The second one that kept beating against my brain was that I shouldn't have warned Aidan that the Alpha's throne was about to explode. I could have ended this tonight, but I'd gotten too caught up in being cocky and trying to get one over on him that I'd missed the big picture.

I'd barely cleared the forest when the percussion from the explosion tore through the night and shook the ground beneath us.

My pack and our allies reconvened at Les Loups-Garous, which had been officially locked down. Aidan's cronies had disappeared, but I knew that tonight had just been the beginning. My stupidity in warning Aidan had assured that this war would continue.

I sent a search party, a mix of Lunata and pack, to go assess the damage. Their findings had been devastating. The clearing had housed over a hundred beings tonight, with harsh losses for all sides. The Alpha's throne and the surrounding cliff had been blasted into the ravine below. Twenty of our people, whether they be allies, pack, or Lunata, had died.

And of course, one of them was Casey. Casey whose body had been blasted down into the ravine along with Moon Bay Cliff.

Des had told me that my life was the only one that mattered. As she sat in a room upstairs with Zee, crying uncontrollably over the loss of her man, I wondered if she would still say the same thing.

I wanted to be there, breaking down with her, but I needed to address the survivors.

Standing in front of them, high up on my podium, I struggled to find the words that would make them feel that their sacrifices had been worth the pain they now felt. Still, I tried.

"Tonight, Aidan Hawthorne and his defectors declared war against me, and those who stand with me. Tonight, our mighty kingdom fell victim to a terrible evil. You all saw what he has, the army that he has created, and I am certain that the force he showed today is only a fraction of the troops he has at his disposal. Tonight, I stand here, and I ask you, will you allow his betrayal to go unpunished, or will you stand with me as I prepare to destroy him?"

I looked down at the crowd, but none of them answered. At least not until Emory's voice rang out. "What do you offer?"

I gave him a small, grateful smile. "I offer the protection of Les Loups-Garous. As you see it is a fortress, impenetrable and safe. In return, I ask that you pledge your packs to me."

"What does that mean for us?" Victor, the Alpha from the Eurasian-Pack, asked.

I swallowed. "It means that you will no longer be an Alpha

of your own pack. If you do this, we will be forging a new bond. One pack, led by the True Alpha."

"We won't all fit here."

"Les Loups-Garous is designed to house many wolves. It may not be the most comfortable living situation, but until this war is over, I feel it's the best course of action."

"And when the war is over? Will you allow us to go back to the old ways? Will you give us back our packs?"

I paused, my she-wolf informing me that we could do amazing things with all that power. I kindly reminded her that I didn't want all that power, and nodded once.

"You have my word. When this is over, I will restore the balance."

"Then you may have my pack."

I smiled graciously at Victor and then listened as the other Alpha's pledged their allegiance to my cause.

When they finished, I thanked them and stepped off the stage, making my way through the crowd to the exit.

Throughout the proceedings, I had been watching Daniel, who hadn't said anything to me since we'd left the clearing. I'd watched as he paced around the bar, pulling various bottles off the shelf and taking drinks before shattering the bottles against the floor. I'd watched as he'd slipped out the front door, and now I intended to talk to him.

I followed him as he cut his way through the forest, back to the clearing that held nothing but sorrow.

"Don't you think it's unsafe here?" I asked once he'd stopped.

Daniel shook his head. "Aidan and his people are long gone. They're off somewhere regrouping."

"What are you doing out here, Daniel?"

"I'm leaving."

I shook my head. "What are you talking about? You can't leave. This is your home. You just need to come back inside. We can go to bed, and you can calm down."

"Leave me alone, Christa."

"No. Let's go home."

Daniel's shoulders hunched as he stared pointedly at the ground. "I don't belong here. I'm no better than him. I couldn't stop him," he mumbled, his defeated tone telling me just how broken he was.

I took a step forward, reaching for him, and felt a pang as he backed away from me. Taking a shaking breath and trying to keep myself from breaking down, I dropped my arm and didn't make another step toward him. "He's your father, Daniel. How could you have stopped him if you didn't even believe he was a threat?"

Daniel scoffed and finally looked up at me, his eyes dark and edging more closely to feral than I had ever seen. I froze, the wildness in him alarming the she-wolf inside as she reminded me that feral wolves are dangerous.

"You warned me. You told me what Cooper Jones said. I ignored you," he paused for just a moment before taking a ragged breath. "I ignored you, and now Casey is dead. His blood is on my hands."

I shook my head while I tried to reason with him. "You made a mistake. But you do belong here. You belong with me." My voice quivered with a plea as I begged him to understand. As I begged to make him see that I needed him here with me. If he left, I didn't know what I would do.

Daniel looked at the ground again. "I don't belong here, and I don't belong with you," he whispered.

"Daniel, of course, you belong with me. After everything we've been through..." I trailed off, trying to find the right thing to say and realizing I didn't know what to say to ease his guilt. The only thing I could offer him was the comfort of our love. "After everything that has happened, I still love you."

Daniel's head shot up, and he met my eyes with a steely, narrowed gaze. "You shouldn't," he growled, and before I could cut in to argue, he said the one thing that could stop me in my tracks. "And I don't love you. Not anymore, anyway. I can't, not after all of this. Not after all the lies and the betrayals."

I stared at him as my eyes brimmed with tears, both of us standing in the middle of the clearing just a few feet from where the first of many battles had just taken place, and I felt my blood turn to ice. His words struck me harder than any hit I had taken tonight. They rocked me to my core, ripping into my heart and tearing it apart.

"That's not true." I cried, but even to my own ears I could hear that doubt had already taken hold, and I was breaking with the realization that it could indeed be true.

As though answering the thoughts in my head, Daniel spoke again, his tone cruel and taunting. "Listen to yourself, Christa. Deep down, you know that it is true."

My mouth went dry as his cutting words dug deep. I licked my lips, my response coming out in a small defeated whisper. "But, I need you. I don't know how to survive this. I don't know how I'll make it through without you."

Daniel cocked his eyebrow, a gesture that I'd always found to be annoying and sexy all at once. This time, that familiar motion was neither. Devoid of the playfulness or affection that usually lit up his face, the simple movement was just cold.

"You're the True Alpha; you'll figure it out."

And without another word, Daniel Hawthorne turned away from me and shifted before running off into the wilderness.

I stared where he had disappeared, waiting for him to come back and tell me he was sorry. My chest ached while my heart beat thunderously, and I realized he wasn't coming back. With one last painful thud, I broke, my heart and soul shattering into millions of jagged shards, and I fell to the ground.

I curled myself into a heap and sobbed, the cries ripping out of me in huge painful gasps. He was gone. The thought repeated itself over and over again until I could think no more.

I don't know how long I laid there, gasping for my life as my world crumbled around me before the soft sound of steps in the grassy clearing alerted me that someone was coming.

My first thought was Des, coming to collect me. She had to be worried; she had to be wondering where I'd gone.

As the person bent low, lips near my ear, I realized that it couldn't possibly be Des. She was somewhere else. Somewhere experiencing her own earth-shattering heartache while she mourned the death of the man *she* loved.

Words, softly spoken but still stern, cut through the fog in my head and the silence around me.

"It's time to get up now, Christa."

I winced as Emory's voice cut through me, and I whimpered. "I can't. He left me. I don't have the strength to pick myself up."

Emory breathed deeply then spoke again. "Daniel's a fool for leaving you," he began, and shock rocked through me. How could Emory have possibly known who I meant? I shouldn't have been surprised, Daniel had been the center of my universe and Emory was well aware, but logic failed me as I battled to regain composure. Before I could say any more, he continued, "But the fact remains, you must get up."

I gritted my teeth, not comprehending why he didn't understand that my will to go on had run off with Daniel. "I can't. I. Don't. Have. The. Strength," I spat out.

Emory went to his knees beside me and brushed my hair away from my face before placing his hand lightly on my cheek. "Then I will lend you mine until you can regain yours."

"You can't lend me your strength. You're not part of my pack," I whispered.

Emory moved his hand from my cheek and placed his wrist on my lips. "Then make me a part of it. I need a pack, and you need a Beta. More importantly, you need someone at your side who will keep you safe while your heart heals."

Understanding coursed through me as I realized what he offered. I looked up, meeting his gold eyes with my questioning look. "Are you sure?"

Emory nodded. "Let me be your Beta."

I nodded back. "I accept your offer," I whispered, and then I bit down, drawing the slightest prick of blood with my canine tooth.

I felt magic surge around us and then through me, connecting Emory to me and what remained of my pack.

He smiled at me and rose to offer his hand down to me. "Now, let me be your strength, Christa. You need to stand, your pack needs their Alpha, now more than ever."

I stared up at him a moment longer before I felt that familiar werewolf magic pulsing through me as Emory lent me his power, and I realized he was right.

I sat up, allowing myself one last tear as I mourned the love I had lost before I pushed it away. Before I pushed it all away. All the guilt, all the doubt, all the sadness. Everything inside me, all of my emotions. I locked them away.

As I took Emory's hand, he pulled me to my feet while I gazed at all the destruction that had taken place. I should have felt sadness, betrayal, heartbreak. Instead, I felt nothing. I had used Emory's borrowed strength to shut myself off from feeling any emotions.

In the back of my mind, the she-wolf told me that I played a dangerous game. An Alpha that felt nothing was in danger of losing sight of what mattered.

I didn't care. I'd done what I needed to do to pick myself up. I told her that I could allow myself time to grieve later when all was said and done.

Right now, I needed to pick myself up.

Right now, I had more important things to do.

I had a war to win.

CHAPTER NINETEEN

Graduation came. I wanted to be happy, but I couldn't. I couldn't feel anything. In the aftermath of everything that had happened, this night seemed inconsequential.

My family didn't come to graduation. After what had happened with my dad, I realized that Aidan would continue to use them as leverage until he destroyed me, so I told my grandparents what I was, and I sent them all away. I told them not to tell me where they were. I told them not to tell anyone associated with me where they were. It was for their own safety.

They cried as we'd said our goodbyes.

I didn't. The defense mechanism I'd put in place made sure I couldn't feel anything that would damage my heart and soul any further than Daniel had.

Currently, Des and I found ourselves crammed into a booth with Emory in the bar area of Les Loups-Garous while my pack threw us a graduation party. It was a kind gesture; I just didn't feel like celebrating.

Along with Casey, my science teacher had died in the clearing. Also three other students. Students who should have been here celebrating with the rest of the pack. The school had honored the memory of the students who fell that night, awarding them all with posthumous diplomas. The principal had prepared a statement, stating how tragic it had been to discover that our science teacher had driven these kids home after prom as a favor, and how their lives had ended because a drunk driver had hit them head-on.

It was a sad story. Not nearly as devastating as the truth.

Brock brought us over a round of shots, and I drank mine without bothering to toast the others before standing and muttering to my friends that I would be back.

My graduation dress was itchy, and I didn't want to wear it anymore.

I made my way up the stairs to my apartment. I could officially call it mine. I owned it, and the whole building. Daniel had managed to transfer the deed into my name. It had come in the mail a couple of weeks after he left.

My apartment was trashed, and I couldn't muster enough care to pick it up. I'd over-turned the couch, the chairs, and the tables one night when I'd accidentally stumbled into Daniel's room after a night of drinking with Des and Emory. It had been a rare moment where I'd allowed the anger I felt to surface as I stared at the bed that hadn't been touched or made since *that* night.

I'd since had a lock put on that door.

I went into my room and rifled around through the pile of clothes on the floor. A pile that had grown so much that I couldn't distinguish between my dirty and clean laundry. Producing a pair of jeans, I slipped them on and then threw on my hoodie sweater.

I shuffled into the bathroom and stared at myself in the mirror. I'd lost weight, my face jutting at hard angles, and I had dark circles under my eyes. The result of a lack of food and sleep, no doubt.

I shook my head at my sad reflection and turned the faucet on, before splashing cold water on my face. I dried my hands on my jeans but paused when I felt something in my pocket.

Confused, I reached in and pulled out the envelope that James had given me weeks ago. Curious, I ripped it open and pulled out the letter.

Christa,

If you're reading this, then I fear that the war has found you. I am an ally of sorts, someone with information that could help you defeat this threat. I only ask that if you seek me out, you do not try to enlist me to your cause. I have my own lives to protect, and they are more precious than you could possibly imagine. This being said, I know what the prophecy says, I know what the lycans truly are and how to save them. Please understand that you must save them. They are the key to restoring the balance. If you choose to gain my knowledge, you may find me where the desert meets the trees, and the river connects two great lakes.

Sincerely,
Pike Sharpova

I re-read the letter twice, my eyes faltering over my mother's surname while I tried to make sense of it.

My geography skills were poor, and I had no clue what his riddle meant. I would have to enlist help, though, because this letter had made one thing clear. Whoever this man was, he held the key to my future.

For the first time since Daniel had left, I felt a surge of excitement, and I tore out of my apartment and down the stairs at break-neck speed.

I reached my friends right as Brock produced another tray of shots. I grabbed one and slid into the booth, lifting the glass into the air. "Cheers," I shouted before downing the drink and staring at Emory and Des excitedly.

My friends noticed the change in me and exchanged quick glances before Des cocked her head. "Is everything okay, Christa?"

I knew Des hurt, too, but that she put on a good show. Even still, once I told her my plan, I had to hope that doing something after weeks of waiting would lift her spirits, too.

I grabbed another shot and poured it down my throat before I launched into an explanation of how I'd obtained the note, and what it had said.

Des leaned forward, already knowing that I had cooked up a plan. "What's your plan, Christa?

I stared at them, my mouth splitting into a mischievous smile of its own accord. "You guys want to go on an adventure?"

****

Thank you for reading *Beta Rising.* I would appreciate it if you would take a few minutes to write an honest review on the web site of the bookseller where you purchased this book. Reviews are very important in the success of a novel because they help other readers to find it. Thank you

Keep reading for a preview of the next book in the *Les Loup-Garous* series.

Teaser for *Survivor's Call*, Book Three in *Les Loups-Garous*.

PROLOGUE

He stared at the phone, the number two beating against his mind.

Two minutes after he left that he'd felt her will break. Two months since he'd abandoned her. Two weeks since he'd tried to call, and heard the message that had broken his heart in... two.

How stupid, he thought to himself, that he'd be so anxious to try the call again. He just didn't want to hear them.

But, he did long to hear her.

Gritting his teeth, he thrust the number into the phone and waited as it rang. One ring. Two rings. Three rings.

The answering machine clicked. "You've reached Christa," her voice sang through the receiver, and he smiled. Then the other voice came on, and he winced. "And Emory."

Their voices in sing-songy unison, the message continued. "We're on an adventure. Don't bother leaving a message; we don't know when we'll be back."

He ended the call, staring angrily at the phone. Two weeks? Surely, in two weeks they would have made it back from whatever romantic destination they'd ventured off to.

Jealousy sang through his veins. How could she?

In the back of his mind his wolf, much more persistent since he'd been living life in animal form, scoffed. "*Why wouldn't she? You left.*"

He bit back his irritation. Of course, the wolf was right. But still, it hurt.

He'd been afraid that she would never be able to make it through what he'd done to her.

Yet, somehow, she'd survived.

She'd survived without him, and now he had to wonder if he could survive without her.

He closed his eyes, and like every time before, he saw her face.

No. He couldn't survive without her.

His howl tore through the night as he shifted and began to run, only one thought guiding him as he went.

He was going home.

Chapter One

"This wasn't what I thought you'd meant when you'd said 'Hey Des, do you want to go on an adventure?'"

I looked up at my best friend, crouched low on the rooftop of a super-tall building and staring down on at least three dark shadows guarding the doorway I needed to get through.

"That's not what I said. I said 'Hey Des, after graduation, we should go on a recon mission,'" I whispered. I was lying. I'd totally told her we were going on an adventure.

From next to me, sunk down just as low, Emory's liquid gold eyes met mine. "Do you guys want to shut the hell up? Or were you hoping that the lycans down there would hear you?"

I ignored his comment outright. "Any ideas? This is like a fourteen-story drop right into the middle of a lycan lair."

Emory considered, and then darted a glance to where our backpacks were leaned against the other side. "We could use the harnesses and repel down?"

I shook my head. "Too much work. Plus, we only have about thirty seconds of surprise to get the drop on these guys. Repelling will take too long."

A devilish grin split across Emory's lips. "We could jump."

I had a smart-ass remark on my lips, but Des beat me to it. "Oh, yeah. Jump fourteen stories and try to fight those guys with your broken legs? Get serious, Em."

That sly grin still lit his face. "As fun as that would be, I meant that we could secure a rope to one of the harnesses, and base-jump. If we measure it right, I can pull the slack on the rope so that instead of dropping to the ground, you guys would hang a few feet up and then be able to stealthily drop the rest of the way."

Des shook her head. "No way. I'm not doing that."

I shrugged. "I'll do it."

Emory's smile widened. "Great. I'll go get the stuff."

As Emory slunk across the rooftop, I stood and turned to Des. She looked at me like I was crazy. "You don't need to do this."

I shrugged, not saying anything.

"Seriously, Christa. That's a long drop," she said, glancing over the edge. I looked, too, gulping as I took that drop in. Despite my calm exterior, a nagging voice in my mind reminded me that base-jumping wasn't really in my skill set.

I jumped as arms closed around me, fastening a harness in place. "You're not chickening out, are you?" Emory whispered, lips inches from my ear.

"Don't encourage this." Des snorted.

I turned my head as much as I could and grinned at Emory. He grinned back and stepped away, turning back to dig through the pack that he'd dragged over.

I peered over the ledge again, trying not to think too hard about what I was going to do.

"Fuck it," I muttered, turning from the ledge and heading for the middle of the roof. I spun back around, shot a prayer to whoever was up there, and took off running toward the edge.

"Christa!" Emory shouted, but I couldn't let him break my concentration. "Christa!" He tried again.

I hit the edge and jumped.

Right as I heard Emory yell..."I didn't clip the rope!"

*****

Look for *Survivor's Call* in 2019.

ABOUT THE AUTHOR

Angelina Fasano lives in Las Vegas Nevada with her husband, daughter, and freedom-seeking dog. *Alpha's Song* was the first novel in a planned series with *Beta Rising* being the second. When she isn't working on a novel, she can be found reading other people's stories or managing the office where she works.

More Books from Pynhavyn Press

THE FUNERAL SINGER SERIES
By Lillian I Wolfe

Music is a passion for Gillian Foster, a struggling musician with dreams of success. When an accident bestows a paranormal talent, her whole life takes an unexpected turn. Getting gigs as a funeral singer, she finds her conscious-self transported to an interim cemetery where she can speak to the recently departed *while she is singing*. Inexplicably, she is bound to help the spirit to complete any unfinished business.

But more than departed spirits haunt the transitional plane, and they pose a threat to not only the souls in transit, but those still living as well. And they've identified Gillian as a danger. She's one soul against hundreds and she needs help.

Can she find others like her and rally enough to stop the spread of evil that can take everyone she loves?

The *Funeral Singer* series of five books explores the overall theme as each thriller takes Gillian deeper into danger as she tries to help the departed souls cross to safety on the next plane.

O'Ceagan's Legacy: Book 1 (O'Ceagan Saga)

by Lillian I Wolfe (Sci-Fi Fantasy Adventure)

Trained by her grandfather to command, Grania O'Ceagan expects to one day inherit the family's space freighter, but first she must prove herself worthy to be captain. Her ambitious brother Liam is nipping at her heels and wants a ship as well.

On the return trip from Earth to their home world, they take on two unplanned passengers and find themselves facing a disaster that could destroy everything. Can Grania muster her crew and apply all she's learned to save her ship and crew from impending destruction?

For Eleven Million Reasons (The Franklin Logs)

by M.L. Weatherington - Police Mystery

If you think that winning the lottery is a dream come true, you need to read the possible dark side of publicized sudden wealth. In For Eleven Million Reasons, mystery author M. L. Weatherington takes you on a suspenseful ride of murder and intrigue as Lt. Arthur Franklin pursues a killer. Don't miss this thrill ride of a first novel.

idewiped! (The Franklin Logs)

by M.L. Weatherington - Police Mystery

Picking up from the first book, Lt. Arthur Franklin of the Lodi Police Department finds himself suffering from doubt and uncertainty as he recuperates from the injury suffered in his last case–the one that nearly took his daughter's life. Melissa has retreated more than Art, who has been seeing a psychiatrist, Amanda Burton, a stunning woman and Art is undeniably attracted.

Meanwhile, a new murder has hit the streets of Lodi. Even though Art is on leave, his partner, Walt, wants to get his input on the case. With few clues to help them, it's a real puzzler. As things begin to escalate, Art is pulled into more than one mystery. Can Art help Walt solve the murder and how does it tie in with a mysterious stalker at his house?

The Gentle Giant Returns (The Franklin Logs)

by M.L. Weatherington - Police Mystery

Crime is news, and everyone's ears perk up when blood is spilt. Art prides himself on solving these few and far between homicides and noting the case resolved in his personal and private Franklin Logs. It is a red spiral-bound notebook he keeps in his home office drawer. There are few entries, but every crime that he solved was personal to him, like finding a long-lost friend and bringing them home.

This is one of those times where Melissa, Amanda, Doc Wexford, Murphy, and Walt are trying to unravel a puzzle. The mystery is the loquacious African Grey Parrot, the tape recording, and, well, you will see as you get into the story. You, like all of them, want answers from Art, but he is not talking.

Find out why in *THE GENTLE GIANT RETURNS*

Bitter Vintage

by Riona Kelly - Suspense Romance

When the heir to the Claremont Vineyards is killed in an accident, his sister Martinique returns home for the funeral. She finds her father reclusive and odd, her estranged half-sister in residence, and a mysterious person skulking around the property. As she learns more about her brother's death, she is convinced there is more to the story and is determined to learn the truth. But can she prove it?

Bitter Vintage brings the suspense of treachery, greed, and ambition along with romance and betrayal as the story unfolds against the California vineyards of the Napa-Sonoma region amid the migrant workers' struggle for fair wages in 1964.

Echoes of the Past

by Riona Kelly - Suspense Romance

A picture perfect morning. A dead woman washed onto the beach. Kathleen Donaghue's summer research trip to Wales turned upside down in that horrible moment when she found the body. Without warning, the intrigue surrounding the victim sucked her into an eddy of unanswered questions. Who was she? How did she come to be washed ashore? Was it murder?

An enigmatic stranger arrives at her hotel, and with a brief encounter, he sets her trouble radar on alert. A man to be avoided. Only he seems to go out of his way to find her as their paths continue to cross. The more Kathleen tries to pull away, the more fate shoves her closer. Has she stumbled into a mystery that might endanger her life?

The first book in a series of international romantic suspense novels, *Echoes of the Past* is set in present-day North Wales with an *American Rose Abroad*.

Alpha's Song (Les Loups-Garous)

by Angelina Fasano- YA Urban Fantasy

In quiet little Kennington, Massachusetts, dark secrets abound and some are buried deeper than others. Mysterious club owner Daniel Hawthorne keeps them close to his heart.

Following the devastating death of her mother, Christa Ellsworth never expected to return to the town where she grew up, but five years later, she finds herself dragged back to the scene of her family's tragedy. Christa's plan to finish high school unnoticed comes to a halt following a chance encounter with the devastatingly handsome club owner she can't get out of her head. She begins to uncover the extraordinary truth about the town she grew up in and an unusual birthright that is now hers. Can she handle it?

www.ingramcontent.com/pod-product-compliance
Lightning Source LLC
Chambersburg PA
CBHW050023180626
46810CB00002B/541